The Scandalous Summerfields

Disgrace is their middle name!

Left destitute by their philandering parents,
the three Summerfield sisters, Lorene, Tess
and Genna, and their half brother, Edmund,
are the talk of the *ton*—for all the wrong reasons!

They are at the mercy of the marriage mart to
transport their family from the fringes of society
to the dizzying heights of respectability.

But with no dowries and a damaged reputation,
only some very special matches can survive the
scandalous Summerfields!

Meet tempestuous Tess in
Bound by Duty
April 2015

And look for the rest of the family's exploits
Coming soon!

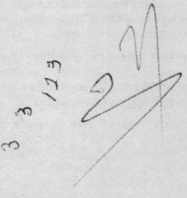

Author Note

An idea for a story may come from anywhere. A random event. A place. A character from history. For my new miniseries, The Scandalous Summerfields, the spark came from the previous generation of my own family—my mother and her sisters and brother.

I did not want to tell their life stories, though. They lived ordinary lives, heroic in ordinary ways and minus the drama and conflict of a romance novel. Instead I took inspiration from them.

Like my mother and her sisters, the Summerfields are left to fend for themselves at a young age. My mother's parents died when my mother was barely in her twenties and her youngest sister was still in high school. Their brother, the oldest, had already married and had children of his own, so the three sisters needed to band together to take care of each other. As a result, my mother and my aunts were extremely close their whole lives. My aunt Loraine even lived with us until I was a teenager. There was not a day that went by that she and my mother did not talk on the phone, nor a week pass without them calling my aunt Gerry, who lived some distance away.

I wanted my Summerfield sisters to have this closeness to each other and to their brother. I wanted to honor that special bond I saw in my mother and aunts, a bond I share with my own two sisters.

I hope you enjoy book one of The Scandalous Summerfields.

Diane Gaston

Bound by Duty

HARLEQUIN®HISTORICAL

Recycling programs
for this product may
not exist in your area.

ISBN-13: 978-0-373-29829-7

Bound by Duty

Printed in U.S.A.

www.Harlequin.com

Diane Gaston always said that if she were not a mental health social worker, she'd want to be a romance novelist, writing the historical romances she loved to read. When this dream came true, she discovered a whole new world of friends and happy endings. Diane lives in Virginia near Washington, DC, with her husband and three very ordinary house cats. She loves to hear from readers! Contact her at dianegaston.com, or on Facebook or Twitter.

Books by Diane Gaston

Harlequin Historical

The Scandalous Summerfields
Bound by Duty

The Masquerade Club
A Reputation for Notoriety
A Marriage of Notoriety
A Lady of Notoriety

Three Soldiers
Gallant Officer, Forbidden Lady
Chivalrous Captain, Rebel Mistress
Valiant Soldier, Beautiful Enemy

Linked by character
The Diamonds of Welbourne Manor
"Justine and the Noble Viscount"
A Not So Respectable Gentleman?

Harlequin Historical *Undone!* ebooks
The Unlacing of Miss Leigh
The Liberation of Miss Finch

Visit the Author Profile page at Harlequin.com for more titles.

To the memory of my mother, Teresa Gaston, a kind and gentle soul who was always quietly there for me, and who would never, ever, hurt anyone's feelings.

Chapter One

February 1815—Lincolnshire, England

The winter wind rattled the windowpanes of Summerfield House as Tess Summerfield answered her older sister's summons.

Come to the morning room immediately, her note said.

More bad news, Tess feared. It seemed lately that the only time Lorene summoned her and their youngest sister, Genna, to that parlour was to hear bad news.

The wind's wail seemed appropriately foreboding.

The morning room on its best sunny days filled with light, but this day it seemed awash in grey. Lorene stood ominously by the fireplace. Genna sat sulkily in a nearby chair.

'What is it, Lorene?' Tess asked.

Lorene had been acting oddly lately, leaving the house on unexplained errands and remaining away for hours.

Their father's sudden death two months ago had seemed the worst of circumstances, but shortly afterwards they'd also discovered that he'd depleted their dowries before he died. Next, the distant cousin who was to inherit their father's title and property made it very clear he had no intention of providing for them. After all, everyone believed the scandalous Summerfield sisters were really not Summerfields at all. Rumour always had it that each had been sired by a different lover.

Before their mother ran off with one, that was.

This heir to their father's baronetcy also made it clear he wished to take possession of the entailed property as soon as possible and that meant the sisters must vacate the house, their home for all their lives.

What more could happen to them?

'Please sit,' Lorene said, her lovely face lined with stress.

Tess exchanged a glance with Genna and sat as instructed.

Lorene paced in front of them. 'I know we all have been worried over what would become of us—'

Worry was too mild a term. Tess expected they would be split apart, forced to take positions as governesses or lady's companions, if they should be so lucky as to find such positions, given the family's reputation.

'I—I have come upon a solution.' Lorene sent them each a worried look.

If it was a solution, why did she appear so worried? 'What is it, Lorene?'

Lorene wrung her hands. 'I—I discovered a way to restore your dowries. A way to make you eligible again.'

It would take a sizeable dowry to erase the scandal that had dogged them their whole lives. If their mother's abandonment were not enough, there was also their father's scandal. Even before their mother left, he'd brought his bastard son home to rear. Of course, Tess and her sisters loved Edmund; he was their brother, after all, even if his presence generated more talk.

'What nonsense,' Genna grumbled. 'Nothing makes us

eligible. Our mother had too many lovers. That is why we look nothing alike.'

That was not entirely true. They all had high foreheads and thin faces, even if Lorene was dark-haired with brown eyes, Genna was blue-eyed and blonde, and Tess was somewhere in between, with chestnut hair and hazel eyes.

Like their mother, Tess was told, although she did not remember precisely what her mother looked like.

A thought occurred to her. 'Lorene, do not say that you found our mother. Is she restoring our dowries?'

Tess had been only nine when their mother left.

Lorene looked surprised. 'Our mother? No. No. That is not it.'

'What is it, then?' Genna asked testily.

Lorene stopped pacing and faced them both. 'I have married.'

'Married!' Tess rose from her chair. 'Married!'

'You cannot have married,' Genna protested. 'There were no bans.'

'It was by special licence.'

No. Impossible! Lorene would never have kept such a big secret from Tess. They shared every confidence—almost.

'Who?' she asked, trying not to feel hurt.

Lorene's voice dropped to a whisper. 'Lord Tinmore.'

'Lord Tinmore?' Tess and Genna exclaimed in unison.

'The recluse?' Tess asked.

Since the deaths of his wife and son years before, Lord Tinmore had secluded himself on his nearby estate in Lincolnshire, not too distant from their village of Yardney. Tess could not think of a time Lorene could have met the man, let alone be courted by him. No one saw Lord Tinmore.

'He must be eighty years old!' cried Genna.

Lorene lifted her chin. 'He is only seventy-six.'

'Seventy-six. So much better.' Genna spoke with sarcasm.

Her adored older sister married to an ancient recluse? This was too much to bear. 'Why, Lorene? Why would you do such a thing?'

Lorene's eyes flashed. 'I did it for you, Tess. For both of you. Lord Tinmore promised to provide you with dowries and host you for a Season in London. He will even send Edmund the funds to purchase an advancement in the army and the means to support its expenses. He is a fine man.'

She married this man so they could have dowries? And Edmund, advancement?

'I never asked you for a dowry,' Genna said. 'And Edmund can earn advancement on his own.'

'You know he cannot, now that the war is over,' Lorene shot back. 'He does not have enough as it is. It costs him money to be an officer, you know.'

Genna shook her head. 'Did our dowries not provide Edmund enough?'

Their father had used the last of their dowry money to purchase the lieutenancy for Edmund.

Lorene leaped to Edmund's defence. 'Edmund has no knowledge of that fact, Genna, and you are never to tell him. He would be sick about it if he knew. Besides, Papa intended to recoup the funds for our dowries. He assured me his latest investment would yield all we would need.'

Of course, it would most likely go the way all his too-good-to-be-true investments went. If it paid off now, which was unlikely, the money would go to the estate's heir. Their father's will provided only for their now non-existent dowries.

But Lorene would say nothing bad about their father. Or

about anyone. She believed the best of everyone. Even their mother. Lorene would insist that abandoning her daughters had been the right thing for their mother, because she'd run off with a man she truly loved.

What of the love a mother should have for her children? Tess wondered.

Now Lorene was making the same mistake as their parents—engaging in a loveless marriage.

She glared at Lorene. 'You cannot possibly love Lord Tinmore.'

'No, I do not love him,' Lorene admitted. 'But that is beside the point.'

'Beside what point?' Tess shot back. 'Did you learn nothing from our parents? You will be miserable. You will make him miserable.'

'I will not.' Lorene straightened her spine. 'I promised I would devote my life to making him happy and I intend to keep my promise.'

'But what of you?' Tess asked.

Lorene averted her gaze. 'I could not think of what else to do. What would become of you and Genna if I did nothing?' Her question required no answer. They all knew what fate had been in store for them.

'Well, you did not have to fall on your sword for us,' Genna said.

'I thought about it a great deal,' Lorene went on, seemingly ignoring Genna's comment. 'It made sense. If I had done nothing, we all would have faced dismal lives. By marrying Lord Tinmore, you and Edmund have hope. With good dowries you can marry as you wish. You will not be desperate.'

What Lorene meant was that she, Genna and even Edmund could now marry for love. They could avoid the unhappiness of their parents and still have security. They had a chance for a happy life and all it had cost Lorene was her own chance for happiness.

A chance for love.

God help her, Tess felt a tiny spark of hope. If she had a dowry, Mr Welton could court her.

She turned her face away. How awful of her! To be glad for Lorene's sacrifice.

She composed herself again. 'How did you accomplish it, Lorene? How did you even meet him?'

'I went to him. I asked him to marry me and he agreed.'

Without telling her sister, the person closest to her? 'Without a courtship?'

Lorene gave Tess an exasperated look. 'What need was there for a courtship? We settled matters in a few meetings and Lord Tinmore arranged for a special licence. When his man of business procured the licence for him, the vicar of his church married us in his parlour.'

'You could have invited us,' Genna chided.

Genna was hurt, as well, obviously.

Lorene swung around to her. 'You would have tried to stop me.'

'Yes. I would have done that.' Genna spoke firmly.

The wind gusted and the windowpanes banged. Would Tess have tried to stop Lorene? She did not know.

The clouds that cast a pall on them parted and light peeked through.

They were saved. Lorene had saved them.

By sacrificing herself.

A mere two weeks later Tess Summerfield lounged on the bed in one of the many bedchambers of Tinmore Hall. This room had been given to Genna who stood behind an easel, facing the window. Lorene again paced nervously back and forth, which seemed to be her new habit.

'It is a lovely house party, is it not?' Lorene asked, looking hopefully at each of them.

'Lovely!' Tess agreed eagerly.

So much had changed so very quickly. Two days after Lorene announced her marriage, they moved out of the only home they'd ever known, taking with them no more than a trunk of belongings each. Now Lord Tinmore had invited several guests in a hastily arranged house party to introduce his new bride to his closest society friends. In another month or so they would travel to London for a whirlwind of dress fittings and hat shopping in order to show them off to best advantage when the Season began. Lorene's marriage was still a shock, but Tess could not help but be excited about what lay ahead.

She was also deeply, deeply grateful to Lorene—as well as feeling guilty.

Genna was not grateful, however. She remained as surly as the day Lorene had told them her secret.

'It is lovely, isn't it, Genna?' Tess, too, reeled from the loss of their home, but she was determined to show Lorene her support.

Genna threw her paintbrush into its jug of water and spun around. 'I hate the house party. I hate everything about it.'

'Genna!' Tess scolded.

Lorene made a placating gesture. 'It is all right. Let her speak her mind.'

Genna's face flushed. 'I cannot bear that you married that man—that *old* man—for money. His guests call you a fortune hunter and they are correct.'

'That is enough, Genna!' Tess cried. 'Especially because Lorene did it for us.'

'I did not ask for it.' Genna turned to Lorene. 'I would never have asked it of you. Ever.'

'No one asked me.' Lorene went to her and placed her hand on Genna's arm. 'Besides, the earl is a good man. Look what he has done for us already.'

He'd given them a new home at Tinmore Hall. He'd had them fitted for new dresses by the village seamstress. He was in the process of arranging dowries for her and for Genna and an allowance for Edmund whose regiment was somewhere on the Continent.

Tess sat up. 'It was a brave sacrifice. Don't you see that, Genna? We have a chance now. Lord Tinmore will provide us with respectable dowries. We're going to have a London Season where we can meet many eligible young men.'

Mr Welton would be in London. He'd said he would be there for the Season. Tess wanted so much to tell him of her changed circumstances.

Lorene squeezed Genna's arm. 'You will be able to have a choice of young men. You won't have to marry merely for a roof over your head and food in your mouth. You will be able to wait for a man you are able to truly esteem.'

'You can make a love match.' It was what Tess desired more than anything. That and to always be close to her sisters.

Lorene's tone turned earnest. 'I want you to have a love match, to have that sort of happiness.'

Tess was known as the practical sister. Sensible and resourceful. Would Lorene and Genna not be surprised to learn that she had a secret *tendre* for a man? To even think of him made her giddy with excitement.

Genna's face contorted as she faced Lorene. 'You married an ugly, smelly old man so that Tess, Edmund and I could marry for love. Bravo, Lorene. We're supposed to be happy knowing that because of us you must share his bed.'

Lorene blanched and her voice deepened. 'That part of

it is not for you to speak of. Ever. That is my private affair and mine alone. Do you hear?'

'What about your life, Lorene? What about your choices? Your love match?' Genna's voice turned shrill.

Lorene put a hand to her forehead. 'I did make a choice. I chose to do this. For you. And Lord Tinmore has been good enough to provide you with this lovely room, with your paints and paper. He's ordered us each a new wardrobe and soon he will take us all to London for even more finery—'

Genna broke in. 'And what must you do in return, Lorene?'

Lorene glared at her. She straightened and turned towards the door. 'I must go now. I must see that everything is in order for our guests. I expect you to behave properly in front of them, Genna.'

'I know how to behave properly,' Genna snapped, still recalcitrant. 'Did Papa not teach us to never behave like our mother?'

Lorene shot her one more scathing—and, Tess thought— pained look and left the room.

Tess leaped off the bed. 'Genna, how could you? That was terrible to say. About…about sharing Lord Tinmore's bed.' And about their mother.

Genna folded her arms across her chest. 'Well, it is what we think about, is it not? What she must do for him? Because of us?'

Tess felt a pang of guilt.

She took it out on Genna, walking over to her and shaking her. 'We cannot speak of it! It hurts her. You saw that.'

Genna pulled away, but looked chagrined.

Tess went on. 'We must make the best of this, for her sake. She's done us an enormous service at great sacrifice. She has given us a gift beyond measure. We are free to choose who we want to marry.' She thought of Mr Welton. 'We must not make her feel bad for it.'

'Oh, very well.' Genna turned back to her watercolour. 'But what are we to say when we hear the guests speak of her marrying Lord Tinmore for his money? Are we to say, "Yes, that is it exactly. She married him for his money and his title. Just like our mother did our father"?'

That was another truth best left unspoken.

'We pretend we do not hear anything.' Tess spoke firmly. 'We act as if Lorene's marriage to Lord Tinmore is a love match and that we are delighted for them both.'

'Hmmph. A love match between a beautiful young woman and a very old, smelly man.' Genna stabbed at her painting. 'And what do we say when they accuse *us* of exploiting Lord Tinmore, as well?'

'Us?' Tess blinked. 'Has anyone said that?'

Genna shrugged. 'Not to my face. Yet. So tell me what I ought to say when they do.'

Tess had not considered that possibility, but it made sense. In a way, she, Genna and Edmund stood to gain more from Lord Tinmore's money than Lorene. His money would open possibilities for them, possibilities that filled Tess with joy.

Until guilt stabbed at her again. 'We simply act grateful for everything he does for us, because we are grateful, are we not?'

Genna made a false smile. 'Very grateful.'

Genna bore watching. She was entirely too impetuous and plain speaking for her own good.

Tess changed the subject. 'I do not think Lord Tinmore has anything planned for us until dinner.'

The guests, all closer to his age than to his bride's, were in need of rest after travelling to Lincolnshire the day before. Tess supposed they had accepted the first invitation to Tinmore Hall in thirty years because they wanted to see what sort of woman caused Lord Tinmore to finally open his doors.

Tess dreaded their second meeting of the guests. The ladies' travelling clothes were finer than her best gown. Their dinner gowns took away her breath. The new gowns Lord Tinmore had ordered would not be ready for a week, but Tess could not bear for her and her sisters to look so shabby in the meantime.

'Would you like to walk to the village with me?' she asked.

Genna looked surprised. 'Why are you going to the village?'

'For lace and ribbons. I believe I can embellish our gowns so it does not appear as if we are wearing the same one, night after night.' They might be charity cases, but they could at least try not to look like ones.

'You are being foolish to go out.' Genna gestured to the window. 'It will rain.'

Tess glanced at the overcast sky. 'The rain should hold off until I return.'

'Well, I am not chancing it.' Genna dipped her brush in some paint.

'Very well. I can walk alone.' Tess always walked alone to Yardney, the village that once had been her home.

But it was only a few short miles from here. Obviously Lorene had walked the distance often enough to get married. Why not walk to Yardney instead of the village nearby? It would take only a little longer. If she went to Yardney she could call upon Mr Welton's aunt. If Mr Welton was still her house guest, she could tell him about having her dowry restored.

'You should take a maid or something,' Genna said. 'Is that not what wealthy wards do?'

If she wanted someone to know where she was bound, perhaps. Besides, Lord Tinmore was not their guardian. They'd not been appointed a guardian after their father died. There had been no property or fortune to protect. They were under Lord Tinmore's protection, though.

'Lord Tinmore will not care if I walk to the village when I've been walking the countryside my whole life.' At least Tess hoped he would not care. She and Genna had hardly seen him, only for a few meals. She opened the door. 'In any event, I am going.' With luck she could change their dresses by dinnertime and see to her future, as well.

Genna did not look away from her watercolour. 'Well, if it pours and you get soaking wet and catch your death of a cold, do not expect *me* to wipe your nose.'

That was much how their father had become ill. Surely Genna did not realise.

'I never catch colds.' Tess walked out of the room, closing the door behind her.

The rain did not begin until Tess left Yardney and was already on the road back to Tinmore Hall. The first drops that splattered the dirt road quickly grew to a heavy downpour. Moments later it was as if the heavens had decided to tip over all their buckets at once. In mere minutes Tess's cloak was soaked through. Even her purchases, wrapped in paper and string and held under her cloak, were becoming wet.

'Genna, you are going to gloat,' she muttered.

But it had been worth it. Tess discovered that Mr Welton had indeed left for London, but he knew about Lorene's marriage. She told his aunt about her changed circumstances.

He would find her when Lord Tinmore took them all to town for the Season. Only a few more weeks.

Mud from the road stuck to Tess's half-boots, and it became an effort merely to lift one foot in front of the other. Water poured from the drooping brim of her hat and the raindrops hit her face like needles of ice. She had at least two miles to go before she'd cross through the gatehouse of the estate.

The mud grabbed at her half-boots like some devious creature bent on stopping her. Trying to quicken her pace was futile, but at last she spied the bridge ahead through the thick sheets of rain.

But the stream now rushed over it.

'No!' Her protest was swallowed by the wind.

What now? She did not know of any other way to reach Tinmore Hall. There was no choice but to walk to the nearby village as she ought to have done in the first place. The rain was cutting into her like knives now, not needles.

She glanced at the wooded area next to the road. If this were home, she'd know precisely how to cut through the woods and cross the fields. She might be home already, sitting in front of a fire, letting the heat penetrate instead of this rain. Here she did not dare leave the road that she knew led to Tinmore Village.

Do not think, she told herself. *Just put one foot in front of the other.* Despair nudged at her resolve.

She walked and walked until she thought she saw a vague outline of the village church tower. She hurried on, but up ahead water was streaming across the road. She could not go forward. She could not go back.

But she could go home, home to Yardney, at least. Perhaps she would seek shelter at Mr Welton's aunt's house. Or knock at the door of Summerfield House.

She turned back, retracing her steps, passing the road leading to the blocked bridge. A short distance from there, the road was flooded. Turning back again, she walked until she found another road, not knowing where it would lead her.

If only she were closer to home. She would be able to turn in any direction and find someone's house who would welcome her, but she no longer knew where she was or how to find her way to anywhere familiar. She was lost, wet and terribly cold.

Chapter Two

Marc Glenville cursed the rain.

Why there must be a downpour while he was on horse-back on his way to London was beyond him. Unless the gods of weather somehow caught his mood.

Returning to London was never a joy.

But there was nothing else for him to do. His business in Scotland was complete.

His horse faltered and his head dipped. A stream of water trickled down his back.

Business in Scotland. Ha!

That was the fiction he told his parents and would tell anyone else who questioned his whereabouts these last long months, but it was not the truth.

He'd been to France. Paris and the countryside, mixing with Bonapartists and others discontented with returning Louis XVIII to the throne, keeping an ear tuned to whether discontent was apt to erupt in insurrection.

All for king and country.

Unrest was not widespread. The French, like the British, were fatigued with war. Mark had made his reports. No more would be asked of him.

It was time to face more personal matters.

Time to face again the fact that his brother would never again grin at him from across the dinner table and his best friend would never again come to call. When he was pretending to be Monsieur Renard, *citoyen ordinaire* of France, he could almost forget that Lucien, his brother, had been gone for four years and Charles, not quite three. Whenever he returned, though, he half-expected to see them walk through the door when he was home.

Grief shot through him like a bolt of lightning.

Foolish Lucien. Reckless Charles. They'd died so needlessly.

Marc willed his emotions to cool, lifting his face to the rain that was already chilling his bones. Best to keep emotions in control. When deep in espionage, it could save his life; back in London, it might save his sanity.

Good God. Was the near-freezing rain begetting gloomy thoughts as well as soaking him to the bone? Concentrate on the road and on his poor horse. Slogging through muddy, rut-filled roads was a battle, even for the sturdy fellow.

The stallion blew out a breath.

'Hard going, eh, Apollo?' Marc patted the horse's neck.

He'd hoped to reach Peterborough by nightfall, but that was not in the cards in this weather. He'd be lucky to make the next village, whatever that was, and hope its inn had a room with a clean bed.

The rain had forced him off the main route and he and Apollo were inching their way through any roads that remained passable.

The delay did not bother him overmuch. No one was expecting him. He'd not informed his parents he was coming to town. Let it be a surprise.

Marc dreaded the family visit, always, but it was time to take his place as heir, now that duty did not call him elsewhere. He'd call upon Doria Caldwell, Charles's sister, and make official what had been implied between them since Charles was killed. He owed that much to Charles.

Besides, the Caldwell family, now consisting only of her and her father, was so ordinary and respectable—and rational—he would relish being a part of it.

Lightning flashed through the sky and thunder boomed. Was he now to be struck by real lightning, instead of being struck figuratively?

He must be near a village; he'd been riding long enough. Gazing up ahead, he hoped to see rooftops in the distance or a road sign or any indication that shelter might be near, but the rain formed a grey curtain that obscured all but a few feet in front of him. What's more, the curtain seemed to move with him, keeping him engulfed in the gloom and making his eyelids grow heavy.

Lightning flashed again and he thought he'd seen someone in the road. He peered harder until through the curtain of rain a figure took form. It was a woman on foot, not yet hearing his horse coming up from behind.

'Halloo, there!' he called out. 'Halloo!'

The woman, shrouded in a dark cloak, turned and waved her hands for him to stop.

As if any gentleman could pass by.

He rode up to her and dismounted. 'Madam, where are you bound? May I offer some assistance?'

She looked up at him. She was a young woman, pretty enough, though her face was stiff with anxiety and exhaustion. 'I want to go to Tinmore Hall.' It seemed an effort for her to speak.

'Point the way,' he responded. 'I'll carry you on my horse.'

She shook her head. 'No use. Floods. Floods everywhere. Cannot get there. Cannot get to the village.' Her voice shook from the cold.

He extended a hand. 'Come. I'll lift you on to my horse.' Her cloak was as wet as if it had been pulled from a laundry bath. Her hat had lost any shape at all. Worse, her lips were blue. 'We'll find a place to get you dry.'

She nodded, but there was no expression in her pale eyes.

She handed him a sodden parcel which he stuffed in one of his saddlebags. He lifted her on to Apollo and mounted behind her. 'Are you comfortable? Do you feel secure?'

She nodded again and shivered from the cold.

He encircled her in his arms, but that offered little relief from the cold. He took the reins. Poor Apollo, even more burdened now, started forward again.

'I am not from here.' He spoke loudly to be heard through the rain's din. 'How far to the next village?'

She turned her head. 'Lost. Yardney—cannot find it.'

Yardney must be a nearby village. 'We'll find it.' He'd been telling himself he'd find a village this last hour or more.

She shivered again. 'Cold,' she said. 'So cold.'

He'd better find her shelter quickly and get her warm. People died of cold.

She leaned against him and her muscles relaxed.

He rode on and found a crossroads with a sign pointing to Kirton.

'See?' he shouted, pointing to the sign. 'Kirton.'

She did not answer him.

A little further on, the road was filled with water. He turned around and backtracked until he came to the crossroads again, taking the other route. Someone was farming the lands here. There must be houses about.

If only he could see them through the rain.

The road led to a narrower, rougher road, until it became little more than a path. He followed it as it wound back and forth. Hoping he was not wasting more precious time, he peered ahead looking for anything with a roof and walls.

A little cottage appeared in front of them. No candles shone in the windows, though. No smoke rose from the chimney. With luck it would be dry.

'Look!' he called to his companion, but she did not answer.

Apollo gained a spurt of energy, cantering to the promise of shelter. As they came closer, a small stable also came into view and he guided Apollo to its door. He dismounted carefully, holding on to her. She slipped off, into his arms. Lifting her over his shoulder, he unlatched the stable door. Apollo walked in immediately.

Marc lay the woman down on a dry patch of floor. 'Cold,' she murmured, curling into a ball.

At least she was alive.

He turned back to his horse, patting him on the neck. 'She comes first, old fellow. I'll tend to you as soon as I can.'

He left the stable and hurried up to the door of the cabin. He pounded on it, but there was no answer and the door was locked. He peered in a window, but the inside was dark. Reaching in a pocket inside his greatcoat, he pulled out a set of skeleton keys—what self-respecting spy would be without skeleton keys? He tried several before one clicked and the latch turned.

The light from outside did little to illuminate the interior of the cabin, but Marc immediately spied a fireplace and a cot with folded blankets atop it. It was enough.

He hurried back to the stable.

Apollo whinnied at his return. 'You'll have to wait a bit longer, old fellow.'

He lifted the woman again, her sodden garments making her an even heavier burden. She groaned as he put her over his shoulder and hurried back through the rain to the cabin door.

His first task was to get her wet clothes off. He placed her on the floor where it would not matter if her clothes left a puddle. After tossing off his greatcoat, he worked as quickly as he could, cutting the laces of her dress and her corset and stripping her down to her bare skin.

She tried to cover herself, but not out of modesty. 'Cold,' she whimpered.

She was a beauty. Full, high breasts, narrow waist and long, shapely legs. He swallowed at the sight, but allowed himself only a glance before grabbing a blanket and wrapping it around her. He carried her to the cot and wrapped the second blanket around her.

By this time his eyes were accustomed to the darkness of the room. He saw a stack of wood and kindling and a scuttle of coal. On top of the fireplace were tapers and a flint. He hurried to make a fire. When it burned well enough, he flung his greatcoat around him again and ran back out in the rain to tend to Apollo.

The stable was well stocked with dry cloths and brushes. He dried off the poor horse as best he could, covering him with a blanket. There was hay, which Apollo ate eagerly, and a pump from which Marc drew fresh water to quench Apollo's thirst.

'There you are, old fellow.' He stroked Apollo's neck. 'That is all I can do for you. Soon the rain must stop and, with luck, we will be on our way before night falls. For now, eat and rest and I will check on you later.'

Marc ran back through the unrelenting rain to the cabin. He checked on his new charge. Her cheeks had some colour, thank God, and her skin seemed a bit warmer to the touch. Her features had relaxed and she slept.

He blew out a relieved breath and, for the first time, realised he, too, was wet and cold and weary. He stripped down to his shirt and breeches and pulled a chair as near to the fire as he could. He really ought to hang up their wet clothes to dry, but the warmth of the fire was too enticing. Instead he stared at the woman.

She was lovely, but who was she?

Hers was a strong face, with full lips and an elegant nose. Her brows arched appealingly and her lashes were thick. He could not tell from her clothing what her station in life might be. What sort of woman would be walking in the rain? She mentioned Tinmore Hall. Lord Tinmore's estate? Perhaps she was in service there.

If he could look at her hands, he might learn more. Were they rough from work? They were tucked beneath the blanket. Her hair was pulled back in a simple knot such as any woman might wear on a walk to the village. It would never dry that way.

He reached over and pulled the pins from her dark hair and unwound it from its knot. He spread it over the pillow as best he could. He leaned back.

Good God, now she looked like some classical goddess. Aphrodite, perhaps. Goddess of love, beauty, pleasure.

When she woke, would she wish for pleasure? His blood raced.

It did more to warm him than the fire.

Tess woke to the crash of a thunderclap and the constant keen of rain. She remembered walking. She remembered the rain soaking into her clothing.

Her clothing!

She sat upright. She was covered by a blanket, nothing more.

'You are awake,' a man's voice said.

He sat on a nearby chair. That was right—a man on a horse. She'd really seen him, then.

'Where am I?' she rasped. Her throat was dry. 'Where are my clothes?'

'I fashioned a clothes line and hung them.' He pointed behind her.

She turned and saw her cloak, her dress, her corset and her shift hanging from a rope strung across the room. Next to her clothes were a man's greatcoat, coat and waistcoat.

He continued talking. 'We are in a cabin somewhere in Lincolnshire, but blast if I know where. You fell victim to the cold. I had to get you dry and warm or...' He ended with a shrug of a shoulder.

'You brought me here?' And removed her clothing? Her cheeks burned at the thought.

'It was shelter. It was dry and stocked with firewood and coal.'

Tess blinked and gazed about her. It was a small cabin with what looked like a scullery in one corner. It was furnished with a table and chairs, the chair he sat upon, and a bed pulled close to the fire.

She was warm, she realised.

The man shifted position and his face was lit by the firelight. His hair was as dark as a raven's wing, with thick brows to match and the shadow of a beard. In contrast, his eyes were a piercing blue. She had never seen a man quite like him and he was dressed in only his shirt and breeches. Even his feet were bare.

A breath caught in her throat. 'Who are you?' The blanket slipped off her shoulder and she pulled it about her again.

He stood. He was taller than her half-brother and Edmund reached six feet. 'I am Marc Glenville.' He bowed. 'At your service.' His thick brows rose. 'And you are?'

Tess swallowed. 'I am Miss Tess Summerfield.' She frowned. She ought to have introduced herself as *Miss Summerfield*. Lorene was Lady Tinmore now, so Tess had become the eldest unmarried sister.

She touched her hair. It was loose! What had happened to her hair?

'I took out your hairpins.' The man—Mr Glenville—sat again. 'I did undress you, Miss Summerfield, but only because you were suffering from the cold. I give you my word as a gentleman, it was necessary. A person can die from the cold.'

He was a gentleman. His accent, his bearing, were that of a gentleman.

'I do not remember any of it.' She shook her head.

'A function of the cold. An indication that there was some urgency in getting you warm.' His voice was deep and smooth and soothing.

She ought to be more frightened, to be in a strange place, with a strange man. Naked. But it had been far more frightening to be wandering for hours in the chilling rain.

'I must thank you, sir,' she murmured. 'It seems I owe you my life.'

He glanced away as if fending off her words. 'It was luck. I found this cabin by luck. A groundskeeper's cabin, I suspect, used only when he works this part of the property.'

She looked around the cabin once more.

He stood again. 'Are you hungry? I have a kettle ready to make tea.'

She nodded. 'Tea would be lovely.'

He hung the kettle above the fire and reached over to pick up what looked like a saddlebag near his chair.

'Your horse!' She remembered a horse.

He smiled again. 'Apollo.'

Was the animal out in the rain? 'You must bring him in here.'

He made a calming gesture with his hand. 'Do not fear. Apollo is warm and dry in a stable, with plenty of water and hay. I've checked on him. He was quite content. I will check on him again in a few minutes.' He carried the saddlebags over to the table, searched inside them and pulled out a tin and an oilskin package.

When he walked to the scullery and his back was turned, Tess rose from the bed and, careful to keep the blankets around her, went to check her clothing. Her dress was still very wet, but her shift was almost dry.

'Mr Glenville?' She pulled her shift from the line.

He turned. 'Yes?'

She clutched her shift to her chest. 'Will you please keep your back turned? I—I wish to don my shift.'

Without saying a word, he turned his back again and faced the window.

Marc watched her reflection in the window. Not very well done of him, but he was unable to resist. Her figure was every bit as tantalising from the back as from the front.

No harm in looking.

Except he could feel his body stir in response. He resumed his search for teacups and a teapot. He found the pot, but had to settle for two Toby jugs.

'You can look now.' Her voice turned low. Did she know how seductive it was?

'Is your shift dry?' he asked, trying to sound matter-of-fact rather than like a man battling his baser urges.

'It is a little damp, but I feel better wearing it.' She was still wrapped up in the blanket.

He lifted the jugs for her to see. 'These will have to do for tea. Who the devil knows why they are here?' He placed them on the table. 'Do you mind waiting for tea? I should check on my horse.'

'Apollo?' She remembered the name. 'Of course I do not mind. I should feel terrible if your horse suffered because of me.'

Was this sarcasm? He peered at her, but saw only concern on her face.

Consideration of his horse's well-being was nearly as seductive as her naked reflection and her lowered voice.

He took his greatcoat off the rope and threw it over his shoulders. 'I will only be a moment. I'll tend to the tea when I return.' He stepped outside.

The mud beneath his bare feet felt painfully cold, but that was preferable to wearing his sodden boots even if he were able to get his feet into them. The rain had slowed, but the sun was low in the sky. Even if the rain stopped, the roads would not improve before dark.

He and Miss Summerfield would spend the night together.

It would be a long, painful night. No matter what his body demanded, he would not take advantage of her. Besides, he well knew a man must keep his passions in check.

On the other hand, if she approached him…?

Apollo whinnied.

'How are you faring, old fellow? Are you warm enough?' He ran his hand down the length of the horse's neck.

He and Apollo had been through adventures more dangerous than this one, but Marc was sorry to have subjected the stallion to one more hardship.

He found a blanket to put over Apollo. 'This will keep

you warm.' He mucked out the stable and replenished the hay and water before returning to the cabin.

When he opened the door Miss Summerfield handed him a towel. 'I found this. You can dry your feet.'

The cabin was brighter. 'You lit lamps.'

'Only two, so I could see to fix the tea.' She walked to the table. 'It has been steeping. It should be ready.'

She fixed the tea?

'Come, we can sit.' She walked over to the table.

She still wore a blanket, but she'd fashioned it like a tunic and belted it with a rope. 'You've made yourself a garment.'

She turned and smiled, making her face even lovelier. 'I devised a way that the blanket will not fall off me if I wish to use my arms. I suppose I should leave a coin to pay for cutting holes in the blanket for my head and for the belt.'

He hung up his greatcoat. 'I would say you are resourceful.'

She smiled again. 'Thank you.'

He sat at the table and she poured him a Toby jug of tea.

'I could not find any sugar,' she said.

'No matter.' His fingers grazed hers as he reached for the jug. He glanced at her hands and saw no evidence of hard work in them.

She sat and poured herself some tea. 'I have never drunk tea from jugs like this. I have never drunk anything from Toby jugs. I have seen some like them in the village shop, though.'

He frowned. A well-bred young lady might not have used a Toby jug. Perhaps a woman in service would not have used a Toby jug either.

Who was this Miss Tess Summerfield?

He took a sip of tea and tapped his jug with his fingers. 'You said something about Tinmore Hall when I picked you up. Are you employed there?'

'Employed there?' She looked puzzled. 'No, I live there. Now, that is. We—my sisters and I—recently moved there.' She paused as if trying to decide to say more. 'My sister Lorene is the new Lady Tinmore.'

But this made no sense. 'I thought the old lord was still alive. He had a grandson?'

She met his eye. 'Lord Tinmore is still alive and he has no grandson. My sister married the old lord.'

His brows shot up. 'The old lord? The man must be in his seventies.'

'He is nearly eighty.' She lifted her chin. 'How do you know Lord Tinmore?'

He took a sip of tea. 'I do not know him. I know of him. My father went to school with his son and I remember my father mentioning the son's death. It was sudden, as I recall.' He stared at her. 'Your sister married a man in his seventies?'

'Yes.' Her gaze did not waver.

She was sister to Lord Tinmore's wife? Well, she certainly was not a housemaid, then.

He'd wager the old earl did not marry below his station—most men of his social stature did not. Most gentlemen were wiser than that.

'Who is Tess Summerfield that an earl would marry your sister?' he asked.

She met his eye. 'I am the second daughter of the late Sir Hollis Summerfield of Yardney.'

Sir Hollis?

Ah, yes. Sir Hollis. He'd heard of him. Or rather, he'd heard of his wife. It was said his wife had had so many lovers her daughters were sired by different men and none of them her husband.

Even so, they must have been reared as respectable

young ladies and now were under the protection of the Earl of Tinmore.

He rubbed his forehead. 'This changes matters. We must be very careful not to be discovered together.'

She sat up straighter. 'I have no intention of being found with you! I assure you I hope to be gone as soon as the rain stops.'

He did not have the heart to tell her that it would likely be dark before then.

She took another sip of tea. 'I am sorry, Mr Glenville. I did not mean to sound so ungrateful. You might have left me in the road.'

He opened his eyes and gazed at her. Her expression was soft and lovely.

'You did not sound ungrateful, Miss Tess Summerfield.' He savoured the sound of her name.

She blushed, as though she had read his thoughts. 'I know what you did for me,' she said quietly. 'You rescued me. And I do realise that being alone with you in this cabin, especially in my state of undress, is a very compromising situation.'

She was direct; he appreciated that.

'I have no wish to see you ruined,' he explained. 'That is all I meant.'

She faced him again. 'All I need is to reach the road back to Tinmore Hall. I will tell no one where I've been or who I've been with. If you can help me get that far, you can trust that I will say nothing of this. Ever.'

'I will see you to safety.' He'd always intended to do so. 'And I, also, will say nothing of this.'

She extended her hand across the table. 'Let us shake on it.'

He placed his large, rough hand in her smaller, smooth one. 'We have a bargain, Miss Summerfield.'

Chapter Three

Up so close, Mr Glenville's blue eyes shone with such intensity Tess could not look away. Nor could she move her hand from his strong grasp. Her face grew warm.

'Are you hungry, Miss Summerfield?' he asked, releasing her.

'A little,' she managed. She was famished.

He pulled the oilskin package towards him. 'I have some bread and cheese here.' He untied the string and unfolded the oilskin. Inside was a small loaf of bread and a wedge of cheese. He tore the bread in half and handed her a piece.

It was damp, but she did not care. She took an eager bite.

He broke off a piece of the cheese for her.

It was all she could do not to gobble it down.

'Do not eat too fast,' he warned, taking a bite of the cheese.

His manner had changed in a way she did not quite understand, but his gaze warmed her as effectively as the fire.

He'd shown her nothing but kindness. Indeed, he'd saved her life. How awful it would be to have someone discover them here. Some women might use such a situation to trap a man into marriage.

It would be dreadful to base a marriage on an accidental mishap. Even Lorene's marriage made more sense than that.

She took sips of tea between bites and held the doughy taste of the flour and the sharp tang of the cheese in her mouth as long as she could. If she had been served wet bread and cheese at someone's dinner table or at an inn, she would have been outraged.

'How can I thank you, Mr Glenville?' she murmured. 'This is ambrosia.'

He glanced at her and his eyes still filled her with heat.

He quickly looked away. 'Tell me why you were out walking in a rainstorm.' It was said conversationally.

She waved a dismissive hand. 'I had an errand in the village.'

'It must have been important.'

It had not been. It had been foolish. She'd hoped to see Mr Welton. And to buy ribbons.

Her ribbons! 'I had a parcel… Was I carrying a parcel when you found me?'

He lifted a finger and leaned down to pull something out of his saddlebags. He held it up to her. 'A parcel.'

She took it.

'The reason for your walk to the village?' He inclined his head towards the parcel.

She felt her cheeks burn. 'Ribbons and lace.'

He responded with surprise.

She shrugged. 'It may not seem important to you, but it was to me.' Even more important had been learning about Mr Welton. 'Besides, I thought the rain would hold off until later in the day.'

He took another bite of cheese.

She pulled off a piece of bread and rolled it into a ball in her fingers. 'So why were you out in the rain?'

He swallowed. 'I am travelling to London.'

She kept up the challenge. 'And set off even though there was threat of rain?'

He lifted his Toby jug, as if in a toast, and smiled. 'Point taken.'

If his eyes had power, so much more did that smile.

Tess lowered her voice. 'I am glad you set off even though there was a threat of rain. What would have happened to me had you been wiser?'

'Someone else would have found you,' he said.

She shook her head. 'I walked for hours. I saw no one else on the road.'

He held her gaze with those riveting eyes.

She glanced away. 'Why were you bound for London?'

'I finished my business in Scotland.' He lifted his Toby jug. 'So I am returning to London.'

'Do you have business in London?'

He sipped his tea. 'Of a sort.'

A sort of which he obviously did not want to discuss.

'I shall be travelling to London soon,' she said, trying to cover her sudden discomfort. 'For the Season. Will you be attending the Season's entertainments?'

His face turned serious. 'I am not certain.'

She felt as though he had withdrawn from her completely, but she did not know why. Perhaps he'd tired of her conversation. She felt suddenly as lonely as she had been when wandering in the storm. She missed her sisters. They would think she was in Tinmore. Tess hoped they would presume she was safe. If only she could get back to them soon.

She finished her piece of bread and cheese, and he wrapped up the rest of his food.

It turned deadly quiet.

'The rain!' she cried. 'I think the rain has stopped!'

She jumped from her chair at the same time as he and they hurried to the door. Both stood there for a moment staring at it.

He reached over and opened it.

The rain had stopped, but it was black outside.

She looked over at him. 'There is no chance we can leave now, is there?'

'None,' he responded. 'It is too wet and too dark. I am afraid we are here all night.'

All night.

Marc wished he could erase the disappointment on her face.

To her credit she said not one word of complaint, even though their situation was now clearly worse than before. Instead she busied herself pouring more hot water from the kettle into the teapot. She did not complain, but, then, she did not say anything.

A cold wind soon rattled the windows and put even more chill into the cabin. Marc rooted through the room again. He found two more blankets, stored in a chest tucked in a far corner. One for her; one for him. He handed her one and they pulled chairs from the table to be near the fire. They wrapped themselves in their blankets, sipped weak, but hot, tea and stared into the fire.

He felt as if he'd lost her company.

He wanted it back. 'Do you go to London for the marriage mart, then?' he asked.

She jumped. He'd startled her.

'I would not choose those words, precisely.' Her voice was hesitant. 'My younger sister and I will come out. We might even be presented to the queen, if Lord Tinmore requests it.'

'I am surprised,' he said.

'Why?' she shot back. 'Why should we not be presented?'

He held up a hand. 'I am surprised any lady would wish all that fuss.'

Miss Summerfield stiffened. 'It would be an honour.'

Did his sister wish it? If so, it would never happen for her.

'An honour, indeed, I suppose,' he said.

'As would procuring vouchers for Almack's,' she went on. 'Will you be getting a voucher for Almack's?'

He gave a dry laugh. 'Not likely.' The London Season was not a good time for his family.

She gazed into the fire. 'Why not? I thought you were high born.'

He sat up straight again. 'Why did you think that?'

'You said your father went to school with Lord Tinmore's son.'

He had said that.

'I am high born.' But he'd been deliberately evasive about who he was. Now that they were to spend the night together, she might as well know. 'You have likely heard of Viscount Northdon?'

She looked blank. 'No.'

She must be the one person in England who had not heard of Viscount Northdon. 'You see, Miss Summerfield, I come from a family with a tarnished reputation. Viscount Northdon is my father and, because he married my mother, our family is not accepted in the highest circles of society.'

He expected to see curiosity in her expression. Instead, he saw sympathy.

It touched him more deeply than he was willing to admit and made him go on. 'My mother is French and came from trade.' It pained him to say the rest. 'But that is not the worst of it. Her father became active in the Terror.' He cleared his throat. 'Hence we are not welcome at Almack's.'

She lowered her gaze and spoke in a quiet voice. 'It is likely our family will not receive vouchers to Almack's, either, even if Lord Tinmore wishes it.' She raised her eyes to him. 'I, too, have a scandalous mother.'

'I have heard of your mother,' he admitted. He'd also heard she'd abandoned her husband and children to run away with one of her lovers.

Pain filled Miss Summerfield's eyes. 'I suppose everyone has heard of our mother.' She pulled her knees up so that her feet rested on the chair's seat. 'I expect they will stare wherever we go. And whisper—'

He knew firsthand she was correct. 'Lord Tinmore's reputation will ease matters for you.'

'Yes.' Her expression filled with resolve. 'Lord Tinmore will do much for us.'

He could reassure her even more. 'Your sister will be seen as having made a brilliant match. No reason you cannot do the same.' Especially with her face and her figure.

'I do not want to wish to make a brilliant match,' she snapped. 'My parents made a brilliant match and look what happened to them.'

And look what happened to his parents for making such an unwise one.

She rested her chin on her knees. 'I do not care about titles or position. I want to marry someone who will love me for myself and who will not care what members of my family have done.'

'Love?' His parents had married for love. Or at least for the physical desire that so often masquerades as love. 'Better to make a marriage of mutual advantage.'

'My parents married for advantage,' she said. 'Believe me, it does not work.'

Such a marriage had a better chance than one made out of love. Love led to rash acts and later regrets.

And constant discord.

'What say you of your sister's marriage, then?' The woman had not married the man out of passion, that was for certain.

She uncurled herself and leaned towards him. 'What can you know about my sister's marriage?'

'I can guess she thought it to her advantage to marry Lord Tinmore.' Why Tinmore might have married her was not a topic for the ears of a young lady.

'That she married him for his money, do you mean?' Her voice rose.

'Of course she married for money. And a title. And Lord Tinmore gained a young wife and a reason to emerge from seclusion. There is no shame in any of that.'

She settled back in her chair and crossed her arms over her chest. 'Lorene had no wish for a title or wealth any more than I do.'

That he very much doubted. 'Then what were her reasons?'

The pain returned to Miss Summerfield's eyes. 'She did it for us. For me and for Genna. And even Edmund. So we—so we could have a chance for decent, happy lives. So Genna and I could have dowries. So we could marry as we wish. And—and not be forced to accept just any offer. So we would not have to become lady's companions or governesses.' She took a breath. 'I assure you, Lorene married Lord Tinmore for the noblest of reasons.'

'Your situation was that dire?' he asked quietly.

She nodded.

'Then I commend your sister even more. I wish her well.' He'd sacrifice for his sister, if he could.

Her brows knitted. 'I fear she will be miserable.' Her

chin set. 'That is why I am determined that I should make a love match and be happy. For my sister.'

He peered at her. 'You would allow your heart to rule your choice?'

'I would insist upon it.'

He tapped his temple. 'Better to use your head, Miss Summerfield.'

She lifted her chin. 'How can you know? You are not married, are you?'

'Married? No.' But he did speak from experience.

When his father had embarked on his Grand Tour as a young man, he met Marc's mother and eloped with her. They continued his tour for a passionate year, but their wedded bliss ended almost immediately when they set foot back on English soil.

'Believe me, Miss Summerfield. A marriage is best contracted by one's brain, not one's heart.' Or one's loins.

She leaned back in her chair again. 'Then I pity the woman who becomes your wife.'

He shrugged. 'On the contrary. She is like-minded.'

She blinked. 'You are betrothed?'

'No.' He rose and put the last of their lumps of coal on the fire. 'But we have an understanding. She is the main reason I am bound for London.'

It ought not to bother Tess that there was a woman he planned to marry. It should not bother her that she might see the woman on his arm in London. Or dancing with him at a ball. She had dreams of dancing with Mr Welton, did she not?

But somehow it would have been a comfort to meet him in London without a woman in tow and to pretend they did not have a huge secret between them.

'Are you certain this woman will marry you, simply

because you offer her—what? That you are a viscount's son?' she asked him.

He shifted in his chair. 'I am heir to the title, not that I ever wished to be.'

'Why would you not wish for the title?' Both their father and Edmund would have been greatly gratified if Edmund had been the legitimate son and heir.

In fact, their father should have married Edmund's mother. She had been the woman he loved.

Mr Glenville turned his blue eyes on her. Grieving blue eyes. 'My brother had to die. Believe me, I would rather have my brother back than a thousand titles.'

She reached over and touched his arm. 'I am so sorry,' she said truthfully. 'It is a terrible thing to earn a title. Someone must always die.'

He smiled, a sad smile. 'Not always. One can earn a title from winning a war, like the Duke of Wellington.'

His smile made her insides flutter. She glanced back to the fire. 'You do not worry that this woman you wish to marry would marry you merely because you will be a viscount someday?'

'Mind?' His smile remained. 'That is what I have to offer. A title. Wealth. Why should she not want those things?'

A title did not keep a man from becoming a bitter person. Wealth could be fleeting, as well she knew.

'Why should you want her, then?' she asked. 'What advantage does she offer you?'

His expression sobered. 'She is the sister of a good friend. We've known each other since childhood. Her family is extremely respectable and that will do much to erase the damage my parents' reputations have done.'

'You will marry her for her family's reputation?' Was that not like marrying for social connections? Her father

had married her mother for her social connections, all of
which disappeared when she ran off with another man.

He gazed at her with understanding. 'Perhaps you and
your sisters never suffered the stigma of your mother's
scandals.'

She glanced away again. 'Our father never took us to
London.' There were, though, a few ladies around Yardney
who whispered when they were in view and a few gentlemen who'd spoken—rudely.

He added, 'You will benefit from Lord Tinmore's reputation in London, no doubt.'

She turned to him. 'I do understand that. Without Tinmore's wealth and reputation, we should be invited no-
where. But that does not mean that I would accept an offer
of marriage from a man for whom I do not feel great regard.'

'I feel regard for my intended bride, but I will not let
emotions dictate my choices.'

'You like her, then?' she asked.

He nodded. 'I like her well enough.'

Well enough. She was beginning to feel very sorry for
his intended. 'But you do not love her?'

He gazed at her and the firelight made his eyes even
more intense. 'Are you asking if I have a passion for her?
If my mind goes blank and my tongue becomes tied when
I am with her? The answer is no.' He turned back to the
fire. 'But I like her well enough.'

Perhaps if Tess's father had loved their mother, she
would not have sought lovers. Perhaps if her mother had
loved her father, he would have indulged her and flattered
her and cosseted her as she wished. Tess and her sisters
had discussed this many times.

'I hope you learn to love her,' Tess told Mr Glenville.
'I hope she loves you.'

His expression remained implacable.

She adjusted her blankets and stared into the fire. The chair felt hard and the wind found its way inside. The fire was losing its battle to keep the place warm.

They were silent for a while until Mr Glenville spoke. 'How old are you, Miss Summerfield?'

'I am two and twenty.'

His brows rose. 'And your sister, Lady Tinmore?'

'She is five and twenty.'

He peered at her. 'In your twenties and you have had no suitors? That is hard to believe.'

She straightened. 'I did not say we had no suitors. Our situation has not been such that those suitors could make an offer. We had no dowries.'

'Your father did not provide you and your sisters with dowries?' he asked.

If he'd heard of their mother, surely he could guess. Their father did not believe they were his daughters.

But she would not speak that out loud. 'Our father was fond of making risky investments. He wanted to be fabulously wealthy so our mother would regret leaving him, but his investments were terrible ones. He used the last of his funds—our dowries—to purchase a commission for Edmund.'

'Edmund is your father's illegitimate son?'

So he also knew that part of her family story, as well.

'Yes.' She added, 'Our half-brother.'

She and her sisters likely shared no blood with Edmund. The sisters shared a mother. He came from their father.

She went on. 'I do not disagree with you that one needs some fortune and reputation in order to make a good match. Lorene has given us this, but wealth and reputation are not enough for a marriage. It is love that is the answer. Love can get one over the inevitable hurdles of life.'

'Now you are sounding philosophic. There are some hurdles that mere emotion can't jump over.' He peered at her. 'Do you have a suitor?'

She felt her face grow red.

He frowned. 'You have a suitor. A man who would not court you because you had no dowry.'

She flushed with anger this time. 'Perhaps I do have such a suitor. Perhaps that is why I say the things I do.'

He threw off his blanket and stood. 'I am going to check on Apollo.' Before he reached the door he turned back to her. 'I hope it all works for you, Miss Summerfield. But before you make that final vow with your suitor, think with your head and forget your heart.'

She wanted to snap back at him, but his tone disturbed her. And what he said was true. Mr Welton could not court her when she had no dowry, but that did not mean his heart could not be engaged.

Did it?

He opened the door and the wind rushed in. The temperature dropped even lower in just that brief moment. Tess forgot about dowries or love matches or reputations. The air was freezing and they'd put the last of the coal on the fire. How would they stay warm through the night?

'I'll look for more firewood,' Mr Glenville said, as if reading her mind. 'What we have won't last the night.'

Chapter Four

Ice crunched under Marc's bare feet as he crossed the yard to the stable. His feet ached from the cold as he tended to Apollo. Why could he not have been stranded in June instead of February?

It was not only the icy cold that disturbed him. His conversation with Miss Summerfield did, as well.

It cut too close. All this talk of marriage. Love.

His parents had fallen in love and where had it led them? To shouting, accusations, recriminations, declarations that they wished they'd never set eyes on each other. They'd ruined their lives, he'd heard over and over.

Then there was Lucien and Charles. Where had love led his brother and his friend?

No falling in love for him. He'd control such runaway emotions.

'That is the sensible way, eh, Apollo?'

His horse snorted in reply and Marc leaned his face against Apollo's warm neck. He found another blanket to help keep Apollo warm and tried not to think of the icy hammers pounding on his feet.

'We'll be on our way in the morning,' Marc murmured. 'Stay steady, old fellow.'

He searched the stable for scraps of wood to burn and found a few pieces to add to the fire. They would burn quickly, though. He and Miss Summerfield were headed for a very cold night, he knew from experience. He'd spent many a cold night in the French countryside, hiding from men whose suspicions about him had been aroused.

Gritting his teeth, he crossed the icy mud again and entered the cabin. She was crouched by the fire, pouring water from the kettle into the teapot.

'I found some wood.' Not enough wood, though. He dropped it by the fireplace, coming close to her.

She looked up at him. 'I thought you might like more tea. It will be even weaker than before, but it might warm you.'

'Tea will be most welcome.'

Her eyes showed some distress. He wanted to touch her, ease her worry. Instead he moved away to hang his greatcoat on the line.

His feet hurt even worse as the blood rushed to them. He hurried back to his chair by the fire and wrapped his feet in the blanket.

'What is wrong?' she asked, gazing at his feet.

'Cold.' He rubbed his feet. 'I believe my wet boots will be preferable at this point.'

She rose and walked over to the clothes line. 'Your socks are fairly dry.' She brought them to him and knelt at his feet. 'I'll put them on for you.'

Her hands felt too soothing and his body came to life, precisely what he did not wish to feel.

'Perhaps this is not the thing for a lady to do,' he managed to protest.

She placed one sock on his foot. 'It is so little, after what you have done for me.'

At least now he felt warmer. He endured the pleasure

of her slipping the second sock on the other foot, gazing down at her as she worked it over his heel. Her hair was in a plait down her back, but tendrils escaped to frame her lovely face.

She was a woman a man could lose his head over. For once he wished he could be like his father had been—blinded by passion and unaware of the disaster ahead of him.

But his eyes were open.

She wrapped his feet in a blanket again and moved away to pour their weak, but hot, tea.

Take care in London, he wanted to tell her. There were men who knew how to play upon a young woman's heart. Love came in many disguises, some even more hurtful than the pain his parents inflicted on each other.

Perhaps he could watch out for her. Perhaps he could warn her away from the worst dangers of love.

No. He needed to stay away from her. She tempted him too much.

She handed him his jug. 'Such as it is.'

He nodded thanks.

She sat in her chair and they sipped the hot liquid that only retained the barest hint of tea. The fire dwindled to embers, but Marc held off on placing the last of their wood on it. He glanced around the room and wondered if he ought to try to break up the furniture.

It seemed an extreme measure and greatly unfair to the owner of the cottage.

Miss Summerfield yawned and curled up in her chair.

He reached over and touched her arm. 'You should lie on the cot and get some sleep. I'll move it closer to the fire.'

'Where will you sleep?' she murmured.

He shrugged. 'The chair will do.' He'd slept in worse places.

The wind found its way through the walls of the cabin. Miss Summerfield shivered. 'It is cold.'

And it would get colder. 'You'll be warmer on the cot.'

She did as he asked and she was soon tucked in under her blanket as close to the fireplace as he could place the bed.

He watched her as she slept and shivered as the temperature dropped even further and the fire consumed the wood. He scavenged the cabin and found a few more lumps of coal, but the room was very, very cold.

She woke, shivering, but not complaining.

There was only one way he could think of to keep her warm now, but it was a proposition that no young lady should accept. It was also a thought that consumed him much too often.

She rolled over and gazed at him. 'You should take a turn on th-the cot. You must be colder than I am.'

'I'm not going to trade places with you, Miss Summerfield.'

She got up and carried her blanket over to her chair. 'I'll sit here, then.'

He raised his voice. 'Get in the cot.'

She looked at him in defiance. 'No. It is your turn.'

'Do not be a damned fool, Miss Summerfield. Get in the cot.' There was no sense in them both sitting up all night, shivering.

She glared at him. 'The only way I'll get in that cot is if you are in it, too.'

The cold was addling her brain, he thought. But this was the answer, the consuming thought. He should not take advantage of it, but, if he did they'd both be warm.

'Very well.' He inclined his head towards the cot. 'Get in the bed and I will join you.'

An anxious look crossed her face and she hesitated,

but she carried her blanket over to the cot and lay down, facing the fire. He covered her with another blanket and crawled underneath it.

'Our bodies will warm each other,' he murmured in her ear. 'Do not fear. This is for warmth and nothing else.'

He hoped he could keep that promise.

Exhaustion helped where desire refused to waver. Even though she was warm and soft against him, the comfort of her had made him fall asleep almost immediately. He did not even wake to feed the fire the last lumps of coal. He knew nothing until the sound of muffled voices reached his ear.

The latch of the door rattled.

The worst had happened. They were discovered.

'Miss Summerfield!' He shook her, but had only time enough to bound from the cot when the door burst open.

'Halloo there!' a man cried.

Miss Summerfield sat up.

'I say,' said the man, a gentleman by appearance. 'What goes here?'

He entered the cabin followed by two men in work-men's dress.

'Is that you, Miss Summerfield?' the gentleman asked.

Marc took charge. 'Who are you?' he demanded.

Miss Summerfield covered herself with the blanket.

'I am Lord Attison,' the gentleman said indignantly. 'And, more to the purpose, who are you?'

Miss Summerfield answered before Marc could speak, 'He is Mr Glenville, sir. Allow us to explain.'

Marc put a stilling hand on her arm. 'First he must explain why he barges in without so much as a knock.' Put him on the defensive.

Lord Attison shot daggers at Marc. 'I was sent to find

Miss Summerfield.' He turned to her. 'You have caused Lord Tinmore much worry, young lady, do you realise that?'

Marc stepped between Miss Summerfield and Lord Attison. 'Do you have some authority here?'

Miss Summerfield answered, 'He is one of Lord Tinmore's guests.'

'Well,' Marc spoke sharply, 'you may tell Lord Tinmore that it is a fine thing to let this young lady nearly freeze to death. You should have come earlier.'

Lord Attison stuck out his chest. 'And you should have returned her home, sir.' His gaze shifted to Miss Summerfield. 'Or would that have ruined your little tryst?'

'You have it wrong—' Miss Summerfield protested.

Marc seized Lord Attison's arm and marched him to the door. 'We will discuss this outside and allow this lady to dress.'

Once all the men were outside, Marc used his size to be as intimidating as possible to the smaller Lord Attison. 'You will make no assumptions here, do you comprehend? This lady has been through enough without your salacious comments.'

'Lord Tinmore—' the man started to say.

Marc interrupted him. 'I will explain to Lord Tinmore and to no one else. And, you, sir, will say nothing of this until you are instructed by your host. Is that understood?'

Possibly, just possibly Lord Tinmore would have sufficient power and influence to allow this incident to blow over without any damage to Miss Summerfield.

Or himself.

The cold of the morning finally hit him and it took all Marc's strength to keep from dissolving into a quivering mess in front of this man. He wore only his shirt and breeches.

And his socks, now damp from the frost on the ground.

Attison looked him up and down. 'Being undressed in front of an innocent young lady—' The man smirked. 'Or is she an innocent?'

Marc seized him again. 'Silence that tongue!'

Attison's eyes flashed with alarm, but he quickly recovered and pursed his lips. 'I will leave you to Lord Tinmore, as you wish.'

Marc released him and turned to the other two men. 'Do you know who owns this cabin?'

One man nodded. 'Lord Tinmore. It is a groundskeeper's cabin.'

'Are we on Lord Tinmore's property?' How close were they to the house?

'We are, sir,' the other man answered. He gestured to the south.

Against the milky-white sky rose a huge Elizabethan house with dozens of windows and three turrets adorning its roof.

They had been that close.

'The roads and bridges were flooded yesterday,' he said.

One of the men nodded. 'The water receded overnight.'

Miss Summerfield opened the door, glancing warily at their three early morning visitors. 'Mr Glenville, may I see you for a moment?'

Attison made a move to speak, but Marc silenced him with a steely glare.

He entered the cabin and closed the door.

'I have no laces,' she said to him, presenting her back.

'I cut them.' He looked around the room and found her packet of ribbons and lace. He pulled a long ribbon from the still-damp package and started lacing it through the eyelets on her corset and her dress.

'What do we do now?' she asked, her voice cracking.

He worked the laces. 'We tell what happened.'

'You will speak to Lord Tinmore?'

He tied the ribbon in a bow. 'I will speak to him. It turns out we are close to Tinmore Hall.' He turned her to face him. 'It is important that we make no apology, Miss Summerfield. We did what we needed to do to get through the storm. We did nothing wrong.'

Her jaw set. 'No apologies.'

At least she had fortitude.

He grabbed his waistcoat and coat and quickly put them on. He shoved his feet into his boots. 'We must leave now.'

She nodded.

They opened the door and walked out into the cold morning air.

Within an hour Marc and Miss Summerfield stood in front of a wizened old man in spectacles who nonetheless had a commanding bearing.

From his large wing-back chair, he glared at Miss Summerfield. 'You have caused your sister great worry, young lady.'

'It was quite unintended, sir.' At least she kept her voice strong.

Lord Tinmore, old and wrinkled, wielded his cane like a sceptre, obviously accustomed to authority.

Marc spoke up. 'We may dispense with this matter quickly if you will listen to what we have to say.' Men of strength usually respected strength.

Lord Tinmore glared at him over his spectacles. 'I want your name, sir.'

Marc bowed. 'Glenville.'

Tinmore tapped his temple. 'Glenville?'

'My father is Viscount Northdon. He was a schoolmate of your son's.' Maybe that connection would help them.

Pain edged the man's eyes, but the look vanished quickly. 'Northdon,' he scoffed. 'I know of him.'

Of course. Everyone, except perhaps Miss Summerfield, knew of his father.

Tinmore scowled at him.

Marc continued. 'Sir. Who I am, who my father is, has no bearing on this matter. I found Miss Summerfield near freezing in the storm. We took shelter in the cabin and it was impossible to leave until morning.'

'That is the truth!' Miss Summerfield added, with a bit too much emotion.

Tinmore's attention swung to her. 'The truth! The truth is you went gallivanting around the countryside without a chaperone, in bad weather, and wound up spending the night with a man!'

'We had no choice,' Miss Summerfield protested, still shivering and wrapping her arms around herself to try to stay warm.

Tinmore wagged a finger at her. 'You are a reckless scapegrace, girl! A discredit to your sister! And to me!'

'Enough!' Marc shouted. 'Miss Summerfield is still cold. And hungry. She needs dry clothing and food, not an undeserved scolding.'

'Do not dictate to me, young man!' Tinmore countered.

Marc glared at him. 'Give her leave to change into warm, dry clothes.'

Lord Tinmore glared back, but Marc refused to waver.

Marc lowered his voice to a firm, dangerous tone. 'Let her go.'

'Oh, very well.' Tinmore waved a hand at Miss Summerfield. 'Leave now, girl. But I am not finished with you.'

Miss Summerfield curtsied and started for the door. Before she reached it, she turned back. 'My lord, Mr Glenville is also cold and hungry—'

Tinmore snapped at her, 'I told you to leave. Do as I say.'

She did not move. 'That is little thanks for what he has done, sir. You could find him dry clothing.'

'Leave!' Tinmore shouted.

She remained where she was.

Marc spoke to her in a soothing tone. 'Do not fret over me, Miss Summerfield. Go now. Change into warm clothes. Eat something.'

She nodded and went out the door.

He turned back to Tinmore. 'That was poorly done of you, sir. She has been through an ordeal.'

Tinmore's eyes nearly popped out of his head. 'I'm out of patience with her. She caused her sister much worry and now more scandal. I will not have scandal in my house.'

Did this man not have any heart? 'She might have lost her life if I had not found her.'

He pursed his lips. 'Would have served her right.'

By God, would he have preferred her to die? 'She needs your help, sir. You have the power to stop any talk. If you stand by her, who would question it?'

'Much you know, Glenville.' Tinmore took off his spectacles and wiped them with a handkerchief. 'Attison is a scandalmonger of the first rate. There is no stopping him.'

'You invited him. And sent him on the search. You are more responsible for any scandal that results than Miss Summerfield. She should not have to pay.'

'Yes, I invited him!' Tinmore cried. 'So he could see firsthand that I am not in my dotage and that my wife is not a fortune hunter who duped me into marriage.'

Was he surprised that was what people would think?

'This chit has made everything worse. I suppose you know what people say about their mother?' He grimaced.

'If she thinks I'm still giving her a Season and providing her a dowry, she has another think coming.'

He would cut her off? 'You are being unfair.'

'It is my money to spend as I wish.' He fixed his gaze on Marc again. 'You are the one who wronged her, not me.'

Marc had not wronged her. He'd rescued her and kept her safe. But Tinmore was right about one thing. None of that would matter in the eyes of polite society, not if Tinmore refused to stand by her.

'If you will not protect her, I will.' Marc stepped closer to the man and glared down at him. 'I will marry her. That will silence the gossip. And she will need nothing from you.'

Tinmore's mouth quirked into a fleeting smile, but his scowl returned and he waved a hand. 'Marry her, then. Get her out of my sight.'

Marc stood in the hallway, outside the closed door of the private sitting room where Lord Tinmore presumably still sat in his throne-like chair.

He should be on his way to London, not offering marriage, but he'd had no choice, had he? It had been his duty.

The honourable thing to do.

Of all the reasons to marry, this must be the most foolish. Not out of passion. Not a love match. Not a well-considered decision.

So much for his pragmatic choice of marrying Doria. So much for paying the debt he owed to Charles. No comfortable life for him. Lost was the serenity marriage to Doria would offer. Lost was the respectability of her family. He, the son of the scandalous Lord and Lady Northdon, would marry the daughter of scandalous Sir Hollis and Lady Summerfield.

Tongues would wag.

He would not save her from gossip, after all. Perhaps he'd not done her so large a favour.

He must find her. Speak to her. Tell her what he'd done.

She needed to make the choice. The discredit of marrying him or the ruin of crying off.

But, if Tinmore made good his threat, she would also be impoverished.

A footman approached him. 'I am to show you to your room, sir.'

'Never mind my room,' he responded. 'I need to speak to Miss Tess Summerfield.'

The man's eyes widened in alarm. 'I cannot take you to Miss Summerfield.'

'Deliver a message to her for me, then.'

The footman shook his head. 'I do not think Lord Tinmore would approve.'

Marc gestured for him to lead the way. 'Lord Tinmore will not mind. The lady and I are going to be married.'

Tess sat in Genna's bedchamber again, like she had done only the day before, her two sisters with her.

It seemed an age ago.

Genna and Lorene had been waiting for her outside Lord Tinmore's drawing room. They'd hugged and cried and Lorene scolded her for giving them such a fright. While they walked to her bedchamber she filled them in on what had happened to her.

In her room a bath awaited. Tess bathed and washed her hair quickly, before dressing in warm, dry clothes. Hot porridge, bread, cheese and tea were set before her and the mere scent of it made her stomach ache with hunger.

Her mind, though, was on Mr Glenville. Would he convince Lord Tinmore that nothing happened between them? Would Tinmore let him go? The whole experience had become like a dream. Would it fade from her memory?

She did not want to forget him.

The maids came to remove the bath and straighten the room. Tess and her sisters retired to Genna's room and her sisters' relief at finding her safe had worn off.

'Tess, how could you have been so foolish?' Lorene paced, as she had paced the previous morning. 'It is one thing to seek shelter. Quite another to share a bed with a man.'

'It was cold,' Tess explained. She remembered Mr Glenville climbing on to the cot, covering them both with his blanket. She remembered the warmth of his body next to hers, both comforting and thrilling.

'Do you know what the guests are saying?' Genna offered. 'They are saying you met by design. That you planned the tryst. Why else would you venture out on an obviously rainy day?'

Lord Attison must have been very busy telling tales.

'That is ridiculous!' Tess cried. 'I told you how it happened. I never even met Mr Glenville before!'

'You might have met him some other time.' Genna settled herself on the window seat. 'You are known to take walks alone.'

Tess glared at her. 'Are you doubting my word, Genna? I went to the village to shop.'

Not to the nearby village, though. To Yardney. To see Mr Welton, had he been there.

'No.' Genna spoke as if this were some interesting problem happening to someone else. 'But you did not bring any lace or ribbon, did you?'

The lace and ribbon. She'd forgotten her parcel. 'I left the parcel at the cabin. We could send someone for it.'

'It would not matter. What really happened does not matter.' Lorene still paced. 'Appearances. That is what matters.' She shook her head. 'I do not know what Lord Tinmore will do. This is such a trial for him and it has already put a strain on the house party.'

'A trial for him? A strain on the house party?' Tess rose off the bed. 'Goodness, Lorene. I did not choose to have this happen. I simply walked to the village and became caught in a horrible storm. Perhaps I should have tried to cross the bridge or continued down the roads even though water was rushing over both. Then I would have drowned. Or perhaps Mr Glenville should have left me on the road to freeze to death. Either way would have been so much less trouble for Lord Tinmore!'

Lorene grabbed Tess and hugged her. 'Do not say that. Never say that. That is what we all thought happened to you.'

Tess hugged her back. 'I had hoped you'd think I stayed in the village.'

There was a knock at the door and a maid stuck her head in. 'Pardon, my lady, but his lordship wishes to speak with Miss Summerfield immediately. In the library.'

Lorene released her. 'You must go.' She turned to the maid. 'Tell Lord Tinmore she will be there directly.'

The maid rushed off.

'I will accompany you,' Lorene said.

Genna rose from the window seat. 'I will come, too.'

'No.' Tess held them back with her arm. 'It is best you stay out of it.' Lord Tinmore would only become upset with them because of her.

Genna sat again and looked sulky. 'Well, you had better come back right away and tell us all about it.'

'I will walk with you, at least,' Lorene said.

As they walked the distance to Lord Tinmore's private

sitting room, Tess tried to quiet her nerves. Would Mr Glenville still be there? Goodness, she hoped Lord Tinmore allowed him to dress in dry clothing and get something to eat.

Had he been able to convince Lord Tinmore to let the incident pass? She hoped so. She prayed so.

'Tinmore is a reasonable man,' Lorene said when they entered the long hallway leading to his private rooms.

Lord Tinmore had seemed fairly unreasonable to Tess. Unlike Glenville, who had come to her defence.

At the stairs, a footman approached and handed Tess a piece of paper. 'A message for you, miss.' He glanced warily at Lorene, the new lady of the house, and hurried away.

Tess unfolded the paper and read the note. 'It is from Mr Glenville. He wishes to speak with me right away.' She folded the paper again and put it in a pocket. 'I should see him first.'

She turned around, but Lorene seized her arm. 'You cannot see Mr Glenville!'

'Why not?' She tried to pull away. 'He is waiting in the morning room. I can see him there.'

'No!' Lorene cried. 'You must attend Lord Tinmore first!' She pulled her along to Lord Tinmore's sitting room. Another footman stood at the door and opened it when they approached.

'Go to him.' Lorene gave her a little push.

Tess entered the room.

Lord Tinmore was alone, seated in the same chair where he had been before. His demeanour had not softened.

Tess curtsied. 'You asked to see me, my lord.'

His lips pursed. 'I trust you are comfortable now.'

'I am, sir. Thank you.' She remembered what Glenville had said. Make no apologies. They had done noth-

ing wrong. 'I hope you allowed the same courtesy to my
rescuer.'

'You need not concern yourself with Mr Glenville,' Tinmore snapped.

She straightened her spine.

He frowned. 'You have created a great deal of trouble
for yourself, for my wife and for your younger sister.'

She looked him directly in the face. 'The rain caused a
great deal of trouble for me. I was in danger and a gentleman rescued me. Surely you can make something sensible
of that without a great deal of trouble.'

'Such as what?' He stiffened in his chair.

'Such as nothing.' Her heart pounded. Perhaps he could
be convinced. 'Declare Mr Glenville a hero and allow him
to go on his way.'

'A hero?' His expression turned shrewd. 'You seem im-
moderately concerned about Mr Glenville.'

Her hopes were shaken. 'Do not try to make something of that, sir. He saved my life and I am not so much
a simpleton as to miss the fact that you are trying to punish him for it.'

'Punish him?' Lord Tinmore's rheumy eyes flashed.
'He was caught in bed with you. That cannot be ignored.'

'It can be ignored if you wish it,' she shot back. 'The
world will believe what you, sir, wish it to believe.'

He stared at her before continuing. 'You have bedded
a man and been caught at it. At least your paramour un-
derstands you must pay the consequences.'

Her heart pounded. 'What do you mean?'

'He will marry you.'

'No!' she cried. 'He will not.'

He half-rose from his chair. 'He will and that is that.'

Fear exploded inside her, but she could not allow it to
show. Instead she moved closer to him and leaned down

into his face. 'You know, sir,' she said in a low voice. 'You know that Mr Glenville and I did nothing wrong, nothing to truly compromise me. You know he rescued me. Saved my life. You know all you have to do is tell your friends the truth. Tell everyone the truth.'

'No.' He sat back in his chair. 'Glenville said he'd marry you and that will resolve matters nicely, with the minimum of scandal tainting my marriage.'

'Your marriage? Why should what happened to me taint your marriage?' she countered.

'It adds scandal to my wife's name,' he said. 'Your mother and father's carnal excesses are bad enough. I'll not tolerate more…' He shook his head. 'Stranded in a storm! Hmmph!'

She glared at him. 'You know it is true, sir.'

He waved her words away. 'You will marry Glenville and that is the final word.'

Her insides felt shredded, but she made herself lift her chin. 'What has Mr Glenville to say to this?'

Tinmore's mouth moved against his gums, an old man's gesture. 'Mr Glenville knows his duty. He made the offer.'

'No.' Her entire body began to shake. 'He does not wish to marry me. I cannot marry a man who does not wish to marry me.'

'He may not wish it.' Lord Tinmore smirked. 'But he'll do it. As will you.'

'You cannot force this marriage on him. Or on me!' she cried.

'Glenville made the offer. It is up to you to accept or not.' He leaned forward. 'But understand this. For you there will be no dowry, no Season.'

His words were a blow.

She swallowed the pain. And loss.

She lifted her chin. 'If you choose to break your bargain with my sister, it is no concern of mine.'

He worked his mouth as if unable to form words.

He finally spoke. 'If you do not marry Mr Glenville, I will also withdraw all funds and support from your sister Genna and your by-blow of a brother. Your sister will not have a dowry and your brother will not see a penny of mine.'

She felt the blood drain from her face. 'You would not be so cruel.'

He stared her directly in the eye. 'You will marry Mr Glenville after all, will you not?'

She fixed her gaze on Lord Tinmore and would not allow her voice to show her utter defeat. 'For my sisters' and brother's sakes, I have no choice. I will marry Mr Glenville.'

'Excellent!' Lord Tinmore clapped. 'Tomorrow I will send you with him to London in my carriage.'

'Tomorrow!'

'I want you out of sight of my guests. Once they know you are to be married, the talk will disappear. By the time I bring my wife and your younger sister to London, all will be forgotten.'

He was sending her away. She'd already lost so much. Her mother. Her father. Her home. Now she was to lose her sisters, as well.

And to be married to a man who would undoubtedly resent her and detest having been trapped into marriage with her.

As soon as Tess left Tinmore, she hurried to the morning room, but Mr Glenville was not there. If only she could speak with him. There must be some way out of this.

She waited there an hour, pacing back and forth. Finally

a footman opened the door and told her Lord Tinmore wished her to return to her room. She was not to come to dinner with her sisters and the house-party guests. She was expected to remain in her room.

And she was forbidden to seek out Mr Glenville.

Chapter Five

The next morning, Tess walked through the cavernous house, her sisters at her side. They made their way to the front door where Lord Tinmore's carriage and Mr Glenville would await her. One of the Tinmore maids, whom she did not know, was to accompany her to London, but return with the carriage.

Lorene had been scolding her every step of the way. 'I gave you the chance to choose who to marry and look what you do.'

Perhaps it was too much to hope that her sister would take her part against her husband.

Tess was beyond defending herself, in any event. She was sick with grief and trepidation. This was the very worst way to be married. Not out of love. Not even for status or financial gain. Mr Glenville was forced to marry her because he'd rescued her in the rain and taken her to a cabin to keep warm and dry.

If only she had been able to talk with him. Why had he not waited for her in the morning room?

Tess could not believe she would walk through Tinmore Hall's great door into a new life among people she did not know, in a place she'd never been before.

Genna had been in tears the whole morning. 'Why do you have to leave now?' She sniffed. 'Why can you not come to London when we go there?'

'It is better this way.' Tess was determined that her sisters not know how devastated she felt. 'Besides, I will see you in London in just a few weeks.' Although she had no assurances that Lord Tinmore would allow it. He might forbid her to call. Her sisters might be totally lost to her, as well.

Lorene had been so wrong about the reclusive earl. He was not reasonable. Nor benevolent. He went back on promises and wielded his power in the cruellest possible way. He had better not treat Lorene with cruelty or Tess would—

What could she do?

Nothing.

'You were supposed to marry happily,' Lorene went on. 'Now what was the use of my—my—' She could not say the words, but Tess knew—they all knew—what she meant.

They reached the hall. The arsenal of swords and pikes and other weapons hung on the wall surrounding the door seemed like a harbinger of pain and destruction.

She turned to Lorene. 'I will do very well, Lorene. I will be a viscountess some day. How grand will that be?'

'You will become like Mama,' Lorene rasped through her tears. 'You will be unhappy.'

She hugged Lorene. 'Do not concern yourself about me.'

Lorene held on to her. 'I meant something so different for you. A London Season. A chance to meet many fine young men, a chance to find your own true love.'

'I will still be there for the Season, will I not?' She pasted on a smile. 'Genna will have more fine young men to fall in love with her this way.'

'Do not look to me.' Genna wiped her eyes. 'I wanted nothing to do with this.' She turned to Lorene. 'This is your fault, you know. None of this would have happened if you had not married, Lorene.'

'I did it for you.' Lorene burst into tears. 'For both of you.'

'Stop. Stop.' Tess could not bear this. 'We must not fight and, for heaven's sake, do not cry. I will be fine. Mr Glenville is not a bad man. He rescued me, did he not? His proposal of marriage was honourable, was it not? I will do very well, I am sure.'

She hoped she convinced them, because she was having a great deal of difficulty convincing herself that all would be well.

The huge front door opened and a footman stepped in. 'The carriage is awaiting you, miss.'

Tess's heart jumped into her throat. 'I must leave.'

Her sisters followed her outside.

Tess looked past the carriage to the man on horseback—Mr Glenville astride his horse. Apollo.

'Is that him?' Genna asked.

His face was shaded by his hat and he sat stiffly in his saddle. What had Lord Tinmore threatened him with to make him offer to marry a woman he did not even know?

'Yes, that is Mr Glenville,' she responded.

Genna sniffed. 'Well, at least he is not fat.'

Nor ugly, Tess thought. On the contrary, he was handsome and tall and strong, and when his blue eyes fixed on her, something stirred deep inside her.

But he did not love her. How could he?

He had already selected his intended bride, a woman who could be an advantage to him, a woman who had the one thing Tess could never give him—a family reputation free from scandal.

He nodded to her and her cheeks burned. She hugged her sisters one last time before allowing the footman to assist her into the coach.

Marc followed the carriage, his mood nothing but dark. Anger seethed inside him. Anger at Lord Tinmore. Anger at Miss Summerfield's sister for marrying such a man.

Anger at himself for not waking before dawn and making certain he and Miss Summerfield were not discovered. Even more, he should have known better than to share her bed, even if he'd done nothing but warm her.

He'd waited as long as he could in the morning room where he'd been served his food, but she had not come. Eventually an elderly butler arrived and insisted he leave.

Not that it would have made any difference, although he might have reassured her in some way.

Damned Tinmore. If the man had stated that he believed them, the scandal would have faded quickly. Instead he'd been unnecessarily cruel. Miss Summerfield did not deserve cruelty. All she'd done was walk to the village to shop. Good God. Shopping was his mother's primary entertainment. How could any woman be faulted for wanting to visit shops? Miss Summerfield had also misjudged the weather. Well, so had he.

They reached Yardney, the village Miss Summerfield had tried to reach in the storm, the village where she had purchased her ribbons. From his seat on Apollo's back, he could see her face peeking out of the carriage window, looking desolate.

Fate was a cruel jokester.

If she had shopped an hour longer or an hour less, maybe even minutes more or minutes less, she would not have been on the road during the storm and she would be free.

Instead she was trapped into marrying him.

* * *

At least the coachman kept up a good speed, considering the roads were not yet dry. This trip would take them at least three days. Apollo was accustomed to hard rides.

The carriage changed horses when necessary and Marc made certain they did not resume the journey until Apollo had rested. When they reached a coaching inn in Bourne, it was past noon and time they stopped long enough to eat a meal.

It would be his first chance to speak to her.

He handed over care of Apollo to one of the stable boys and walked over to help her from the coach.

'Thank you,' she said. She looked tense and fatigued.

'Miss Summerfield, will you dine with me?' he asked.

She nodded.

A maid who'd seen the better part of her forties had accompanied her in the coach. The woman scowled and sniffed impatiently. 'Will you be needing my services, miss?' She spoke in an overly solicitous and distinctly unpleasant manner.

'No, Ivers,' Miss Summerfield replied in a tight voice. 'Please have a pleasant repast. Do—do you need any money?'

Did Miss Summerfield have any money? Marc wondered. Had Lord Tinmore cut her off that completely?

The maid lifted her nose. 'His lordship provided for me.' The woman marched away.

Miss Summerfield blew out a breath.

'Well, she is certainly unpleasant,' Marc said.

Miss Summerfield sighed. 'That is couching it in the mildest terms.'

Marc did not offer his arm, because he did not think she would wish to take it, but she walked next to him into the inn. The public room was not crowded.

The innkeeper greeted them.

'Do you have a private dining room?' Marc asked him.

'I do indeed, sir,' the man said. 'Follow me.'

He led them past other tables and chairs, some with diners, some not, through a short hallway to a private room. It had a window overlooking the yard and a small round table with four chairs.

The innkeeper took their meal orders. Tea for Miss Summerfield, ale for Marc and meat pie for them both.

When the innkeeper left, Marc pulled out a chair for Miss Summerfield. 'Does the room suit you? It seems comfortable enough.'

She sat. 'It is wonderful. That detestable maid is not here.'

'Why is she accompanying you?' He took a chair across from her.

'Lord Tinmore sent her to travel with me.' Her voice was stressed. 'I do not know her at all. She is not one of the maids I'd met before.'

'You'd not met her?' Tinmore made her take this journey with a stranger?

She pulled off her gloves. 'She is quite disapproving. I suppose she was treated to the most sordid version of our time together.'

'Why did Tinmore not allow your own maid to accompany you?' he asked.

She met his eye only briefly. 'I shared a maid with my sister and I would not ask her to leave her home for me.' She glanced away again. 'Had I been given a choice, I mean.'

Damned Tinmore. 'Do you want to be rid of this one?'

'It is useless for me to want anything,' she said.

Their food and drink arrived and he remembered the last meal they'd shared. Sodden bread and cheese and Toby jugs. That day seemed pleasant compared to their present situation.

She looked up at him. 'Why did you offer to marry me?'

Her blunt question took him aback, but he had to admire that she did not shrink from the topic.

'It was my duty,' he replied.

She closed her eyes and averted her face as if his words had been a blow.

He softened his voice. 'It was the only solution. We were caught in a compromising situation, after all.' And, of course, Tinmore threatened to banish her and leave her penniless. Did she know that? If not, he would not tell her.

Her eyes grew bright with tears. 'I am so sorry, Mr Glenville.'

He was seized with a strong impulse to enfold her in his arms and assure her all would be well. He wanted to kiss away her tears and make her forget any unhappiness she'd ever experienced—

Wait. This would never do. No woman had ever stirred him the way she had done. He needed to keep a clear head.

She took a breath and smiled wanly. 'Do you think perhaps if we had a long engagement everyone would forget about us and you could marry the woman you wanted to marry?'

Was that her worry? Odd. He'd not thought of Doria since he'd made his decision. 'I doubt Tinmore is the sort who would forget.' He drank his ale. 'What would he do to you if we did not marry?'

'It does not matter what he would do to me.' Angry tears glittered in her eyes. 'Lord Tinmore said he would cut off Genna and Edmund without a penny. He would go back on his promise to my sister. Likely he'd make her life even more miserable.' She swiped at her eyes and took a sip of tea.

'Damned Tinmore.'

She glanced at him in surprise.

He took another long sip of his drink. 'Let's be rid of him and his threats.' He leaned across the table towards her. 'What say you to sending away Tinmore's carriage and with it that vile woman he inflicted on you? We do not need his transportation to London. I will arrange something for you.'

Her eyes widened. 'You would do that?'

He grinned. 'With pleasure.'

Mr Glenville acted quickly. As soon as he finished eating, he discharged the maid and sent her and the carriage back to Tinmore Hall. They'd reach there before the end of the day.

Tess wished she could see Lord Tinmore's face when they arrived. She hoped he choked on his outrage.

She'd not expected Glenville to be so kind. Certainly he must resent this forced marriage, although he'd be too much of a gentleman to say so.

He'd never wanted a marriage with love, he'd said, so perhaps it did not matter to him as much. But he did wish for respectability and that was something already lost. How long would his kindness last, as a result? Would he not begin to resent her as her father had resented her mother?

He secured rooms in the inn and found a village girl who worked for the local seamstress, but was eager to improve her situation. She presented herself to Tess for Tess's approval.

'Good afternoon, miss.' The girl, a pert, curly-haired blonde, curtsied. 'I'm Nancy Peters. What would you like to know about me? I would so like to be a lady's maid, if you find me to your likin'.'

The girl was bright-eyed and fresh-faced and so very eager.

'Do you want to go to London, Miss Peters?' Tess asked.

The girl pressed her hands to her cheeks. 'It is Nancy, miss. I am not old enough to be Miss Peters. Sounds like you are speaking of my aunt. She's old. Thirty, I think.' She took a breath. 'But you want to know if I want to go to London?' Her eyes grew huge. 'My dream is to go to London!' Her expression changed again. 'But do you not want to know if I know how to care for your clothing? And to dress your hair?'

Tess almost smiled. 'Do you know those things?'

Nancy looked earnest. 'I have been sewing clothes for as long as I can remember. I know how to care for cloth.' She frowned. 'I know a little about hair, but I can learn. Surely I will learn much in London just by looking at the ladies. I have good references and I'm an honest girl, I promise.'

Nancy made it feel as if spring had come early. She was so fresh. So happy.

'I believe you will do very nicely, Nancy.'

She jumped up and down. 'Oh, thank you, miss! Thank you! I—I must tell my mother and pack. But may I do something for you now?'

'Nothing now. Take your time.'

The young girl curtsied, grinned and danced out of the room.

Mr Glenville knocked and poked his head in. He'd been standing outside the room. 'Will she do?'

'Yes,' Tess said. 'Thank you, Mr Glenville.'

He walked towards her. 'It is Marc, miss,' he said, mimicking the new maid's voice. 'I'm not old enough to be Mr Glenville.'

'Marc.' She smiled, but her smile fled. 'I suppose it is acceptable to use given names since we are betrothed.' She looked up at him. 'I am Tess.'

'Tess,' he repeated in a low voice. 'I believe I've found a coach for hire that should be available tomorrow. We can proceed then.'

She met his gaze again. 'I feel as if you have rescued me again.' A third time, really. Was his offer of marriage not another rescue? He could have ridden away and forgotten her. 'Nancy is as delightful as Ivers was unpleasant.'

'I dislike being under someone else's thumb,' he said in a low voice. 'And I'd be a fool if I let that thumb's lackey spy on me.'

He was correct, of course. She'd not thought of it before, but obviously Ivers was supposed to report on her.

Glenville walked back to the doorway, but turned and faced her again. 'Shall I have your dinner sent up to this room?'

Did he not wish to dine with her? She felt disappointed. But she would not show him. 'Very well.'

The next two days on the road were much more pleasant for Tess with Nancy as a companion, but Marc spent little time with her. She rode with Nancy, ate with her, shared rooms with her at the inns where they stopped for the night. Nancy was so open and curious and eager to please that Tess was tempted to tell her everything about her family, her sisters and how it came about that she was going to marry. She missed her sisters so desperately. Confiding in someone would ease the loneliness, but it would not be fair to burden a servant with her trials. She told Nancy only that her betrothal had been sudden and that Marc's parents knew nothing of it. To the village girl it sounded all romantic and exciting.

It was exciting, Tess could not disagree, but obviously romance was not a part of it.

* * *

The morning of the third day, Marc appeared when Tess and Nancy entered the public room for breakfast.

He smiled at her. 'Good morning, Tess.'

Her heart skipped a beat. When had her heart skipped beats? With Mr Welton, perhaps, but that seemed an eon ago.

'Good morning.' She lowered her lashes.

He turned to Nancy. 'Nancy, I would like to dine with Miss Summerfield alone. Would you mind?'

Imagine him asking a maid.

Nancy curtsied. 'Not at all, Mr Glenville.' She grinned. 'Do not worry over me. I'll take care of myself.' She entered the room and took a seat at one of the tables.

Tess glanced at Marc. 'May we keep her in view? I do not like to leave her alone.'

'Indeed,' he responded.

He led her to a table nearby the maid.

Why did Tess feel so breathless? As if she'd run down the stairs to this room?

A tavern maid arrived and they ordered their food.

From across the table he gazed at her with his startling blue eyes. 'I expect we will reach London today.' His demeanour was serious. 'I should tell you what to expect.'

Her eyes widened. She'd worried about what would happen when they reached London. Would he leave her alone someplace, like in a hotel for ladies? Would she be alone in a city she knew only from magazines and books?

'I plan to take you to my parents' house.'

Tess released a relieved breath.

This plan appeared to make his brow furrow deeper, though. 'I cannot predict how they will welcome you. I can only warn you that my parents are...' He paused as if he had to consider carefully what to say. 'Well, their situation—not being as socially connected as you might wish—'

She interrupted him. 'Do not concern yourself over that. I am not at all certain I wish to be connected to society.' Not if such people were as unreasonable as Lord Tinmore.

A defensive tone entered his voice. 'I told you that my mother was not born to society. She may not be accepted by the *ton*, but she is a fine person.'

Tess almost reached for his hand, only inches from hers on the table. 'Yes, you did tell me. I am the last person who would judge your mother from the situation of her parents. I can only hope your parents do not hold it against me for being the daughter of Sir Hollis and Lady Summerfield.'

He shook his head. 'That is what I cannot predict.'

She blinked. 'You had hoped to marry a respectable woman. I expect that was their wish, as well. I am so sorry.'

He frowned, but his blue eyes still pierced her. 'No more apologies, Tess. What is past is done. We can only look to the future.'

But the future was like the sheets of rain from the storm that led to this day. She could not see where she was headed. To Tess the future seemed grey and cold, a place where she would be lost and alone.

By midday, much to Nancy's sheer glee, the buildings of London came into view. Tess recognised the dome of St Paul's Cathedral from engravings of the church in books. She'd imagined this moment, her first sight of London, many times, but her actual arrival brought trepidation.

Not that Nancy noticed. Nancy leaned out the window and remarked on everything she saw. A building with a red door! A street vendor selling ginger cakes! A man dressed in purple livery!

Tess glimpsed Marc from time to time as he led the

coachman to his parents' house. It was located in Mayfair, he'd told her. An excellent address on Grosvenor Street near the square.

She was nervous about meeting his parents. Perhaps it would be better to leave her at a hotel, or even at a bench in the park to wait while he explained to his parents that he was forced to marry the daughter of the infamous Sir Hollis and Lady Summerfield.

The rows of shops turned into rows of town houses with doors painted bright red, green or blue. The carriages on these streets were of finer make. Fashionable phaetons were driven by elegantly dressed men, a young boy perched on the back, ready to attend to the horses.

'Have you ever seen the like!' exclaimed Nancy.

'I never have,' Tess answered truthfully. The genteel people who called upon her family were neighbours or friends of her father's passing through and they wore travelling clothes. Lord Tinmore's carriages came from another age—nothing she'd ever seen outside of books or fashion plates was as sporting and new as what passed them.

'We must be in Mayfair,' Tess said.

They were close to the end of her journey and the beginning of a life of unknowns. Would Lord and Lady Northdon accept her or would they be furious that their son was forced to marry her?

The carriage came to a stop by a row of town houses.

They had arrived.

Marc dismounted from Apollo and opened the door of the carriage. 'We are here,' he said.

He looked as grim as she felt.

She nodded and gave him her hand so he could assist her from the carriage. Could he feel how her hand shook?

He gazed directly into her eyes, a silent communication that might have been intended to reassure her, but merely revealed he was as uncertain of their reception here as she was. It was a scant second of intimacy, though, and that in itself heartened her a little.

'Wait here,' he said before he walked up to the door and pounded the wrought-iron knocker.

A footman answered. 'Mr Glenville! Welcome. Were his lordship and her ladyship expecting you?'

'Not at all,' Glenville said. 'Good to see you, Staines.'

Why had he not written his parents that he was coming? He could have sent a letter from any of the inns where they'd stayed. He could have prevented making her presence such a surprise.

'Are they at home?' he asked.

'They are, sir.' He opened the door wider for Marc to enter.

'I am not alone.' He gestured to Tess and Nancy and to the coachman who was lowering trunks and travelling bags on to the pavement. 'I will discharge the carriage, but I need someone to bring in the luggage and tend to my horse.'

'Indeed, sir.' Staines stared wide-eyed at them before disappearing inside the house. Soon two other footmen hurried out. One took Apollo's reins and the other picked up one of the trunks and headed for a servants' entrance below street level.

Marc returned to Tess. 'Come inside.' He turned to Staines again. 'Do you know where in the house my parents are?'

'I cannot say for certain, sir, but your father is likely in the library and your mother in her sitting room.' Staines picked up two of the smaller bags. 'Shall I announce you?'

'No,' Marc replied. 'I'll find them.'

He took Tess's elbow and escorted her inside. He helped her off with her cloak and laid it on a chair in the hall. 'Come this way to the drawing room. I should not be long.'

Nancy stared up at the painted-and-plasterwork ceiling as she followed.

They entered an elegant drawing room that looked straight out of Ackermann's prints of the latest furnishings. Not the worn but genteel furniture of Summerfield House, nor the opulence of a bygone era in Tinmore Hall.

'I'll return soon.' He hurried out the door before Tess could say a word.

She closed her eyes and tried to quiet her nerves.

'This room is so grand!' Nancy twirled around. 'And it is so big.' She walked around, peering at everything. 'Look! Little porcelain people.'

There were Meissen figurines on a side table.

Tess only half-listened to her inventory of items in the room.

'I cannot believe I will live in this house!' Nancy exclaimed.

'Do not be hasty,' Tess said. 'We may not be able to stay. Remember Lord and Lady Northdon know nothing of us.'

Nancy spun around to face the door, as if Lord and Lady Northdon might enter at any moment. 'I wonder what Mr Glenville is saying to them.'

Chapter Six

Marc knocked on his mother's sitting-room door.

'Qui est là?'

The familiarity of her voice warmed him. *'C'est moi, Maman.'*

'Marc?'

She was already on her feet when he opened the door. Still thin, still white-haired, still beautifully fine-boned. As lovely a woman as ever.

'Marc!' She threw her arms around him.

Her embrace was strong and firm, the embrace of the woman who had soothed all his childhood hurts, the woman who valiantly did not complain of having no friends and few social contacts.

She continued to speak in French. 'We did not expect you. Come. Sit with me and tell me all about where you have been and what you have been doing. You spent Christmas in Scotland, no?'

He answered in French. *'Oui.'* That was about as much as he could tell her of his doings. 'Come with me to Papa. He is in the library. I have something to tell you.'

'Must we, Marc?' Her mouth pursed. 'Tell me here, *s'il vous plaît*. I do not wish to leave this room.'

'No. I want to speak with you and Papa together, Maman.' Here he was, in the middle of them again.

'He does not like to be disturbed, *cher*.' She frowned.

She meant they spent their days apart as much as possible.

'I insist, Maman.' He extended his hand to the door. 'Come with me. It is important.'

'Very well. If it is important.' She sighed, taking his arm.

When they reached the library, she walked in first.

'John!' she snapped, switching to English. 'Look who is here.'

Her father scowled at her sharp tone, but broke into a smile when he saw Marc. 'My boy! What a pleasant surprise. A pleasant surprise.'

Again Marc was engulfed in a hug. 'Papa.'

His father seemed smaller than Marc remembered. Marc embraced him back, but the old resentments nagged at him.

'What brings you here? Are you staying? You have not been home in a very long time.' His tone, of course, turned to a scold. 'You should stay awhile.'

He'd been in his father's presence for less than a minute and already the man was scolding and issuing orders and reminding Marc he was not his brother who could do no wrong in their father's eyes.

Marc moved out of his father's embrace and tried to keep the rancour out of his voice. 'I might extend my visit.' He gestured to the sofa nearby. 'Please, both of you sit. I have something to tell you.'

They sat—in separate chairs.

Marc sat on the sofa. He'd had nearly three days to prepare for this conversation and still had not decided what to say.

Better to lunge than parry. 'I have brought a lady with me, a lady I will marry…'

Both his parents stared back in shock.

'Marry!' his mother cried, but her eyes kindled with excitement.

His father frowned. 'Who is this lady?'

Marc took a breath and began his explanation. His father would know who Tess's parents were, so there was no sense withholding that information. He would withhold the reason he and Tess were marrying, though. Eventually, when Lord Tinmore's guests made their way to London, the story might come out, but telling it now would only make Tess's introduction to his parents more difficult for her.

'She is Sir Hollis and Lady Summerfield's daughter?' his father cried when Marc finished.

'Who is this Sir Hollis and Lady Summerfield?' his mother demanded.

His father gave her a peeved look. 'Sir Hollis was a fool who threw away a fortune on bad investments, but not before marrying a wife who cuckolded him repeatedly before she finally ran away with one of her lovers. She had so many lovers, no one knows who fathered her children.'

'Pfft!' Marc's mother waved away her husband's words. 'Lovers. What does that matter?'

'Fidelity matters very much to some people,' he countered.

'Does it?' His mother glared at his father.

Good God. Was one of them—or both—taking lovers now?

His father cleared his throat. 'In this situation, however, it matters that we don't know what blood flows in this young lady's veins.'

'Yes!' His mother nearly bounded from her seat. 'She

might have common blood in her. Would that not be *très tragique*!'

His father's face turned red. 'I did not mean that and you know it. I meant there could be insanity in the family. Or deformity.'

Marc stood. 'Silence!'

They both looked at him as if surprised he was there.

'It does not matter who her parents were or what blood is in her, I am marrying Miss Summerfield, not her parents.' He glared at them both.

'Good God.' His father rubbed his face. 'It is bad enough your brother—' He broke off and it took a moment for him to renew his attack on Marc. 'What is the urgency of this marriage? Is she increasing?'

'Increasing? Say what you mean.' His mother turned to him. 'Is she *enceinte*?'

'No!' Marc responded. 'There is no child. She is a virtuous, respectable young lady and I have treated her as such.'

'Well, her family is not respectable.' His father huffed. 'Her mother. Her father. And did I not read that a sister married old Tinmore? That could not be respectable.'

'Pah.' His mother's eyes flashed at his father. 'You put too much on respectable. You always did.'

He glared back at her. 'Not always.'

They stared at each other and Marc felt he might as well not be in the room.

'You could have stopped Lucien,' she whispered.

This again. Were they still battling over his brother's death? This was the most painful of all.

His mother, though, returned to the topic at hand. 'What is it with this Tinmore? Is he not *respectable*?'

His father's tone turned almost civil. 'He is eighty, if he's a day, and he's been a recluse for years.' He glanced away in thought. 'I wonder if he is in his right mind. Must not be if some chit duped him into marriage.'

'You think it is the woman who is at fault?' his mother countered. 'More likely this Tinmore forced her to marry him.'

Marc broke in. 'Never mind Tinmore! Will you welcome Miss Summerfield into this house or must I put her up in a hotel some place until I can arrange to marry her? I need to know this minute because she is waiting in the drawing room.'

Nancy finally settled in a chair against the wall and Tess sat where she could view the drawing-room door. From the window she'd seen the last of their luggage carried away and the carriage driving off. It was disconcerting to not know precisely where she was or how to get anywhere. If she were on the streets of Mayfair, she'd be as lost as she'd been in the storm.

The door opened and she braced herself.

But it was not Marc, nor his parents who entered. It was a young blonde beauty, so much Genna's size and colouring that Tess ached to see her sister again. The girl, though, looked even younger than Genna's nineteen.

Tess stood and Nancy popped up, as well.

'Hello,' the girl said. She had the same piercing blue eyes as Mr Glenville, complimented by a stylish day dress of nearly the same hue. 'Staines told me my brother was here. And that we had visitors.' She walked over to Tess and curtsied. 'I am Amelie Glenville.'

Brother? Marc had not mentioned he had a younger sister.

Tess curtsied in return. 'I am Miss Summerfield. Tess Summerfield.' She gestured to Nancy. 'This is my maid, Nancy.'

Nancy's curtsy was deep. 'Miss.'

'You came with my brother, did you not?' Miss Glenville asked, her tone hesitant.

She was shy, Tess guessed. 'Yes. Yes, we did.'

'I ordered some tea for you.' Miss Glenville lowered her gaze. 'Please do sit. Both of you.'

Tess lowered herself into the chair again.

Miss Glenville took a seat nearby. 'Where is my brother now?' she asked.

'With your parents, I think.' He'd seemed gone a long time. A bad sign.

Staines entered carrying a tea tray with some little cakes. Miss Glenville, with the deliberateness of an unpractised hostess, poured for them both. Nancy, still wide-eyed, but suddenly bashful and perhaps even more desirous of refreshment than Tess, retreated to a far chair along the wall to consume her tea and cakes.

'You came in a carriage,' Miss Glenville said timidly. 'Where did you come from?'

'From Lincolnshire, actually,' Tess responded.

'Lincolnshire!' the girl exclaimed. 'You must have travelled for days.'

'Yes.' Home was very far away.

Miss Glenville seemed to search for what else to say. 'You must be very tired.'

They'd left with the morning's first light and the clock in this room just chimed three times. 'We stopped along the way.'

Miss Glenville fell silent, but she looked as if she were trying to decide something. She finally blurted out, 'Are—are you a friend of my brother's? Why did he leave you in the drawing room alone?'

Tess would not take it upon herself to explain why Glenville arrived at her home with a strange woman, luggage in tow. 'He wished to speak with your parents first.'

Miss Glenville made a puzzled frown, then smiled shyly. 'It is nice to have a visitor, in any event. We do not have many when we come to London.'

Tess very much wanted to put the girl at ease. 'Then many people are missing a lovely house. This room looks the very height of fashion.'

'It is.' Miss Glenville brightened. 'Maman likes very much to make a room pretty.'

'She succeeds very well.'

There was another long silence. Tess felt the pain of Miss Glenville's meekness. She had Genna's beauty, but lacked Genna's confident outspokenness.

Finally Miss Glenville stood. 'Shall I see what is keeping my brother?'

Tess smiled. 'Yes, please. I would so appreciate that.'

Miss Glenville curtsied again and fled the room.

When the door was closed, Nancy spoke in a hushed tone. 'She is a beautiful lady!'

'Very beautiful.' Amelie Glenville was as beautiful as her brother was handsome, as fair-haired as he was dark.

Tess considered herself passable, but not a beauty like honey-blonde Genna or mahogany-haired Lorene. Or like their mother, who was renowned for her beauty, even though Tess could barely remember what she looked like.

Was the woman Marc wanted to marry a great beauty?

Tess sighed. There was no use dwelling on such matters. She would do what she must for Genna and Edmund. And Lorene.

Footsteps sounded outside the door. Several footsteps. Tess stood again.

The door opened and Marc entered first. His gaze caught Tess's right away, and she saw no reassurance in it. Behind him came an unsmiling but graceful lady whose white hair showed the vestiges of having been blonde like Miss Glenville. Next entered an equally sober grey-haired gentleman. Miss Glenville, who walked in last, was the only one smiling.

Mr Glenville came to Tess's side. 'Let me present you to my parents.'

She raised her chin as his parents came to stand in front of her. They exchanged glances, their expressions grim.

'May I present Miss Tess Summerfield.' He gestured to his parents. 'My parents, Lord and Lady Northdon.'

She curtsied. 'I am honoured.'

'Yes,' uttered Lord Northdon.

Lady Northdon made a nervous laugh.

This was a horrible moment. Tess was desperate to survive it. 'I realise I am a great surprise to you. For that I apologise. I assure you I will certainly endeavour not to be a problem—'

'Problem?' Lady Northdon responded in a French accent. 'A surprise, yes, but we are quite able to accommodate a guest, even on short notice.'

'Then I am to stay?' she asked.

Lord Northdon cleared his throat. 'We did not even expect our son, so you will forgive us if we need time to accustom ourselves to you.'

Or was she not to stay?

Tess glanced at them both. 'Your son has told you of… me.'

To her surprise Marc took her hand and squeezed it. 'I old them of our betrothal. That we wish to marry as soon s I can arrange it.'

Even though her senses flared at his touch, she knew the gesture had been a signal, nothing more. He was trying to tell her he'd not explained everything.

Miss Glenville's eyes grew huge. 'You are to be married?'

Tess smiled at her. 'Yes. I could not tell you before your parents knew.'

'Married.' The girl's voice turned dreamy.

Lord Northdon scowled.

Lady Northdon glanced at him and laughed. 'My husband thought you were *enceinte.*'

'What was I supposed to think?' Lord Northdon snapped.

'It would have explained much, would it not, sir?' Tess mollified. 'But, no, I am not *enceinte.*'

The word hung in the air until Lord Northdon said, 'Well, are we going to sit or are we going to stand here all day?'

Lady Northdon swooped over. 'That is no way to speak to a guest, John.' She took Tess's arm. 'Come, sit with Amelie and me. Would you like some refreshment?'

Tess felt as if she'd fallen between two fighting cats. 'Miss Glenville served us tea.' She sat where Lady Northdon asked her to sit. 'May I ask if my maid and I are to stay in this house?'

'Oui.' Lady Northdon pursed her lips. 'If my son asks it, you must stay.'

That was not precisely a welcome. 'Then may I request my maid be shown our rooms? And be introduced to the rest of the staff and to the customs of the house?'

Miss Glenville piped up. 'I can take her to the housekeeper, Maman.'

Her mother waved her hand. 'Yes. Do that, Amelie.'

Nancy sent Tess an anxious but excited look before following Miss Glenville out of the room.

'Pour me some brandy,' Lord Northdon demanded of his son.

Marc crossed the room to a cabinet. He turned. 'Maman, some claret?' He paused. 'Tess?'

Tess waited for Lady Northdon to say yes before she agreed. 'I would very much like some claret.' A whole bottle of it, perhaps.

With glasses poured, Lady Northdon clapped her hands. 'Now we must plan a wedding, no? What church? Grosvenor Chapel? I know the fashion is to marry at St George's, but Grosvenor is closer.'

'They do not want a church wedding, Ines,' Lord Northdon shot back. 'The fashion is to marry at home by special licence.'

'I do not know such things.' She pouted. 'Marry at home. Pah! A wedding is for a church.'

'A church wedding is for the country where there might be many guests,' Lord Northdon countered. 'There will be no guests here.'

Marc drained his brandy in one gulp. 'Tess and I will decide, but we are not deciding now.'

Had Tess landed in Bedlam by mistake? 'Perhaps I might retire to my room until dinnertime?' she asked. 'I am a little fatigued from the journey.'

'Bien sûr,' Lady Northdon said. 'The room should be ready.'

Marc strode over to Tess. 'I will take you.'

Marc nearly pulled her out of her seat and out of the room.

Once in the hall, he slowed. 'I am so sorry, Tess. They were even worse than I feared.'

'How could you expect them to approve of me?' Tess asked.

'There is no reason they should not approve of you.'

Did he truly think that?

He led her up the stairs. 'My father knows of your parents, of course, but he is not in a position to object on that score.' He stopped at the first landing and faced her, holding her arms almost as if she were a true fiancée. 'I did not tell them the whole story. I said only that we were betrothed and will be married as soon as possible.'

She gave him an ironic smile. 'And that I am not *enceinte*.'

He rolled his eyes, but flashed a smile. 'That, as well.'

She could feel the tension in him even after he released her. He was trying so very hard to ease matters for her. Marc Glenville was a kind man.

'Come. I'll show you to the room.' They continued to the third floor. 'Your room is likely to be rather plain, I'm afraid. I do not think my mother's interest in decorating reached this floor.'

'I need nothing fancy.' Her room at Summerfield House had been very pleasant, but had not approached the opulence of the one Lord Tinmore allotted to her. 'Am I alone on this floor?' she asked.

'My room is here, too.'

Her insides fluttered.

As they approached the door, they heard voices. Nancy talking happily to someone.

When they opened the door, Nancy looked up. She and another maid were making the bed. A third girl was wiping the furniture.

'Goodness, miss!' Nancy exclaimed. 'We are almost done with the room, if you do not mind.'

Passing the time watching two cheerful maids doing their work seemed the best the day had to offer. 'I do not mind. I just wish to rest from the trip.'

'I will leave you.' Marc merely nodded and walked away.

Tess lowered herself into a chair by the window and rubbed her brow and wished she could be back in Lincolnshire.

* * *

Marc left Tess and went in search of Staines to help him change into fresh clothes. Clean linen and a coat and waistcoat not covered with the dirt of the road were almost reviving, but he was too stirred up to savour the experience. He wanted fresh air. A quick turn in the park would calm him enough to face the rest of the day.

On his way out, he met Amelie on the stairs. He embraced her. 'I did not have a chance to say a proper hello, little sister.'

'I am so glad you are here,' she answered, hugging him back so tightly his guilt at leaving her alone with their parents rushed back at him.

'I was away too long, I know.' He held on to her.

'I understand, Marc. Really, I do.'

She did not know any of it. His reasons for leaving his family, usually without a word, were hidden from them.

He released her, but held her at arm's length. 'By God, I believe I've been gone longer than I thought. You have turned into a beautiful woman while I was away.'

She blushed. 'Do not say such silly things.'

'I mean it.' He examined her again. How could she miss attracting suitors with a face like that? 'You should have a Season.'

Her smile turned sad. 'Maman and Papa do not receive many invitations.'

None, she meant.

'I'll do something about that, I promise.' He was filled with resolve.

Doria Caldwell, the woman he'd planned to marry, would have opened doors for Amelie. The Caldwells were not in the highest circles, but they received plenty of invitations. What he could do for Amelie now, he did not know. He'd brought on more scandal, not less.

Amelie pulled on his arm. 'Come. Talk to me a little. Tell me about Miss Summerfield. How you met her. Everything.'

He glanced away. 'There is little to tell. We met in Lincolnshire and I decided to marry her.'

Her pretty mouth opened, as if she were going to ask another question, but she shut it again. After a moment or two, she smiled again. 'Tell me about Scotland and anywhere else you've been.'

He put an arm around her. 'I have a better idea. Fetch a warm cloak. Let us take a walk in the park. Who knows? Perhaps you will catch the eye of some handsome young man.'

She pushed him away. 'I do not care about that, but I would love to walk in the park with you.'

It was the fashionable hour, but too early in the year for a turn in the park to be considered a social event. Too bad, maybe all she needed was to be seen in the park.

Marc resolved to think of some way for Amelie to be introduced to society. In the meantime, he would merely enjoy a walk with her.

Chapter Seven

When it was time for dinner, Marc knocked on Tess's door. The least he could do was save her from having to walk to the drawing room and face his parents alone.

Nancy opened the door and greeted him with a smile. 'Mr Glenville! Have you come to collect Miss Summerfield for dinner? She is ready.' She stepped away and revealed Tess. 'I tried to dress her hair like your mother's and your sister's, but different. And did we select the right dress?'

The maid had succeeded very well. Tess was a vision. Her hair was pulled high on her head and cascaded around her face in shiny chestnut curls. Her gown was simple and unembellished, a pale pink that might have been worn many times, but it flattered her. In fact, it made him all too aware she was a woman and that he soon would share a wedding night with her.

'You look…nice, Tess,' he managed.

She looked down at herself. 'This was one of the dresses I intended to alter with that lamentable lace and ribbon.'

The lace and ribbon she'd purchased on the day of the storm.

'I could alter your dress!' Nancy piped up. 'If I had

lace, I could put it around the neckline and perhaps at the sleeves and maybe around the skirt in some way. Beading would look wonderful sewn into the lace. If I had beading.'

Bless this maid. Her diversion interrupted Marc's too-carnal thoughts. 'I will ask my sister. I suspect there is plenty of lace and ribbon and beading in this house.'

'That would be wonderful!' Nancy beamed.

'I will ask her tonight.' Marc offered Tess his arm. 'Shall we go?'

She nodded, her expression a cross between tense and sad. He could not make this right for her, no matter how hard he tried.

When they entered the corridor, Tess sighed. 'She is so effortlessly happy.'

'Nancy, you mean?'

She nodded.

Unlike the two of them, he thought.

They reached the stairs and she hesitated. 'Are you certain I will not be underdressed? Your mother's and sister's day dresses were finer than this.'

He gazed at her and again was stirred into baser urges that turned his voice raw. 'It flatters you.'

Her eyes grew wide.

Finally she moved forward. 'I do not know why I asked. It was my only choice.'

They walked down the stairs.

'If it pleases you, buy as many new dresses as you desire. I am well able to pay for them.' His father provided an allowance made even more generous because of his brother's death but, even without that, he had money of his own.

She stopped and stared at him again. 'Thank you, Marc,' she murmured.

She looked so vulnerable at this moment all he wished

was to hold her in his arms. At this moment she could ask him for anything and he would provide it for her.

She affected him. Strongly.

He pulled away. 'It is the least I can do since we are to marry.'

She lowered her lashes and continued to walk down the stairs.

Tess entered the drawing room with emotions disordered. She'd felt drawn to Marc in those few moments together, almost as though they'd regained the camaraderie they'd shared in the cabin, but, inexplicably, he withdrew from her again.

She might have spent the entire evening disturbed by his manner, but, as soon as Marc's mother discovered Tess needed a new wardrobe, there was no chance to think of anything besides fabrics, modistes and the latest fashions, which Lady Northdon was determined Tess should have. Fashion, it turned out, was Lady Northdon's consuming interest.

She said, 'My father was—what is the word in English—'

'A linen-draper, Maman,' her daughter responded.

'*Oui*. A linen-draper.' She made a sound of disgust. 'Before he entered politics, that is.' Her expression brightened again. 'I grew up around the most marvellous fabrics and I knew all the best modistes in Paris, because they purchased only from my father, you know. I always wore dresses that were *au courant*.'

During the meal Lady Northdon and her daughter talked of nothing else but Tess's new wardrobe. Marc and his father held their own conversation and Tess could almost forget he was there.

Almost.

After dinner when the men remained in the dining room with their brandy, Lady Northdon sent tea up to her private sitting room where she pulled out a collection of fashion prints that would put Yardney's lending library to shame. She had the latest issues of *La Belle Assemblée*, and *The Ladies' Fashionable Repository*, as well as the *Journal des Dames et des Modes* from France.

Marc and his father never joined them. Tess told herself it was easier that way. She could almost pretend she was with her sisters, planning their next gowns, talking of what hats and shoes would go with them. Unlike discussing fashion with her sisters, however, this time no one ever discussed how much it would cost.

By the time Tess retired to her bedchamber, Lady Northdon and Miss Glenville were calling her Tess and she was calling Miss Glenville Amelie. She would not dream of addressing Lady Northdon as anything but Lady Northdon, but dropping the formality made it a little like having a family again. It should have given her enough peace to fall easily asleep.

Sleep did not come so easy, though. Alone, under the bedcovers, she thought again of Marc.

Perhaps love was impossible, under the circumstances, but could they at least be the friends they'd become when stranded in the cabin?

The next morning Tess found her way to the breakfast room with some assistance from the footman attending the hall. When she entered, though, she was alone.

Another footman stepped into the room.

'Am I too late or too early?' she asked him. 'When does the family eat?'

'Lord Northdon rises quite early and has already break-
fasted,' the man responded. 'The ladies tend to eat late.'

'And Mr Glenville?' Why must her heart pound when
she spoke his name?

'I believe he rose early and went out without eating,
miss.'

What could it mean that he left early?

'Thank you.' She approached the buffet and glanced at
the food. 'I am happy to serve myself, but I would love a
cup of hot tea.'

He nodded. 'Right away, miss.'

A generous array of breakfast foods was spread out on
the sideboard. Not only the breads, butter and jams she
was used to at home, but also oatmeal with cream, pound
cakes, ham and kippers. It was almost as varied and generous as the breakfasts at Tinmore Hall. She took a little
of each offering, which filled her plate rather fully.

She sat and the footman poured her tea and withdrew.

The good spirits with which she'd filled her plate ebbed
in the stillness and loneliness. She picked at her food and
wondered if she could abandon her plate without the footman reporting it to the cook and housekeeper and ulti-
mately reaching the ear of Lady Northdon.

The door opened and Marc entered the room.

She flushed with pleasure.

He paused and in that moment her spirits plummeted
again. He might not be pleased to see her.

Then he smiled.

'Tess, you surprised me.' He bowed to her. 'How nice
to see you up this early.'

His pleasure sounded genuine. She relaxed a little. 'I
am used to country hours, I fear.'

He glanced at the footman. 'Coffee, Wilson, if you
would be so good.'

Marc walked to the buffet and filled his plate. 'I rarely sleep late.'

They shared that trait, at least. Of course they'd both slept too late that morning in the cabin. How different everything would have been, if they had not.

He sat adjacent from her. 'I've given Apollo a bit of a run on Rotten Row.'

Dear Apollo, who'd carried them both through the storm and who'd travelled three days to reach London. 'Poor Apollo. Did he not deserve a day of rest?'

He glanced at her, but she could not read his expression. 'I think he appreciated the run. He dislikes holding back.'

She looked down at her food. Why could she not hold her tongue?

He started eating. The footman came with a pot of coffee for him and withdrew again.

He took a sip, then smiled at her again. 'I must tell Apollo sometime that he has a champion in you.'

When he smiled like that, he made it hard for her to breathe.

He cut a piece of ham. 'I have an errand to perform this morning. I am sorry to leave you alone.'

He did not sound all that sorry. 'Do not concern yourself. Your mother and sister are taking me to the shops for new clothes.'

'Are they?' He nodded. 'That should please Maman very much. There is nothing she enjoys more.'

'She is very knowledgeable.' Tess took a sip of her tea. 'She is taking me to a modiste on Petticoat Lane. A Madame LeClaire. Apparently Madame LeClaire is someone she knew in France when she was a girl.'

He frowned. 'Poor Maman. I did not realise she once knew the modiste. No wonder she likes to buy new dresses.' He speared a piece of ham and chewed it. After he'd swallowed it, he went on. 'She's had a difficult time of it.'

'It is a shame, really,' Tess said. 'She is a lovely person and so fashionable. There is much other ladies could learn from her.'

'You like her?' he asked.

Of course she liked her. 'She's been very kind to me.'

He reached over and took her hand. 'Let her order all the clothes she wants for you. As I said before, the cost is of no consequence.'

He cared about his mother. Another thing to like about him.

He released her and she was unsure what the gesture had meant.

'I am certain I will enjoy your mother's company and assistance. I only hope that I will look well enough for London.'

His blue eyes pierced her. 'You look well enough for London already.'

After breakfast, Marc set off on the first of his errands of the day. A visit to Horse Guards to an office of a gentleman he'd called upon several times before. The visit was a formality, an official end to the clandestine activities of which Marc had been a part these last few years of the war. Now that Napoleon had abdicated, though, his days as a British spy in France were over.

When Marc's brother died his father insisted he not return to his regiment. Marc had been forced to give up the dream he and his friend Charles shared since they were boys. But not long after, he'd been recruited for another sort of service to his country—as a spy.

On several occasions he crossed the Channel in secret and entered enemy territory. He watched the coast for naval activity, spent time in Paris meeting French contacts, keeping his eyes and ears open, passing for a Frenchman named Renard. Thanks to his French mother, Marc spoke the language without an accent and, with a simple change of clothes, he easily passed for a common Frenchman. The information he had gathered saved many a British soldier's life.

It was some consolation for not being at Ciudad Rodrigo to keep Charles from volunteering for the Forlorn Hope. Charles was one of the first to storm the walls; one of the first to die.

Marc walked up to the office of Lord Greybury, his superior, to say his final goodbye and receive his official release from duty. Only a select few, no more than he could count on one hand, knew what Marc had done for the war effort. That was all well and good. Marc had not risked his life for the glory of it.

He'd always known his days as a spy would come to an end. How different this end was than what he'd planned. He'd planned to help take Charles's place in Charles's family, and, in return, abide in a house that scandal had never touched, where rational thinking and calm discourse existed instead of shouted words and deliberate misunderstandings.

He and Tess would begin their marriage in scandal. Would they, like his own parents, wind up without having a civil word to say to each other?

The mere thought of her, though, stirred him. His rational mind might bemoan this scandalous marriage, but another part of him was in a hurry to wed her.

His next stop would be to Doctors' Commons at the office of the Archbishop of Canterbury where he would arrange a special licence. He and Tess would be able to marry within days.

He told himself this would be the best way to minimise the gossip that would ensue when word escaped that they'd been caught in a compromising situation. When they presented themselves as a married couple, there would be little to talk about.

Was that truly his reason? Or was he merely eager for the wedding night?

After his visit to Doctors' Commons, Marc had one more call to make.

He walked through Mayfair to the street where Mr Caldwell's town house was located. Likely Caldwell would be at the Home Office where he worked for Lord Sidmouth. That was for the best. It was his daughter Marc needed to see.

This house had been as familiar as his own ever since his school days when he and Charles became the best of friends. They'd both been mad for the army and obsessed by anything to do with it. Even as young boys they plotted to purchase commissions in the same regiment. For years the two of them had debated which regiment it should be and what part of the world they most wanted to see. India? The Colonies? When the time came, though, the Battle of Trafalgar had just been fought and both Charles and he were keen to fight Napoleon.

He and Charles joined the Eighty-Eighth Regiment of Foot, Connaught Rangers. The Devil's Own.

Marc reached the town-house door and sounded the knocker. The butler, who'd known him since those early school days, greeted him warmly. 'Glenville. Come in. Come in.'

A few minutes later, he was in the drawing room waiting for Doria. He'd known her nearly as long as Charles.

She entered the room as serene as always. 'Marc. How delightful. You are back in London. It is good to see you.'

She was, he realised, quite an attractive woman, dark and intense, with thick, grave brows framing fine, intelligent eyes. There was no reason for her not to stir his blood.

But she did not.

She extended both hands and he clasped them. 'Are you well, Doria?'

'Very well.' She smiled and led him to the sofa.

'And your father?' he asked.

She sat. 'He is in good health. But tell me about you. Did you enjoy Scotland?'

Her question seemed more out of politeness than genuine interest. 'Scotland was pleasant.'

'Would you like some tea?' she asked.

He joined her on the sofa. 'No. I cannot stay long.'

He'd never discussed marriage with her, not specifically, not since they were children and she had insisted in all seriousness that she would marry him. She was much like her father. Practical, intelligent and impassive. Their house had always been serene—unlike his—and he'd always preferred being there instead of his own home.

Charles had been equally as quiet on the outside, but his heart had always been full of big dreams and strong emotions admirably held in check—unless Marc pushed him to unleash them. Marc's emotions always seemed to burst from the seams, exploding from him like they constantly did from his mother and father. He taught Charles to let loose sometimes, to get into adventures. And scrapes. They'd had great fun.

And when they went too far, they could always return to this house. Here Marc learned he could keep his emotions in check, as well as his wild schemes. Charles, his father and Doria were masters of control. They taught him serenity.

So what had happened that Charles so lost his good sense? How had he allowed his emotions to go unchecked? Too soon after losing his brother, Marc had lost Charles, as well.

The grief of losing Charles washed over him, but Marc tamped it down. It was in this house where he'd gained that skill.

'I have something to tell you,' he said to Doria.

She gazed at him in friendly interest.

He took a breath. 'I am to be married.' He paused. 'Soon.'

Her thick brows rose. 'Married? What a surprise.'

Did she have any emotion beyond surprise? He could not tell. 'It is sudden, I realise.'

She blinked, then shook her head as if tossing away an unwanted thought. 'Who are you marrying?'

Had he hurt her? She would never allow him to see it, if he had. 'She is Miss Summerfield, daughter of Sir Hollis Summerfield of Yardney. You do not know her. She has not been to town before.'

'No, I do not know her.' She spoke so softly he barely heard her.

Her father would certainly have heard of the scandalous Sir Hollis and Lady Summerfield. She'd soon learn of it from him.

'I wanted to tell you before an announcement is made.' He wanted to spare her feelings as much as possible.

'How kind of you.' Her voice seemed composed. 'Is Miss Summerfield in town now?' she asked.

He nodded. 'She is staying at my parents' town house. We will be married by special licence.'

Her brows rose again. Whatever she assumed was his reason to act with such haste, she would soon learn, as well.

'Yardney is in Lincolnshire, is it not?' Doria was well versed in geography as well as most other subjects. She was well practised in making conversation, too. 'Will you be returning there or staying in town?'

'I do not know.'

A silence fell between them, a silence he had no idea how to fill. Had she been Charles he would have told the whole story, even down to his confused emotions regarding Tess Summerfield, but he and Doria had never been confidantes, and the very thing he most valued about her made it impossible for him to tell how his news had affected her.

She smiled politely. 'My father is giving a dinner party. Perhaps you and Miss Summerfield might join us.'

He could not think of anything worse. 'I could not attend and leave my sister and parents.'

'Then they must attend, as well,' she said.

'Please do not feel obligated, Doria.' The Caldwells had kindly included Marc's parents in invitations before. They were among the very few who did.

'Nonsense. They will be welcome,' she said. 'Your sister, too, of course. Is Amelie not of an age to be out?'

'She is.' Amelie had turned eighteen, an age most society daughters made their come-out.

'Then coming to my party will be a treat for her. There will be other young people there. My cousin and some of her friends. It will be good for Amelie to be introduced to them.'

He could not refuse. This party might be the very thing for his sister. It might lead to more invitations and more opportunities to meet potential suitors.

'Very well, Doria. We will attend your dinner party. It is exceedingly kind of you to extend the invitation.'

'It is tomorrow night,' she said.

Tomorrow night?

'Do you have another engagement?' she asked.

'No. No.' Certainly no other engagements.

'Good.'

'I must go.' He stood, suddenly too uncomfortable in the place he'd once always felt at ease.

She stood, as well. 'Wait a moment. I will pen a note to your parents and Miss Summerfield.'

She walked out.

He glanced around the room. He'd once counted on spending many more peaceful hours in this room. He'd always imagined he'd feel Charles's presence here, but the room seemed empty and strange.

She returned and handed him a folded piece of paper. 'We will see you tomorrow, then.'

He placed it in his pocket said goodbye to her there, walking out to the hall alone. The footman brought him his hat and greatcoat and he stepped out into the street.

He'd thought perhaps this was to be his last visit to the house where so many of his happy childhood memories resided. Now he would return. This time he'd squire his new bride to the home of his once-intended bride, with his parents in tow.

All for the sake of his sister.

Tess's morning had been filled with trying on dresses, discussing alterations and embellishments, and planning for other gowns. Lady Northdon and Amelie took her first to the modiste, who had several dresses already sewn that could be altered to fit her. After purchasing four gowns and ordering more, they went on to a linen-draper, a hat shop, a glove shop, a shoe shop.

In each shop, Lady Northdon knew the shopkeepers. She conversed with them happily, asked after their families, oohed and ahhed over their merchandise and appeared to thoroughly enjoy herself.

They were her friends, Tess realised, although the lady was not free to invite them to her home or call upon them at theirs. Tess's heart went out to her, a woman caught between two rungs of society and not belonging to either one.

It was a shame, really, that the aristocracy would not give Lady Northdon a chance. Amelie, as well, could be such a success with her beauty and style and pleasant manners. Gentlemen on the street noticed her. Some even turned around for a second look at her. In a ballroom, how could she not fail to have gentlemen standing in line to be her dance partner?

If Tess thought about it, her own place in London society was equally in question. She already felt as though she did not belong in this fashionable, busy city. She no longer belonged in Lincolnshire, either, though.

It was nearing two o'clock when they stumbled back into the Grosvenor Street town house. The three ladies retired to their bedchambers for a much-needed rest. Only Nancy, who had accompanied them at Tess's request, seemed to have gained energy from the expedition.

She'd been a proper servant during the expedition, staying in the background, not speaking unless spoken to, carrying parcels. Now, however, she was bursting with words.

'I never saw such beautiful fabrics!' Nancy gushed. 'And the designs! So clever! I could make you one of those dresses, miss. The modiste gave me so many wonderful ideas.' Her eyes grew huge. 'Perhaps I could make your wedding dress! I could make it out of some of those lovely silks we saw. An ivory-silk gown with a silver net over it? And beading. And lace! I know I could make it.'

A wedding dress? Tess had not thought about what she would wear. 'I am sure you could make a delightful dress, but you have your maid duties and you will not have much time.'

'I will. I know I will.' Nancy's eyes pleaded. 'All your dresses will be new. They will not require much care. Everything will be new. I will not have enough to do, I am sure of it. Will you please allow me to sew the wedding dress?'

Tess did not care what she wore—that was not true. She wanted Marc to admire her in it.

And it would make Nancy happy—happier, she meant. 'Very well. I will ask Mr Glenville for the money and you may go purchase everything you need.'

'Oh, thank you, miss!' Nancy jumped up and down. 'If I had paper and a pencil, I could make a sketch to show you.'

Paper and pencil. If Tess had paper and ink, she could write to her sisters. She should at least let them know she had arrived safely in London. 'Perhaps you could ask one of the servants how I might have paper and pencil for sketching and pen and ink, as well. Tell them both are for me.'

Nancy bobbed into a curtsy. 'Right away, miss!' She rushed out the door.

After she left, Tess collapsed in a chair and pressed a hand against her forehead. Wedding dresses. Writing to her sisters. The reality of her situation struck Tess anew. She was to be married to Marc Glenville, a man trapped into marrying her, a man she hardly knew.

A knock sounded at the door.

'Come in.' She expected Lady Northdon or Amelie.

The door opened. 'Tess?'

She spun around. It was Marc.

'I heard you were back,' he asked from the doorway. 'How was your shopping expedition?'

Her heart pounded. 'Expensive for you, I am afraid. I purchased a great deal of everything.'

He held up a hand. 'Do not worry over the cost. Enjoy your purchases.'

'At least I will not look shabby.' She gestured to herself. 'Your mother made certain I will wear the latest fashions.'

He smiled. 'She would know.'

His smile gladdened her.

She liked that he cared about his mother and was protective of her. Tess could not pretend to know Lady Northdon well, but after only a day, she knew that Lady Northdon was fiercely devoted to her son and daughter.

What would it be like to have such a mother? Marc spoke. 'I was about to take a walk in the park. Would you care to join me?'

Her fatigue fled. 'Certainly.' She grabbed her bonnet, gloves and pelisse.

Soon they were out of doors, walking down the pavement to the Grosvenor Gate of Hyde Park. He led her through the gate and on to one of the walking paths. The afternoon sky was bright, but overcast. The air was chilly, but Tess did not mind. It felt wonderful to walk with him. Such a normal thing to do. There were a few other people in the park, but so far away it was as if they were alone.

'It is a bit early for the fashionable hour,' he explained as if reading her thoughts. 'Both in the day and for the Season.'

The path took them across a long expanse of grass edged with trees and shrubbery.

'It is almost like a walk in the country,' she said.

He glanced at the sky. 'But one without a rainstorm.'

She smiled at him. 'I sometimes do take walks when there is not a raging storm.'

He smiled back. 'As do I.'

Her heart lifted.

'Do you know about the park?' he asked.

'Only that it is where London society goes to be seen.'
She'd learned that from magazines.

'It was created by Henry VIII in the fifteen hundreds
for hunting and was not open to the public until more than
a century later. Most of the landscaping, including the Serpentine, was created about one hundred years ago. We'll
walk to the Serpentine.'

The Serpentine was the small lake in the park.

They reached the water. It was serene, cool, rippling
gently in the light breeze. Such a contrast to the rushing,
white-foamed water flooding the bridge to Tinmore Hall
that fateful stormy day.

'It is peaceful here,' she commented.

'I should tell you of my errands today,' he said.

Somehow Tess's sense of peace fled. 'Where did you
go?' she asked politely.

'To the Archbishop of Canterbury's office for the special licence.'

The licence for them to marry. 'Oh?' she responded.

'It will take a few days.'

She did not know if that was good news or not. She
could not tell what he thought of it, either.

'I also called upon a friend,' he added in an ominous
tone.

'A friend.'

His words came in a rush. 'Miss Caldwell. Doria. The
sister of a school friend of mine who died at Ciudad Rodrigo.' The terrible siege where so many soldiers died.

She turned to him, now understanding completely.
'Speak plainly, Marc. Was this the woman you planned to
marry? The sister of a friend you spoke about in the cabin?'

He met her gaze. His eyes, reflecting the sky and water, appeared grey. 'Yes.'

She turned away and watched a brown-and-white duck swim in circles near the shore.

He spoke softly. 'I needed to tell her…about us. I could not chance her finding out in another way.'

'Of course you could not.' She understood. Really, she did. 'It must have been a difficult speech to make to her. And for her to hear.'

He rubbed his forehead. 'The whole experience was unsettling. It was like being in a strange place, but one that was once as familiar as my own image in a mirror.'

That was precisely how she had felt when Tinmore's carriage drove through Yardney. Everything familiar had suddenly turned foreign.

He went on. 'I cannot tell you how she reacted. She was completely self-contained. But I must tell you, she has invited our family—and you—to a dinner party tomorrow night. I do not know how many guests are expected, but several, I imagine. Her cousin and some friends among them.'

'A dinner party!' She turned to face him. 'Did you accept?'

'I did.'

She turned away again.

He touched her arm. 'We can cry off, if you wish it, but let me explain why I accepted.' He wrapped her arm around his and started walking again. 'Miss Caldwell's cousin is around Amelie's age. If we attend, it will give Amelie some social time with people her own age. I have no doubt Amelie will be a great success, so this might lead to more invitations.' He paused. 'You must know my family does not receive many invitations. I cannot stand in the way of her having some enjoyment, like other girls her age.'

Or the chance to meet potential suitors, Tess thought.

'Besides this, my mother and father so rarely are seen out socially. This would be good for them, as well.' He stopped and looked down at her. 'What say you?'

She did not want to attend any dinner party, especially one given by the woman he wished to marry. 'You do not think it cruel for me to attend? You were to marry her, Marc.'

'I would not be cruel to you, Tess. If it would be too uncomfortable for you, I will send word we will not attend.'

And have her be the means of depriving his sister of a party? 'I meant cruel to her, not to me.'

He shrugged. 'She extended the invitation, which she certainly did not have to do.'

Perhaps this Miss Caldwell wanted a look at the woman who'd stolen her prospective husband. She straightened her spine. 'I suppose I must face people sometime.'

Chapter Eight

The next day was a flurry of dressmaking.

Marc had not considered that Tess might not yet have a suitable dinner dress. Or that his mother and Amelie would tear through their wardrobes searching for the perfect gown to wear. Nothing they had was perfect. Everything required work.

Worse, his father loudly protested the commotion, insisting all the fuss was nonsense. That simply fired up his mother's temper. There had been nothing to do but insist his father take him to his club and introduce him to his cronies.

His father sometimes retreated to Brooks's Gentlemen's Club, the club that attracted members of the Whig party and others a bit more tolerant of his choice of a wife and his liberal political views. Not that their tolerance resulted in the club members' wives inviting the Northdons to many social events, but at least Marc's father was accepted and comfortable among the other gentlemen in the club.

They sat in the dining room where three or four other gentlemen sat alone with their faces hidden behind the *Morning Post*. Marc ordered a coffee; his father, a Spanish brandy.

'Not too many members here today,' Marc commented.

'Hmmph.' His father sipped his drink. 'I'd wager there are still some tables full in the game room.'

Brooks's was known for its gambling. At least his father never gambled. In fact, his father did not practise any vices, not that Marc knew of.

His father swallowed and took another drink. 'I cannot abide all that fuss about dresses.'

'It makes Maman happy, you know. What else has she to be happy about?'

His father frowned. 'She is not happy. She blames me.' He downed the brandy.

Marc peered at him, still a handsome man even with his silver hair and sagging skin. An unhappy man. 'Is there more trouble between you and Maman?' he asked.

'More trouble?' His father scoffed. 'Do you mean her accusing me of your brother's death? That is hardly new. How was I to know he would be so reckless?'

Lucien had fallen in love with an earl's daughter, but her father refused his suit and the foolish couple eloped to Gretna Green. They never made it, however. Her father's men went in mad pursuit and Lucien overturned his phaeton.

His father's complexion turned grey and he stared into his drink. 'She is right, though. I should have stopped him.'

'Enough, Papa,' Marc said gently. 'Do not blame yourself.' He put his hand on his father's arm.

His father pulled away and took another sip of his brandy.

Marc felt the slap of rejection, but, then, nothing Marc did pleased his father.

He lifted his mug of coffee in both hands and leaned back in his chair. 'The trouble I meant was—when I came home—you and Maman seemed to be accusing each other of infidelity.'

His father waved a dismissive hand. 'Words.' He signalled for another brandy. 'There is no infidelity.' He leaned closer to Marc. 'What about you? Hmm? Why the devil are you marrying Sir Hollis's daughter? You are being as foolish as your brother.'

Was he being as foolish as his brother? Perhaps, but he'd had no other choice, had he?

His father pointed a finger at him. 'Have you lost your senses over her?'

No. But he certainly had the feeling he was battling against losing his senses over her.

The servant returned with more brandy and poured it in his father's glass. His father swirled the nut-brown liquid. *'Thus grief still treads upon the heels of pleasure: Married in haste, we may repent at leisure.'* He downed the entire contents of the glass and gazed up at Marc with a bleak expression. 'At least your brother was spared the repentance.'

That evening Marc's father nursed another glass of brandy in the drawing room while he and Marc waited for the ladies to be ready.

His father tapped impatiently on the side table. 'Your mother will probably change gowns ten times. We'll be late. God knows how long your sister will be.'

'I'm certain someone will be more fashionably late than we are.' Marc felt anxious, too, but one family member needed to at least appear to be calm. His mother and Amelie would be nervous. And Tess? How could she not be?

His sister walked in the room. Her white dress seemed to float about her. Her blonde hair was all in curls like a halo around her head.

His father stopped in his tracks. 'Amelie.' His voice

was hushed. 'You look like—like your— You look like an angel.'

Marc rose and approached his sister to put a kiss on her cheek. 'Papa is right. You are a vision.'

Amelie blushed. 'You are both speaking nonsense, of course, but it is kind of you.'

His father continued to stare at her, almost as if he were seeing a ghost.

The door opened again and this time his mother entered. His father, for an instant, looked upon his mother with that same awed expression. It changed quickly to one that seemed devoid of all emotion.

Marc greeted his mother with a kiss, as well. 'You are in fine looks, Maman. You look glorious.'

His mother's dress was very simple and understated. It relied on colour for its beauty, a deep blue that accented her pale skin and blue eyes.

His mother smiled, but her smile turned uncertain when she glanced at his father.

'Mother looks as lovely as Amelie, wouldn't you say, Papa?' Marc asked.

'They both look fine,' his father answered, but his gaze was averted.

Curse his father! One kind word and his mother would have been over the moon. Marc turned away and saw Tess slip into the room.

He lost his breath.

She did not appear ethereal like Amelie, nor elegant like his mother, but something that pleased him more, something real and warm and female. Her gown was simple, like his mother's, but suited her perfectly, causing nothing to distract from her beauty and her presence. It was a deep, rich green that turned her eyes the same shade and accented the red tones in her hair. Perhaps he had nothing to worry over at this dinner. Surely when this woman entered the room, no one could possibly find fault with her.

There was no fault with her.

'You look beautiful, Tess.' His voice felt raw.

'Thank you,' she said tightly, obviously not believing him. 'I am sorry to keep everyone waiting.'

The others noticed her then.

'Ma chérie!' his mother exclaimed. 'You are perfection.'

Amelie smiled. 'Tess, the dress looks so lovely on you. I am sure everyone will be impressed.'

'Do you think so?' Tess gazed at Amelie and her mother. 'I think no one will notice me with the two of you there.'

Tess was kind to his mother and sister. How could Marc not value that?

He smiled. 'Papa and I will be the envy of all the gentlemen at the party.'

His father started for the door. 'Let us get underway, then.'

His mother held back. 'We will not look out of place?'

Marc put an arm around her. 'Maman, your taste in fashion is unsurpassed. You will not look out of place.'

'I agree,' said Tess with a reassuring smile. 'Although I cannot know what ladies wear to a London dinner party, I would wager you have struck the perfect tone.'

His mother looked mildly heartened.

'Come on,' his father snapped. 'We do not want to be the last ones arriving.'

The ride to the Caldwell town house was silent and thick with tension. Tess was nervous enough, but it made her sad to see Lord and Lady Northdon and Amelie this frightened to attend a dinner party, all because Lady Northdon had been a merchant's daughter and the daughter of French Jacobins.

Would the guests at this dinner party be willing to overlook Tess's scandalous family? Surely someone there would know all about her mother's many lovers and her father's foolish financial dealings. How many would have read of Lorene's marriage to Lord Tinmore? Tess provided plenty for the guests to whisper about even if they would not yet know the circumstances of her betrothal to Marc.

At the town-house door a footman ran out to open the carriage door and help them alight. This was not as prestigious an address as Grosvenor Street, even Tess could tell. The town houses were smaller, the streets narrower. Another footman met them at the door and took their cloaks and the men's topcoats and hats.

The butler walked them to the drawing-room door where he announced them. 'Lord and Lady Northdon, Mr Glenville, Miss Glenville and Miss Summerfield.'

All heads turned and some turned quickly away.

A pleasant-looking man in his fifties approached them and right behind him, a pretty young woman.

'Ah, Lord Northdon. Lady Northdon. How good of you to come. You know my daughter, Doria? Of course you do...' The man's smile was a little forced.

This was Mr Caldwell, obviously, and the young woman, his daughter.

Miss Caldwell looked at Tess with some interest. She was lovely. Dark-haired, fair-skinned, intelligent.

Mr Caldwell fussed over Amelie and the girl's face turned bright pink. Miss Caldwell greeted the family warmly, as if these were old, dear friends.

Finally they came to Tess.

Marc presented her. 'Mr Caldwell, Doria, may I present Miss Summerfield.'

'How nice to meet you.' The young woman seemed remarkably composed. She quickly turned to her father.

'Father, do you recall I told you Miss Summerfield and Marc are to be married?'

'Yes. Yes.' Mr Caldwell's cordial tone turned a bit sharp. 'Welcome, Miss Summerfield.' He turned to Lord and Lady Northdon, quickly dismissing Tess. 'Come meet the other guests.'

Marc offered his arm to Tess and leaned close to her ear. 'I apologise for Mr Caldwell. He was rude to you.'

'Perhaps he is disappointed,' she whispered back.

Marc looked exceptionally handsome in his black coat. His blue eyes were even more riveting than usual in the candlelight of the drawing room. How could Miss Caldwell not despise Tess for taking him away?

They followed Marc's parents and Amelie to where the guests were gathered. During the introductions, some people were kind and polite; some barely acknowledged them. Some guests' faces sparked with recognition when meeting Tess. Were they remembering her scandalous mother? Or her father? Or the new Lady Tinmore?

Amelie earned surprised stares and some frankly admiring ones from the gentlemen present, some envious ones from the ladies. Miss Caldwell's cousin took Amelie under her wing and included her in the group of younger people amusing themselves with a peg board in a corner of the room. Lord Northdon crossed the room to speak to someone and Marc was pulled away by Mr Caldwell.

Miss Caldwell found seats for Lady Northdon and Tess and sat with them, making pleasant conversation, mostly to Lady Northdon. She asked about Lady Northdon's gown and soon drew another lady into the conversation about modistes and linen-drapers and the latest dress designs.

That left her alone with Tess. She smiled politely. 'How long have you known Marc?'

Tess thought perhaps the question was not asked out

of politeness. 'Not very long.' Less than a week, actually. 'And you? You and your father seem like old friends of the Glenvilles.'

Miss Caldwell's smile faltered a bit. 'Old friends of Marc's. He and my brother were in school together as boys and were inseparable. Marc spent as much time in our house as his own, I think. Through him we have been acquainted with his family.'

'Yes,' Tess said. 'Marc told me of your brother and about his tragic loss.'

The young woman lowered her gaze. 'He died at Ciudad Rodrigo.'

'I am so sorry,' Tess said honestly. 'My brother is a soldier and I worry over him constantly.'

Miss Caldwell's gaze shot up. One brow lifted. 'Yes. Of course you do.'

Tess met her eye. 'You have heard of my brother, I see.' Her half-brother, that was. Tess could not remember a time when people did not talk about *Lord Summerfield's bastard* growing up with them.

Miss Caldwell looked almost approving. It was not the reaction Tess expected.

'Do you have any sisters?' Tess asked, grasping for conversation.

Miss Caldwell seemed lost in her own thoughts for a moment. 'Sisters? No. It was just my brother and me.'

At that moment two gentlemen appeared in the doorway, their faces not visible.

'Excuse me. More guests.' Miss Caldwell rose to greet them.

'Mr Pemperton and Mr Welton,' the butler announced.

Tess's gaze snapped to the doorway. Mr Welton—*her* Mr Welton—stepped into the room to be greeted by Miss Caldwell and her father. Tess's heart pounded. She'd heard that everyone knew everyone in Mayfair, but to encounter Mr Welton at her first party? Impossible.

But there he was.

She turned towards Lady Northdon again and pretended to listen to a conversation about sleeve length.

What was she to do? Walk up to him and say hello? Or avoid him?

She was saved from the decision by the dinner announcement.

Marc and his father came to escort Tess and Lady Northdon to the dining room. Amelie had a couple of gentlemen vying for her arm. Mr Welton disappeared somewhere behind Tess and she was certain he had not seen her.

As the group of about thirty people assembled, Miss Caldwell raised her voice. 'We are not being strict about precedence at the table, you will notice. We sat people where they might find most enjoyment.'

Once inside the dining room, though, Lord and Lady Northdon earned places at the high end of the table. How very astute of Miss Caldwell. To have placed them anywhere else would have felt like a snub, even with the caveat of her announcement. Tess's name was further down, but she was seated next to Marc. Again, Miss Caldwell had been exceedingly kind—and generous—to seat Tess next to Marc.

Luckily, Tess was not in Mr Welton's direct line of sight. He sat on the other side of the table, but several seats away from her.

As the dinner progressed, Marc seemed to be doing his best to make conversation with her. He talked about the food and the wine and was solicitous of her needs. He also included her in conversations with the guests who sat next to them.

When those guests were occupied in other conversations, Tess leaned towards him. 'Your mother seems to be doing well. I was worried for her.'

He nodded. 'I was worried, too.'

Tess looked to where Marc's parents sat. 'Miss Caldwell has been kind to me and to your family. She seems to be a fine person.'

He glanced down at his plate. 'Yes, she is.'

Tess gripped her fork. 'Oh, Marc. I feel dreadful. She would make you a fine wife.'

Marc stabbed at a piece of meat. 'Do not think about it, Tess.'

Tess attended to her own plate. How could she not think about it?

Another course was served and they fell into silence with each other, speaking only when the guests next to them required it.

After some time, Marc lightly touched her arm. 'There is a gentleman who keeps looking at you.'

She knew whom he must mean. 'Oh?'

'Blond dandy-looking fellow on the other side of the table.' He tilted his head in the man's direction.

She glanced quickly. 'Mr Welton.' Welton's fine tailoring did seem a bit excessive. Especially if compared to Marc's ease in his clothes. 'I am acquainted with him. He visited his aunt recently in Yardney.'

'In Yardney.' Marc frowned.

He made her feel as if she'd been caught in some indiscretion, which was ridiculous.

'He might not recognise me,' she said. 'Your mother and Nancy have transformed me.'

His gaze pierced her. 'You would not be so easy to forget.'

She felt her cheeks flush with pleasure.

* * *

After dinner the ladies returned to the drawing room for tea. This time the ladies grouped themselves with their friends. Tess sat with Amelie and Lady Northdon.

Amelie was bursting with talk. 'The people here are so kind. I've felt so very welcome.'

'They ought to welcome you, *chérie*.' Her mother patted her arm.

'Some of the young men seem to enjoy your company,' Tess added.

Amelie, as isolated as she was, must not be used to such attention. If only Genna were here to help her.

Amelie coloured and lowered her lashes. 'I have been paid some pretty compliments, but surely the gentlemen are merely being polite.'

'Pah!' Her mother's eyes flashed. 'You are a beauty, but you must be on guard. If they are gentlemen, they will court you properly, no?'

'Oh, no one has said anything untoward, I assure you, Maman,' Amelie responded. 'I do not think I have ever felt so much friendship.'

Was it genuine friendship or some goodwill manufactured by Miss Caldwell?

Tess turned to Lady Northdon. 'You have been received with kindness, have you not?'

Lady Northdon lifted her teacup. 'For the most part.'

Miss Caldwell joined them. 'Is there anything you need, ladies?'

'*Non,*' answered Lady Northdon.

Good for Lady Northdon. She maintained her dignity.

Miss Caldwell smiled at Amelie. 'You have been quite a success, have you not? My cousin assures me several of the gentlemen are smitten already.'

Amelie blushed again. 'Surely you exaggerate.'

What man would not admire Amelie? The girl outshone all the other young ladies.

'I assure you they were lovestruck.' Miss Caldwell glanced at each of them. 'In fact, the ladies are all impressed by your fashion. What is your secret, *madame*? A new modiste?'

'Not new to me,' Lady Northdon replied.

'Well, you all look very lovely.' Miss Caldwell pressed Lady Northdon's hand and moved on to another group of ladies.

After she walked away, Lady Northdon took another sip of tea. With the cup next to her lips, she murmured, '*Quelle horreur!* She feels obliged to be kind to us.'

Amelie's eyes widened. 'Maman! What a horrid thing to say.'

Lady Northdon lifted a shoulder. 'I do not like to feel someone needs to make an effort to be civil to me.'

Yes. There was an air of forced solicitude when Miss Caldwell spoke to them, now that Lady Northdon called her attention to it. Even so, Tess wondered if she could have forced herself to be as kind as Miss Caldwell had the tables been turned.

Amelie protested more and listed all the nice things Miss Caldwell and her friends had said or done this night. Tess could hear no more praise for this fine woman.

She rose. 'Excuse me for a moment.'

Let them think she was in need of the lady's retiring room, but all she truly wanted was a few moments alone. She peeked inside the room set aside for the ladies and found several others there. She tried another door and found a small library where she sank into a chair.

She must not think only of herself and the strain of this evening. She must also think of Marc. How much worse it must be for him. And for Miss Caldwell. Tess had ruined their plans.

The truth of it was, she could see a marriage between Marc and Miss Caldwell working very well. Miss Caldwell would never impetuously walk to the village when rain threatened. She would never become besotted by a gentleman from London visiting his aunt in Lincolnshire. Miss Caldwell could provide the serene, respectable married life Marc desired.

What could Tess offer him?

More scandal.

She heard men's voices in the hallway. They must be rejoining the women. She waited until the voices died away to return to the drawing room. She tried to slip in unnoticed. As soon as she walked through the door, though, Mr Welton approached her.

'Miss Summerfield?' He bowed.

'Mr Welton.' She curtsied.

She'd once felt breathless at just the sight of him in Yardney; giddy when he spoke to her. She felt nothing now. His handsome face, blond hair and pale brown eyes were still striking, but she was unaffected.

He smiled. 'I confess I did not know you at first.'

'I am newly arrived in London,' she said.

'Did I not hear your sister married old Lord Tinmore?' He gave her a knowing look. 'Such a change of fortune for your family.'

His tone was polite and conversational. And utterly indifferent, such a contrast to his flirtation and pretty words in Yardney.

'I understand you are betrothed to Mr Glenville,' he continued in that uninterested manner. 'My very best wishes to you.'

'Thank you,' she managed to say.

He glanced over to Amelie. 'Is Miss Glenville out, I wonder? She is a lovely young lady. If only—' He cut himself off. 'Well, never mind that. Is your sister in town? Your younger sister?'

Genna. Beautiful Genna. 'No, she is not.'

'Tinmore has been generous to your family, I hear.' He meant Tinmore had restored Genna's dowry, she'd wager. 'I heard he planned to break his exile and come to town for the Season. Your sister will come as well, will she not?'

'Yes,' she answered through gritted teeth. 'But, I assure you, Mr Welton, my sister will be looking so much higher than you. After all, Lorene married an earl and I will be a viscountess some day. I believe Genna has hopes to best us with a marquess.'

He was the mere younger son of a baronet.

She curtsied again. 'If you will excuse me, sir. I must return to Lady Northdon.'

She turned away and crossed the room, taking her seat next to Lady Northdon again and attempting to look as unaffected by the interview as possible.

Mr Welton was nothing but a fortune hunter. He'd been toying with her in Yardney. It all had meant nothing to him. How could she have been so fooled?

Across the room Marc sat with Doria Caldwell, watching the scene between Tess and Welton.

'They appear to know each other,' Doria said, as impassive as always.

'She is acquainted with him.' Marc felt consumed with jealousy. 'They met in Lincolnshire.'

'Did they?' She turned to him. 'My father told me about her mother and father. And of her sister's recent marriage.'

He nodded. 'Both our families have scandal in them.

I'll not fault her for the sins of her mother and father if she does not fault me for mine.'

She placed her hand on his arm. 'You are quite right.' She lowered her voice. 'Our family has always loved you for yourself.'

The truth of that felt like a stab in the heart.

He wanted to apologise to her, but that would imply that he'd made her a promise and he had not, not when he'd known he'd be riding into danger at any moment. He'd been careful not to make any promises, although he'd wanted to when Charles died.

He averted his gaze from her and saw Tess return to sit next to his mother.

From the moment Tess said she'd met Welton in Yardney, Marc realised who the man was. Welton was the man Tess had wanted to marry, the man who needed her to have a big dowry to make it worth his while. Marc disliked Welton on sight—well—as soon as he'd seen the man looking at Tess.

Marc's father, standing across the room, gestured for Marc to come.

He rose. 'You'll have to pardon me, Doria. I believe my father wishes to leave.'

'So soon?' She stood, as well. 'I am glad you and your family came. And Miss Summerfield, too, of course. I wish you happiness.'

He took her hand. 'You are a fine lady, Doria. Charles would be proud of the woman you've become.'

Tears filled her eyes. 'Say no more.'

He squeezed her hand and turned away from her.

His father reached him before he'd taken more than a few steps. 'Your mother is ready to leave.'

Marc would bet it was his father who'd tired of the party, who'd tired of pretending the guests weren't forcing themselves to be civil to him. His mother was made of sterner stuff.

'I will say goodnight to Mr Caldwell and arrange for the footman to get our coats.'

A few minutes later they stood outside the town house in the chilly February air, waiting for their carriage. Marc's father was pacing the street, impatient for its arrival. Amelie was excitedly talking with their mother about all the people she'd met—all the young men who'd noticed her.

Marc's thoughts were with Tess, though. It was all he could do not to demand she tell him what she and Welton spoke about.

'How was it for you?' he asked instead.

'The party?' she responded. 'Quite splendid for my first town entertainment.' She did not sound as if it were so splendid. 'How was it for you? It must not have been so easy.'

He gazed down at her, her lovely face illuminated by the rushlights mounted outside the town-house door. 'Not so easy for you, either.'

She glanced away. 'I assure you. It was a lovely party.' Her eyes darted back. 'Not nearly as difficult as a freezing cabin with dwindling firewood.'

He laughed softly and his heart warmed to her. 'I believe I would have preferred the cabin.'

Her brows rose. 'Would you?'

He took a breath. 'There is something to be said about shutting out the rest of the world for a brief time.'

She seemed to search his face. 'Especially when the world outside is so cold.'

Was she talking about the party or the cabin?

'I shall always remember the cabin. It was the place you brought me after saving my life.' She held his gaze.

'Although your life might have been better if you had ridden right by me.'

'I could not have done so.'

She nodded. 'Yes. That would not be in your character, would it? And look how I thank you for it.'

'We are both in this fix.' He touched her arm. 'Do you wish to marry him?'

'Who?'

'Mr Welton.' He spat out the name.

She blinked in surprise. 'Mr Welton? Not at all.' She paused, then lowered her voice. 'What of you? Your attachment to Miss Caldwell was the stronger.'

Truth was, he could not imagine marrying Doria now. He was sensible that he'd broken a promise to her, though, even if it was a promise unspoken.

'Do you wish me to cry off?' she asked, her voice no more than a whisper. 'Because I will, if you wish it.'

He closed the short distance between them and gently touched her face. 'I am marrying you, Tess.'

She looked up at him, her eyes dark, her breath quickening.

'Where the devil is the carriage?' his father bellowed.

Tess jumped back.

Chapter Nine

Marc could not sleep.

He was on fire for her.

Tess had looked so beautiful this night, like a jewel cut
and polished to perfection. His eyes kept straying to her
and it had been all he could do to remain composed. He'd
wanted to take her by the arm and leave the Caldwell town
house, return here and make love to her. When that dan-
dified Welton approached her, he'd wanted to plant the
man a facer. He'd managed to hide his runaway emotions
until they were waiting for the carriage. Then he'd almost
kissed her.

How would it have felt, to seize the woman to whom he
was betrothed and take possession of her mouth?

His father's words pounded in his head—*Thus grief
still treads upon the heels of pleasure...*

Did any good come from so totally losing one's head
and acting out of passion?

Not for his father, certainly.

Nor his brother.

Nor Charles.

How could this work to marry her? She did not wish
to marry him, after all. She had been forced into it. She'd
wanted a husband to love her.

Marc knew this consuming desire for her was not love, but something more primal, something that had robbed his father and mother of happiness and robbed his brother and friend of their lives.

He must conquer this, control it before it controlled him.

He glanced out the window into the starless night. If it were dawn, he'd dress and take Apollo for a long run in the park. Dawn was a few hours away, however.

He paced in his room.

He'd wanted a peaceful and scandal-free life, hadn't he? He'd wanted to marry Doria. They each had an esteem for the other, an admiration. Marriage to her would have been calm and sane, without this churning lust that did him no credit at all.

The memory of Tess's hazel eyes flew into his head. Her eyes were so beautifully expressive. How might those eyes appear in the heat of passion?

He went to the window again and opened the sash. The cool air rushed in like a good slap on the face.

This was madness. Stop thinking, for God's sake.

Marc shut the window again and strode to the door. He left his bedchamber and made his way to the drawing room. A decanter of brandy might quiet his insanity. Make him sleep. He opened the cabinet. The decanter was full. He poured a glass and downed it right there. He grabbed the decanter and glass and returned to his room. Two glasses later, he was only more restless.

He remembered the reflection of her lithe body in the glass of the cabin's window as she had donned her shift. He remembered her creamy, smooth skin, her full breasts and narrow waist.

He poured another glass and downed it in one gulp.

Damnation!

There was only one way out of this. Call off the wed-

ding. So what if Tinmore withheld funds from her sister
and her brother? Marc could make up for that. He could
support Tess, if she so desired. He could give her an in-
come and a dowry. Enable her to marry a man she could
love.

He'd do it!

Marc threw the glass down, wanting to hear it shatter,
but, instead, it bounced off the curtain and rolled across
the carpet. He retrieved it and poured the remains of the
brandy into it, finishing it off.

Why had he not thought of this before? Give them
money. Free Tess and free himself from this insanity.

He'd tell her. Tell her now. It seemed as good a time as
any. Why not? Her room was just a few feet away from
his door.

He placed the empty glass on the table and walked carefully out of his room, his gait unsteady from the brandy.
Still in bare feet, he padded over to Tess's door and raised
his arm to pound on it.

That would not do. He'd wake the whole house.

He rapped lightly. 'Tess. Are you awake? Want to speak
with you.'

He heard her voice faintly through the closed door.
'Marc?'

'Let me in. Need to say something.' He swayed and
steadied himself against the door jamb.

'One minute,' she said.

His head spun, but he ignored it.

Finally she opened the door. 'What is it?'

In the dim light of the hall sconce, she appeared little
more than a shadow. The scent of lavender wafted around
her and intoxicated him even more than the brandy. Lavender. The laundress always scented the bed linens with
lavender. Now whenever he lay between the sheets, he'd

think of her. Her feet were bare, too. Like in the cabin. The memory of her warm against his body slammed into him.

He lowered his voice. 'May I enter?'

She opened the door wider and he stepped inside.

The only light in the room was from the fireplace. It turned her nightdress and robe a ghostly white, like an apparition. A dream. A pleasant dream. Marc shook his head.

He watched as the apparition took a taper to the fire and used it to light a lamp on a nearby table.

She blew out the taper. 'What is it, Marc?'

She was so lovely, so much like the woman in the cabin and the beauty who'd dressed in green for the dinner party. His senses flared with desire.

Why had he come to her bedchamber? He tried to remember. All he could think of was making love to her. She looked like a woman who needed to be well loved.

He shook his head and remembered. He'd come to talk about money.

He came closer. 'Wanted to tell you…' The scent of the bed linens reached his nostrils again and the words disappeared.

He touched her shoulder and fingered a lock of her hair. 'You look lovely, Tess.'

What would it feel like to slide his hand down her body and explore the softness beneath her nightclothes? He remembered her curves when they'd lain together on the cot in the cabin.

A sound of discomfort came from her throat. 'You came to tell me something?'

He nodded. By God, the drink affected him. He couldn't stand without swaying. He couldn't think. 'We have to marry, Tess.'

She stood very still. 'Did you come here to tell me that?'

No, it felt more likely he'd come to feel her hair beneath his fingers. To taste her lips.

He leaned close, so close those lips were a mere touch away. He had almost tasted her lips earlier. If he kissed her, would it ease this sudden hunger for her? How would she taste if he plunged his tongue inside her mouth? If he plunged himself inside her?

Why not? They'd be married within days.

He closed his eyes and his mind cleared for a moment. He leaned away.

She stepped back. 'I think you should go back to your room, Marc.'

He nodded and, still gazing at her, backed away.

'We will marry,' he said again when his hand was on the latch of the door. Before he weakened and changed his mind, he walked out and closed the door behind him.

Tess stared at the closed door, her body a-tremble. What had happened?

He'd been drinking, clearly.

What did it mean that he'd come so close, touching her hair, her arm, making her senses come alive? She was quivering with the mere memory of his touch.

Had he wanted to bed her? Before marriage? Her old governess used to lecture Tess and her sisters to beware of men who'd imbibed too much wine or brandy. Too much drink drove men and women into bed with each other, the governess said.

It was true. Tess had seen her mother drinking wine with a gentleman who'd called upon her. She'd been in her mother's sitting room, a place she'd been forbidden to enter, so she'd hidden behind the curtains. Through a slit in the curtains, she'd seen them kiss. And undress. And—and—

She'd never told anyone of that.

But now all she could think was that Marc had wanted to do that with her. She should have been shocked. Appalled.

Instead, she'd wanted to feel *his* hair between her fingers, put her hand on his shoulders. She'd wanted him to kiss her. She'd wanted him to lie with her in the bed like her mother had lain with her gentleman.

Perhaps she was more like her mother than she ever dreamed she could be.

Tess extinguished the lamp and walked back to her bed. She climbed in. Sleep would be difficult to achieve when every part of her seemed on fire. Was this what her mother had felt when gentlemen came near?

She had never felt this way when Mr Welton shook her hand or leaned close. This was something carnal, something with a power all its own. Something she wanted.

It was unforgivable for Marc to come to her in such a state, was it not? Tess tried to muster up anger or outrage or even embarrassment, but, even now, she wished he would come back.

If Marc Glenville returned to her room this moment and wished to be carnal with her, she would not stop him.

The next morning Marc slept later than usual. When he roused himself, his head ached and his stomach roiled. He washed, shaved and dressed, all the while hoping Staines could not tell he was trying not to cast up his accounts.

In the dining room, the smell of kippers and cheese nearly set him off. He quickly took a piece of toast and poured a cup of coffee and was very glad he was alone in the room.

Not for long, however.

Tess entered.

He thought he must look like hell, but she was as fresh as the air after a storm. Her hair was simply dressed atop her head. She wore a dress of sprigged muslin, blue on white, with blue flowers embroidered on the shoulders and around the hem.

She paused when she saw him.

He stood. 'Good morning, Tess.'

She did not look at him. 'Good morning.' She went directly to the sideboard.

The footman appeared, but only long enough to bring her a pot of tea. Marc was drinking coffee. Lots of coffee.

She sat not too close to him, but not as far away as she might have. She kept her attention on her food, a piece of bread with jam.

He needed to say something. 'I owe you an apology, Tess.'

She gave him the briefest glance.

'I came to your room last night.'

She finally gave him a direct gaze. 'I know.'

He met her eye. 'It was unforgivable of me to wake you and to come to your room. I had too much to drink.'

'Why did you come?' she asked.

He did not wish to tell her of his brandy-laced plan to buy her off. It would not have worked. It would have left her in more scandal, with a ruined reputation and little chance of making a respectable marriage.

He shook his head. 'I do not remember.'

Her brows rose.

'I will say,' he went on, 'that I am not in the habit of drinking to excess. It will not happen again.'

She nodded and glanced back to her food.

A footman came in. 'Lord Northdon wishes to see you in the library, sir.'

A summons from his father never meant anything good. 'Thank you. I'll see him directly.'

He stood again. 'What are your plans today?' he asked Tess.

She looked up at him. 'Your mother wishes to take me shopping again.'

'Do you mind?' Not everyone shared his mother's passion for shopping.

'No. I enjoy it.'

He was not sure if she was being completely honest, but her kindness to his mother meant a great deal to him.

He walked over to her, needing to touch her, just a little, before he left the room.

He touched her shoulder. 'You should have spending money of your own. I will make sure you have some before you leave.'

She grew quite still under his hand. 'Thank you.'

He lifted his hand, his fingers still feeling the warmth of her. He bowed to her and left the room and made his way to the library.

When he stepped into the room, his father swung around in his chair. 'About time. What took so long?'

'Eating breakfast.' And touching Tess.

His father looked him up and down. 'Your colour is poor. Are you ill?'

'Not ill.' He was not going to explain that he'd consumed an entire decanter of brandy and almost seduced his fiancée. 'You have need of me, sir?'

His father picked up a rolled document and handed it to Marc. 'A messenger brought this earlier. Your special licence.'

Marc's stomach protested.

He took the document into his hand and unrolled it. 'It

seems in order.' He took a deep breath. 'I must tell Tess it is here.' He turned to the door.

'Wait,' his father cried. His expression looked strained. 'No one else knows. If you need more time—'

Marc shook his head. 'There's no need to wait.'

Truth was, he did not want to wait. He'd search today to find a clergyman to perform the ceremony as soon as possible.

'Why the devil are you marrying this woman, Marc?' His father sounded exasperated. 'Why the hurry if she is not with child? It does not make sense. There is something you are not telling me.'

He owed it to his father to hear the truth from him. 'There is more to it.' He hoped his breakfast would stay down. 'When I was riding back from Scotland, I came across Tess on the road in a rainstorm. She was suffering greatly from the wet and the cold. I found a cabin and took her there to get her warm. We were forced to spend the night. In the morning Lord Tinmore's men found us and Tinmore declared I had compromised her.'

His father's face turned red. 'You compromised her? How could you be so foolish?'

Marc stared at him. 'I did nothing you would object to. If I had not taken her to the cabin, she would have died from the elements.'

His father averted his gaze, then gave Marc a sceptical look. 'There must be more to it than that.'

Only that Tinmore had threatened to impoverish her, her sister and brother, but what purpose would it serve for his father to know that? 'I am honour bound to marry her.'

'How many knew of this? Could it not have been kept quiet?'

Marc shook his head. 'Tinmore was having a house party at the time. With luck most will have forgotten it by the time those guests and Tinmore arrive in town, but there may be some gossip about it.'

'More talk…' His father spoke more to himself than to Marc.

'I am sorry, Father.' Marc meant it. He never wanted to cause anyone to talk of his family.

'You need to do this, then.' His father's voice sounded more resigned than dictatorial.

'I do, Papa.'

His father rose from his chair. 'If only she came from a better family. Her parents—'

Marc cut him off. 'Do not say a word about her parents.' Surely his father could see the hypocrisy in complaining about *her* parents.

His father walked up to him and gripped his upper arms. 'I did not mean that. I meant—well, I thought—I thought you were marrying her because she had a pretty face.' He looked earnestly into Marc's eyes. 'I feared you would make the same mistake.'

'As you did with Maman?' Marc shrugged him off. 'You have told me many times of your regret at marrying my mother. I do not need to hear it again.'

His father shot back, 'Credit me with wanting to save you pain.'

Marc grimaced. 'Now you are saying marriage to my mother gives you pain. You cause her pain, too, you know.'

His father looked as if Marc had slapped him. 'I think of it. Every day.' His expression turned to concern. 'I do not wish you to have regrets, my son. Perhaps if I had said these things to your brother—' He broke off and waved those words away. He pointed to the special licence. 'Let me lock the paper up in a drawer. We can think of a way out of this.'

'I will marry her. It is the only way.' Marc rolled up the

special licence again and put it in a pocket inside his coat. 'We'll be married as soon as I can arrange it.'

His father nodded. The man suddenly looked smaller and older than he had a moment before.

Marc patted him on the back. 'It will work out, Papa. It is not like Lucien.'

He wanted to marry Tess and there was nothing impetuous about it. He must marry her to spare her reputation. There was no reason they could not do well together.

Especially if he banked his passion and kept it under tight control. There was no reason they could not have the rational sort of marriage he'd planned with Doria.

If he could indeed bank his passion and keep it under tight control.

He left his father and went to get Tess some spending money. He'd venture out that very morning and search for a clergyman to perform the ceremony.

Later that day Marc walked through Mayfair on his way back to his parents' town house. He'd spent hours searching for a clergyman. Finally he found a man from St Clement Danes who agreed to perform the ceremony in three days' time.

It should not have been so difficult, but, as it turned out, many men of the cloth were not eager to perform a service for Lord and Lady Northdon's son. He did not know why he should have expected a different reaction. Such treatment he'd experienced his whole life.

He turned down Berkeley Street from Piccadilly and decided to stop in Gunter's Tea Shop for some sweets for his mother, sister…and Tess. He entered the shop and who should be there, peering into the glass-covered cases displaying treats of all kinds and colours, but Doria, attended by her maid.

He had not expected to see her so soon. Or even at all, for that matter.

She looked over and smiled. 'Marc. What a surprise.'

'Indeed.' He walked over to her. 'How are you, Doria?'

She continued to smile. 'I am well.'

They stared at each other until he turned to the case. 'I came in for some sweets.'

'As did I,' she said.

A clerk approached and she made her order.

Another waited on Marc.

Their packages were ready at the same time and he walked out with her, her maid following.

'What did you select?' she asked.

'Ginger candy, sugar drops and some French nougat,' he responded. 'My mother is particularly fond of French nougat.'

She gestured to the maid who carried her package. 'And my father adores liquor comfits.'

They stood outside the shop. 'I want to thank you again for inviting my family to your dinner party. I think Amelie will talk of nothing else for weeks.'

'I am glad,' Doria responded.

They stepped aside for a gentleman and lady to enter the shop.

She went on. 'Your Miss Summerfield seems like a lovely person.'

He did not know what to make of that. 'I am glad you think so.'

She glanced across the street to the square where there were benches for Gunter's customers to enjoy his ices during the summer months. Most were empty this day.

'Would you sit with me for a minute?' she asked. 'I wish to say something to you.'

'Of course.' He escorted her across the street.

Her maid sat a discreet distance while he shared a bench with Doria.

She seemed to steel herself. 'I think you realise that everyone expected you to make an offer to me—'

He interrupted her. 'We never spoke of it. I never offered marriage to you.'

She held up a hand. 'Yes, I know you did not. There was a time I assumed it would happen, though.'

'I am sorry, Doria,' he said.

'Wait.' She shifted her posture. 'This is difficult to say. I want you to know that I would have refused you.'

He leaned back in surprise.

Her brows furrowed and her voice turned very low. 'The truth is, you are too much a reminder of Charles. Every time I look at you, I remember he is gone. My father very much wanted me to marry you, but he and I must move on from Charles's death. I know we cannot do that if you—if you are constantly present.'

He took her hand. 'I miss Charles, too.' He quickly released her. 'I want you to know, no matter what gossip you hear, that I want to marry Tess. We will be married in three days.' He gave her a wan smile. 'You are the first to know that.'

She took his hand back. 'I am genuinely happy for you.'

Tess gazed out of the carriage window as Lady Northdon and Amelie discussed what to do with the pieces of fabric they'd purchased. Nancy sat in rapt attention to their every word. Tess could barely attend to any of it. She was tired from a fitful night's sleep and a lot of shopping. This day they had visited a corset maker and ordered several types of corsets for her, as well as looking in on yet another linen-draper where Nancy found a silk ivory fabric she declared perfect for Tess's wedding dress. To Nancy's great pleasure, Lady Northdon and Amelie heartily agreed.

Tess's thoughts drifted to Marc. How it felt for him to be so close, to touch her, to have his blue eyes look at her in such a way that made her know he wanted to bed her. Could a man who did not want to marry her still want to bed her?

It must have been the drink. That was the only explanation.

The carriage drove slowly by one of the squares that seemed to be everywhere in Mayfair. This was Berkeley Square, she remembered. They were only a short distance from the town house, thank goodness.

The square was lovely, with trees starting to sprout leaves and plenty of grass and benches for people to sit on.

A lady and gentleman sat on one of the benches, their hands clasped.

Tess gasped.

It was Marc and Miss Caldwell.

Chapter Ten

Tess quickly glanced at Lady Northdon and Amelie to see if they noticed the couple, but both ladies and even Nancy were still wrapped up in the discussion about fabric.

Her throat tightened.

Why would Marc be with Miss Caldwell?

Why else but that he still felt an attachment to her?

How often had she heard her father lament that he'd married her mother instead of the woman he truly loved—Edmund's mother. He'd kept Edmund's mother as a mistress and she'd borne him a son. He'd spent more time with her than with his own wife, more time with his son than the children his wife eventually bore, the ones everyone said were fathered by her lovers.

They all wound up unhappy. That is what happened when two people did not marry for love.

That is what would happen to her and Marc.

The carriage entered Grosvenor Street and brought them to the door.

When they were inside the town house, Tess said, 'I am suddenly very tired. I believe I will retire to my room for a little while.'

'*Mon Dieu, ma chérie,*' exclaimed Lady Northdon. 'You do look pale. Go. Rest. We do not wish you a *maladie.*'

Her kindness made Tess's eyes prick with tears.

She gave Lady Northdon a quick hug. 'Thank you, *madame.*'

She felt like running up the stairs and flinging herself on the bed as she did when she was little and Lorene or Edmund teased her. Instead she forced herself to walk at a normal pace.

Once in the room, she still could not dissemble. Nancy would enter any minute and how would she explain her tears to the maid?

Nancy came into the room, carrying the packages from the shopping trip. 'Oh, miss, I must say that I adore London! I had no idea there could be so many shops. I do believe Lady Northdon knows them all!' She set the packages on a table. 'So many corsets! Did you ever see the like? I understand now how the right corset might enhance a gown. It is like discovering the New World, is it not?'

'A whole new world.' Tess sank into a chair. 'Of corsets.'

'So.' Nancy faced her, arms akimbo. 'What may I do for you? You look very tired.'

'Help me into a morning dress.' She rubbed her eyes. 'I may even nap a little.'

Nancy sprang into action, pulling one of Tess's new morning dresses from the wardrobe.

As she helped Tess out of her walking dress, Tess asked, 'Did the shopping not even tire you today, Nancy?'

'Oh, no, miss!' Nancy pulled the dress over her head. 'There is too much to see.'

She helped Tess into the morning dress and brushed out her hair and put it into a plait. 'There. That should be more comfortable for you. When you are finished resting,

summon me and I'll rearrange your hair. I'll come to help
you dress for dinner, as well.'

It was comforting to be fussed over.

The girl tied a ribbon to hold her plait. 'Unless there is
something else you need for me to do, I'll work on your
wedding dress.'

Her wedding dress. A dress she should not wear.

'It will be so pretty,' Nancy went on. 'I hope you will
like it. It will be the best gown I've ever made.'

'I am certain it will be lovely.'

How could she let Marc marry her, if the woman he
wanted was Miss Caldwell?

'Then I'll go,' said Nancy brightly. 'Have a nice rest.'

Tess remained in the chair, gazing out the window that
looked down upon the small garden in the back, the stor-
age sheds and the gated wall. There was a bench facing
flower beds, a nice place to sit when the weather was warm
and dry, like the bench in Berkeley Square.

She rose from the chair and climbed on to the bed, bury-
ing her face in the pillow.

Be strong, she told herself.

Refuse to marry him. It was her right to cry off, after
all, and his reputation would not suffer overmuch for re-
fusing, not under the circumstances. She would seek em-
ployment. She would put her name in with an agency that
found positions for governesses and ladies' companions.
There were many such agencies in London, she'd heard.

She rolled on to her back and covered her eyes with
her arm.

But what of Genna and Edmund? And Lorene?

A rap on the door made her jump.

'Who is it?' Please, not Amelie or Lady Northdon. She
could not pretend to be cheerful.

'It is Marc,' came the voice from the other side. 'May I speak with you?'

Marc?

This was too much like the night before, waking to his knock. Her senses flared with the memory.

And plummeted and hardened in resolve.

She climbed out of bed and walked to the door.

Like the night before, she opened it a crack. 'What is it?'

'May I come in?' He smelled of fresh air. He must have come straight from Berkeley Square.

She opened the door wider and he entered the room. She left the door ajar.

His demeanour was altered from the night before. Then he'd looked wild, emotional, sensual. Now he appeared steady and calm.

'Forgive my appearance,' she said. 'I was resting.'

'I woke you?' He frowned. 'I am sorry.'

'I was not asleep.' She took a chair. 'What do you want?'

He sat in an adjacent one and handed her a small wrapped package. 'I bought you something. A trifle.'

She untied the string and unfolded the paper. 'Oh. Sweets. How nice.' Her voice rang flat in her own ears.

'I walked by Gunter's Tea Shop and purchased some for you, and for Maman and Amelie.' He smiled.

'Gunter's,' she repeated woodenly.

'On Berkeley Square,' he added.

Berkeley Square. She tried not to flinch.

She set the sweetmeats aside. 'I shall save them for later.'

He reached into a pocket in his coat. 'I also have the special licence.' He pulled out the paper.

'Oh' was all she could manage.

'And I've arranged for a clergyman to perform the ceremony here in three days, if that is to your liking.'

'Three days?' She rose and faced the window. 'Are you certain this is what you want?'

'How many times must I say it, Tess?' He left his chair and stood behind her. 'I know this is not the sort of marriage you desired. I know you marry me for your sisters' and brother's sakes and for no other reason. I know it is not your choice.'

'It is not your choice, either,' she said.

He turned her to face him. 'You are wrong there. I did have a choice and I chose to offer you marriage.'

She would not look at him.

'What is it, Tess?' He shook her gently. 'Is this about my behaviour last night? I told you, it will not happen again.'

'It is not about last night.' The look of him coming to her room, wanting her, was too painful to remember. She raised her gaze to him. 'I know last night was nothing to you, nothing but drink. Please be honest with me now. Do you still wish you could marry Miss Caldwell?'

His expression turned exasperated. 'Why ask this of me again? I told you, that was in the past. I do not think of it now.'

'But you met her at Berkeley Square.' It still hurt. 'I saw you.'

A muscle in his cheek twitched. 'I met her by happenstance and we spoke together a short while. Nothing more.'

Her mother's excuses to her father rang in her ears. *I just happened to encounter him. It was nothing.* Or that day her mother's lover visited her sitting room. *He came to call upon you. I offered him some sherry.*

Lies.

Was Marc lying to her? She'd been completely fooled by Mr Welton, after all. And Lord Tinmore lied about giving her a dowry. Even Lorene had kept the truth from her, the truth about getting married to Tinmore.

Their father lied to them so many times, it became a joke among her and her sisters.

Her own mother had lied to her. She said she'd come to their bedroom to say goodnight. She said she would see Tess the next day.

She never came back.

How was Tess to believe Marc?

Somehow Tess managed to get through the next three days. Marc was especially attentive to her, making time to show her some of the sights of London. They walked through the tombs at Westminster Abbey. Toured the Tower. He even took her to Gunter's Tea Shop where she again saw the bench upon which he had sat with Miss Caldwell.

The wedding was set to take place in the afternoon, because the clergyman Marc found to do the ceremony was not available until the afternoon. Because of the special licence, they did not need to be married in the morning, though, so the time was of no consequence. Tess's preparation for the ceremony started two hours before the scheduled time. As Nancy and Amelie joined her in her bedchamber, it started to rain outside, a heavy, constant rain that reminded Tess of the storm not even a fortnight before, the one that brought her and Marc together.

It seemed fitting that it should rain for this day, as well.

Amelie had begged to help her dress so Tess had to keep up a facade of good cheer for both Amelie and Nancy. Nancy spent at least an hour arranging Tess's hair in curls tied up with ribbon that matched her dress. Amelie tinted Tess's cheeks and lips the lightest pink, which was good because otherwise Tess feared she would have no colour in her face at all.

She felt as if this were someone else's hair being arranged, someone else being dressed like a doll. A part of her was again lost in the storm, wandering one road after another.

Nancy's hands shook as she helped Tess step into her wedding gown and put her arms through its sleeves. Nancy buttoned the long row of buttons she'd sewn on the back of the dress. Then Amelie turned the mirror on Tess.

'Do you like it?' Nancy asked nervously as Tess shook herself back to reality.

In the full-length mirror was the image of a woman dressed in a beautiful ivory-silk gown with embroidery and lace adorning the bodice, sleeves and hem. Tess gasped.

'It is quite the loveliest gown I have ever worn,' she answered truthfully. 'I hardly know myself.'

Amelie clasped her hands together. 'My brother will love it, I am certain, and Maman will be so very impressed.'

Nancy looked awed. 'If her ladyship approves, I can ask for no greater compliment.'

'She will approve, do not worry, Nancy,' Amelie said.

Tess slipped her feet into shoes that matched the ivory silk and picked up her prayer book, the one piece of her past that could accompany her to her wedding. 'I suppose we should go.'

Already waiting in the drawing room were the clergyman, Lord and Lady Northdon, and Marc. The only other people who would witness the wedding would be the servants, who were included as members of the household. Tess was glad for Nancy, who had always been much more excited about the wedding than Tess could ever be.

Nancy fussed with the dress one more time, then nodded and smiled. 'I am ready, miss!' She laughed. 'This is the last time I shall call you miss. You will be ma'am from now on!'

She'd be Mrs Marc Glenville and, someday, Lady Northdon. It felt like the end of Tess Summerfield, the end of her connection to home, a fraying of her ties to her family, who were not even present to see her married.

Her past washed away in the rain.

Amelie walked down the stairs first and Nancy trailed behind Tess, attending to the train of the dress. Amelie slipped into the drawing room to alert them that they were ready. Nancy peeked in and gestured to Tess when they all stood in their places. Nancy opened the door and everyone turned.

The furniture had been moved out of the way and Tess's path to where the clergyman and Marc stood was lined with jardinières of flowers. Lady Northdon's idea, no doubt, and such a dear gesture that a lump formed in Tess's throat.

The servants stood along the walls and Lord and Lady Northdon were joined by Amelie near where Marc stood waiting for her. He was dressed in buff-coloured breeches and a black coat and waistcoat. He might have been attending the finest ball, he looked so handsome, but the expression on his face was unreadable and she faltered before making the inevitable walk towards him. His gaze followed her every step. She clutched her prayer book tighter as she took her place next to him. Marc turned to face the clergyman, a kind-faced man with a smiling demeanour that was almost enough to put her at ease.

'Dearly Beloved,' he began. 'We are gathered together here in the sight of God, and in the face of this congregation, to join together this man and this woman in holy matrimony; which is an honourable estate...'

An honourable estate? It wasn't honour that brought

Tess to this moment. It was love. Not the romantic love for which she once yearned, but love of her sisters and brother. Perhaps there was honour in that.

He went on, not in a style as if he were reciting some memorised passage, but as if he were talking to them in conversation, serious at times, smiling at others. All the while, Tess heard the rain in the background.

The clergyman spoke to Marc as if he'd known Marc for years. 'Wilt thou have this woman to thy wedded wife, to live together after God's ordinance in the holy estate of matrimony? Wilt thou love her, comfort her, honour and keep her, in sickness and in health and, forsaking all other, keep thee only unto her, so long as ye both shall live?'

Marc answered, 'I will.'

Did he hear the rain, as well?

It was her turn.

'Wilt thou have this man to thy wedded husband, to live together after God's ordinance in the holy estate of matrimony? Wilt thou obey him, and serve him, love, honour and keep him, in sickness and in health and, forsaking all other, keep thee only unto him, so long as ye both shall live?'

She answered, 'I will.'

In the distance, thunder rumbled.

The ceremony continued. It was astonishingly personal, and very intimate with just Marc's parents, sister and servants there, all cocooned by the rain.

At the end, the clergyman smiled. 'I pronounce that they be man and wife together.' He finished with the blessing, in like manner, as if he were a friend come to have conversation with them.

And it was over.

After the ceremony, there was punch and cake for the servants. Marc had known some of them since childhood and their congratulations were heartfelt. His mother seemed in her element, basking in praise for how she'd transformed the room into something special for the occasion. She and his father were on good behaviour for once, but, then, they did not speak to each other overmuch. His father talked mostly to Reverend Cane, and his mother, to Amelie.

He and Tess accepted the good wishes of the household, but said little to each other.

She looked stunningly beautiful. No woman on her wedding day could have looked more beautiful. Her silk gown caught the candlelight, making it shimmer as she moved. Her hair was a luxury of curls that appeared as if they would all tumble down with one tug on the ribbon threaded through them.

Tess smiled and accepted the servants' congratulations with grace. She thanked his mother and Reverend Cane for making the ceremony special.

How sad, though, that this was not the wedding of her dreams, a wedding to a man she could love. Marc would try to make it up to her. He vowed to do whatever was in his power to make her life pleasant.

'How are you faring?' he asked her during a break in the congratulations.

'Very well,' she said unconvincingly. 'I am touched by all the care that was taken by your mother and the servants to make this—this—special.'

'You have given my mother a great deal of happiness. And doing this for you brings her much pleasure.' Marc was grateful, so very grateful to Tess for accepting his mother and befriending her. His mother knew so little of friendship.

'I should add Nancy,' Tess said. 'Nancy made this splendid dress.'

His gaze swept over her. 'You look magnificent in it.'

Her expression stiffened. 'That is kind of you to say.'

Any compliment he gave her seemed to have the opposite of what one would expect. Instead of helping her to warm towards him, it made her withdraw even more. At least her distance cooled his ardour, like a cold rain cooled the warm earth.

It was good, though. It helped his head rule his heart. Only by using his head would he avoid any missteps. He was determined to make this marriage pleasant for both of them. He wanted them to regain the camaraderie they had shared when stranded in the cabin.

Eventually the cake and punch were consumed and the servants returned to their duties. Marc, Tess, his parents, the reverend and Amelie sat together in the drawing room until dinner was announced. The wedding breakfast of tradition became a wedding dinner, not unlike dinner every other night of the week, except they had Reverend Cane as a guest and Marc's father served his best wine. The reverend had a gift of making everyone comfortable and Marc experienced perhaps the most pleasant dinner ever with his family. Tess was polite but reserved, but perhaps no one noticed except him.

When dinner was over, it was quite like any other night. The men stayed in the dining room for brandy and the women retired to the drawing room for tea. The reverend did not stay long after the men rejoined the women. He bid them all goodnight and wished Marc and Tess a happy life together. Marc walked him out to the hall where he donned his greatcoat and hat and armed himself with his umbrella. Marc's father had ordered the carriage for the man. When it pulled up to the door, he said goodnight and left.

Marc returned to the drawing room and his father suggested they all retire.

They walked up the stairs together, Marc and Tess leaving his parents and Amelie on the first floor. He followed Tess up to the second floor. Staines was waiting for him as, Marc expected, Nancy would be waiting for Tess. Let the servants ready them for bed. Let them think this would be a typical wedding night.

But nothing was typical about this marriage.

Chapter Eleven

'Here you are, miss—ma'am!' Nancy clapped her hands in excitement when Tess entered the bedchamber. 'This is the wedding night!'

Tess wished she could feel such high spirits. She wished she could feel anything but gut-turning anxiety. She made herself smile. 'I am glad you are here to help me out of my dress.'

Nancy grinned. 'Oh, I'll help you out of your dress and make you very presentable to your new husband!'

Tess did not even know if she would see her husband this night. She pressed her fingers on her brow.

Nancy peered at her, a look of concern on her face. 'Miss—ma'am! Do you know about the wedding night?'

Daughter of the infamous Lady Summerfield not know of such carnal matters? She squeezed Nancy's hand. 'I'm a country girl. I do know about the wedding night.'

She'd seen the act performed, after all.

'Whew!' Nancy's eyes grew wide. 'I was afraid I'd have to tell you. That would have been very strange, would it not?'

'Very strange.' Tess smiled, this time in genuine amusement.

Nancy chattered on while she undid the buttons down

the back of the dress, helped Tess out of it and unlaced her corset.

Dressed in just her shift, Tess washed her face and hands and sat at the dressing table so Nancy could pull the pins from her hair. 'I'll brush out your hair and tie it in a ribbon.'

Having her hair brushed was so soothing that Tess thought she might actually sleep this night. Would it not be wonderful if she could wake up in the morning in her room at Summerfield House? Her sisters would be there and all would be as it had been before their father died. She closed her eyes and again saw that room, bright with sunlight, its pale blue walls and white-skirted tables, her keepsakes lovingly arranged on a shelf. Where were her little treasures now? She'd packed them for Tinmore Hall, but never unpacked them. Would they be lost, like the life she'd once enjoyed?

Nancy wrapped her hair tightly with the ribbon and tied it in a bow. 'I have something for you, ma'am,' she said as she dabbed some lavender scent on Tess's neck and arms. 'Stay right there.'

From the reflection in the mirror, Tess watched Nancy remove a white, neatly folded garment from the clothes press.

'Turn around,' Nancy said.

Tess swivelled in her chair and Nancy held up the white garment and let it loose of its folds. It fluttered down like a billowing cloud.

It was a nightdress made from soft, thin muslin and adorned with lace around the neckline and hem.

'Oh, my!' Tess exclaimed. 'It is lovely! Where did you get it?'

'Lady Northdon gave me the muslin and lace and told me exactly how she wanted it made.' She threw it over her arm and returned to the clothes press for another garment in the same fabric. 'It has a robe to match it!'

Tess rose from her seat and fingered the fabric. 'I cannot imagine how you sewed all these garments. You are a marvel, Nancy.'

Nancy beamed with pride. 'It was a pleasure, ma'am, truly it was.'

Tess hugged the girl. 'I do not know how to thank you. First the beautiful wedding dress and now this. I must also thank Lady Northdon for suggesting it.'

'Let's put you in it,' cried Nancy. 'You want to be ready. Your husband might come any time now.'

Tess took off her shift and Nancy helped her into the nightdress. She turned to the full-length mirror.

It was so sheer that she could see her flesh beneath it.

She added the robe and it was marginally better, but even by lamplight in her room, she could see the outline of her body under the gown and robe.

'What do you think of it?' Nancy asked as she picked up Tess's shift and put it away.

It is too sheer, she wanted to say. Instead, she said, 'I think it is the loveliest nightdress there ever could be.'

Nancy grinned. 'Now, is there anything else I can do for you? I've turned down the bed already.'

Tess did not want the girl to go, but there was no reason for her to stay, except to keep Tess from thinking too much. 'You've done more than enough.'

Nancy stepped forward and gave Tess a quick hug. It was not the proper sort of behaviour for a maid, but Tess found she was hungry for such warmth.

'I'll bid you goodnight, then,' the girl said. She winked. 'A very good night!'

She was gone and Tess was alone. She remained where she stood. As still as a statue, she listened to the sounds of the house. The hiss of the fire, footsteps above her—Nancy going to her room, no doubt. No sound of rain, though. It must have stopped.

He would not come to her, she knew. She wore a woman's nightdress, as alluring as any her mother had possessed, but he would not see it, because theirs was a forced marriage.

All the days in her future stretched before her, empty like land washed bare by a flood.

She strode over to the window and opened it, sucking in the cool air. The air retained that damp chill that so reminded her of their night in the cabin. She stood at the open window until the chill seeped into her skin. She could feel it on her cheeks, in her lungs, on her eyelashes.

They'd worked together well in the cabin, had they not? Of course, Marc had done most of the work, but she had made herself useful, fixing tea and such. The point was, she could act now. She'd not remained passive and helpless in the cabin and she did not need to think of herself as helpless now.

They were husband and wife. It was time she started acting like a wife and not like a little girl pining for her dolls and wishing for things to be different. So what if her keepsakes were lost to her? She could find new ones in her life with him.

She also did not have to wait for him to cross the hall and knock on her door. She could cross the hall and knock on his. He might refuse her this night, but she could offer herself. Or perhaps they could lie together as they'd done in the cabin?

It would be a start.

Tess closed the window and touched her face, reassured that it still felt the bracing chill. She strode to the door and opened it.

As she stepped into the hall she saw him coming to-

wards her, not in breeches and coat, but the loose fabric of
a banyan. He was almost as apparition-like as he'd been
riding towards her in the rain those few days ago, just
the silhouette of him, but she felt that same rush of relief
she'd felt that day.

If he welcomed her, she would no longer be alone.

Marc hesitated when Tess appeared before him. She
looked as alluring as she'd appeared the night he visited
her bedchamber. Only this time he was clear-headed. It
helped a little. Only a little.

'What is it, Tess?' He'd not expected her to seek him
out. He'd been on his way to her door to reassure her he
would not expect anything from her until she was ready.

'I wanted to see you.' She reached out her hand. 'Talk
with me, Marc. Please. For a little while?' Her voice was
uncertain. 'In—in my room or yours.'

He took her hand. 'I have some claret in my room.' He'd
had Staines bring it up earlier in the day when he'd been
dressing. A little wine right now might be a good thing.

'Your room, then,' she said.

He held her hand as they entered his room. He had only
two candles lit, which bathed the room in a soft light. He
led her to a chair near the window. It rattled in the wind
like the window of the cabin they shared. He poured the
claret and handed it to her.

'You wanted to talk?' Perhaps he would like what she
wished to say.

She took a sip of the wine. 'We should—' She began
determinedly, but her courage seemed to flag. She gazed
out the window. 'Did you hear the rain earlier? It sounded
so much like that rain at the cabin.'

'I was reminded of the cabin when I heard it.' He was

reminded of the cabin right now and all his resolve to let his head rule was rapidly being washed away.

She turned her lovely eyes on him. What colour were they at this moment? At the wedding ceremony they had been grey. Like the rain. 'We did well in the cabin, did we not?'

Until he overslept and allowed them to be caught in bed together. 'You did well,' he said.

Her scent distracted him, the lavender scent of bed linens. She looked soft and warm, like she belonged between the sheets, but he'd already promised himself he would not consummate their marriage this night. His head said he would wait until she wanted it, if she ever did, but now the idea of waiting did not appeal to him at all.

He sipped his drink.

She toyed with her glass. 'At the cabin you said you would marry sensibly, that marriage should be to the man and woman's advantage.'

Had he said that? He could not feel less like being sensible right now.

She went on. 'You cautioned me about marrying for love.'

'I remember that.' Men and women mistook love for passion and passion meant allowing one's emotions to dictate actions, as his parents had done.

'If you had married sensibly.' She smiled faintly. 'I assume you intended to—to have a real marriage.'

Of course he had. He was obligated to produce an heir, was he not? 'Certainly.'

She rose and moved towards him, kneeling at his feet. 'Then I think we should have a real marriage. We could make something good of this. What, after all, is the difference between having a sensible marriage and a forced one?'

Was the question rhetorical?

She rested her hands on his knees and gazed up at him. She was offering herself to him? Good Lord, he wanted her beyond all sense. He tried to pull back. Did she truly wish this?

'Tess, you must not feel under any obligation—'

She pushed away and stood, glaring down at him. 'I did not come out of obligation. I wanted to try to make something good out of this, but I can do nothing alone. You must also want me, which you obviously do not.'

She turned on her heel and headed towards the door.

'Wait!' he cried.

He bounded from the chair and caught her by the wrist. He pulled her back and made her face him. Having her in his arms drove words right out of his head.

He took a breath and gazed down at her. 'I never said I did not want you.'

'Then why not?' Her mouth parted and her lashes fluttered. 'I am willing, Marc.'

She had pluck, he must say.

'You want me to show you about making love, Tess?' His blood was surging through his veins as he spoke.

She looked him right in the eye. 'Yes. That is what I want.'

Those words were the only permission he needed. He picked her up and she wrapped her arms around him and did not break her gaze while he carried her to his bed.

He sat her on the bed and stood in front of her. 'How much do you know of this, Tess?'

Her breath quickened. 'Enough. More, than most, I think. I know what happens.'

He still was unsure of her. His head said she offered herself out of duty. His heart wanted to make something good of this, as she suggested.

Her fingers untied the ribbon of her robe. 'I know I must undress for you.'

He watched as she took off her robe. As she moved, the thin cloth of her nightdress clung to her skin. It was so sheer he could see her flesh beneath it. His fingers longed to touch that smooth skin.

Her look was more determined than passionate as she reached for the skirt of her nightdress, but he felt proud of her courage. Slowly she raised the skirt, revealing herself in inches. Glorious inches. Finally she lifted the nightdress over her head and tossed it away and, still looking directly into his face, sat before him, fully revealed.

His eyes drank in the sight of her. Her breasts were high and firm, her nipples dark against her pale skin. Her waist was accented by the fullness of her breasts and hips. The triangle between her legs was tinged with auburn, like her hair. Her legs were long and shaped as if a sculptor had carved them.

She displayed her nakedness almost defiantly. This woman he married would face any situation with admirable fearlessness. She'd already done so and was doing so now. Would she be as bold in lovemaking?

His blood surged in his veins in anticipation of it.

He stepped back and mimicked her undressing, removing his banyan and letting it fall to the floor. He, too, revealed his nakedness, his arousal. She, as he expected, did not avert her gaze.

'Lie back on the bed, Tess,' he instructed.

As she did so, he climbed on to the bed and lay next to her. 'I must touch you, to help ready you.'

She nodded, her eyes widening as he stroked her arms and shoulders. His head was still working enough that he knew it would be best for her to become used to his touch. His loins wished to awaken her body, like his had awakened. He wanted to join her. They were made one in matrimony; now let them be made one in the flesh. Put the past behind them and forge something together.

Her limbs relaxed and he grew bolder.

She gasped as his hand slipped over her breast. He moved gently, though it cost him something. His desire was pushing him and her skin felt so very soft. He moved his hand further down.

Tess did not expect a man's touch to feel this way. His hand was strong and sure, but gentle, and the sensations he created radiated throughout her. She thought she would come apart when he stroked her breasts. The intimacy of it astounded her. Who had touched her there since she'd been a little girl in need of help bathing?

The touch was not all pleasant. His fingers, no matter on what part of her body, created an ache at the womanly parts between her legs. With each stroke the ache grew more intense. Not a pain, exactly.

A need.

His hand moved down her body, closer, and she wanted to push it down *there*, as if his touch would relieve the ache.

Finally his fingers reached the place.

'I need to touch you here. To make you ready. To make it easier for you,' he explained.

He fingered her most sensitive place and the aching surged. Her back arched and she moaned, the sound not unlike those her mother made when Tess had watched her with her lover.

'Do you feel the pleasure?' he asked, his voice rough.

'Not pleasure.' How could she explain? 'Not quite.' She did not have the words.

He was a magnificent man. Tall and as well formed as the Greek statue at Tinmore Hall. Better formed, in fact.

Leaner and hard-muscled. Was it wanton of her to think so? To enjoy his touch so very much?

He rose above her. 'Now,' he uttered, 'I will enter you.'

A wave of fear joined the potpourri of emotion and sensation flowing through her. His male member was large; she could well imagine pain, but she did not want him to stop. She wanted this need, this aching to come to its end, even though she did not know what that end would be.

'Don't stop,' she cried. 'Don't stop.'

It seemed as if her body opened to him and he eased himself inside her, with stroke after stroke. Her muscles responded of their own volition, moving with him, meeting and separating, meeting and separating.

The ache grew even more intense, so all consuming, so needful, that she lost the capacity to think. She was all feeling, all sensation, all merged with this glorious man. Her husband.

He moved faster, his breath came faster and she moved with him, wanting to cry out with each thrust.

Then something remarkable happened. Sensation exploded inside her, filling her with an unimagined pleasure. A moment later, a growl escaped his lips and he trembled inside her. Spilling his seed, she realised.

This was consummation, she thought, as her body drifted into a pleasant languor. Joining.

He collapsed atop her, but immediately lifted his weight off her and rolled to her side. 'You felt it,' he said.

She could not speak, so she nodded her head, and blinked back tears that suddenly filled her eyes.

He rose on an elbow and peered at her, looking puzzled.

She swiped at her cheeks. 'I'm not weeping. Not hurt. Not sad.' She couldn't explain.

He wiped the tears with his thumb and stared into her face. She tried to smile. She wanted to smile.

His expression turned soft and tender. He leaned closer and placed his lips on hers.

She realised then that this was her first kiss. By him. By any man.

And it had come after lovemaking.

Chapter Twelve

Tess woke with the dawn's first light. Through the window she could see a piece of sky, a glorious and joyful shade of pink.

She smiled. Even the sky matched her mood.

After that tumultuous first time of making love, Marc made love to her again. To her delight, the sensations were every bit as wonderful. Different, though. Slower and sweeter.

She, Lorene and Genna had been warned of the temptations of the flesh by every governess they'd had. Considering their parents' excesses in such temptations, it had been good advice. When Tess watched her mother and her mother's lover on the sofa in her sitting room, she'd not understood the appeal. It had not looked at all like something one would desire to do.

Now she understood, though. She understood her mother better, as well, how her mother could crave this wonderful experience, how she could want to repeat it, over and over. She understood precisely how like her mother she was.

Tess gazed at her husband, face relaxed in sleep, hair tousled, thick, dark lashes casting shadows on his cheeks. He took her breath away. She could not imagine lovemaking with anyone else. Ever. She felt connected to him in a way even stronger than her connections to her sisters, as if the consummation of their marriage had indeed made them one.

Did he feel that, as well? How could he not?

She'd felt herself open to him in their lovemaking. Surely now he knew everything there was to know about her; she'd felt that unguarded.

Her heart surged with hope. Surely such a profound experience provided a strong foundation for a marriage. They could build upon this night and perhaps create a marvellous future together. He was a decent man, after all, a good man.

He stirred and opened his eyes. To merely call them blue did them no justice. They were rimmed in navy with flecks of light and dark radiating from the pupil. Having his eyes focused on her was like being pinned with a sabre to the chest.

She could not tell what he hid in the depths of those eyes. Would he open himself to her?

'Good morning,' he murmured, his lashes lowering. 'How do you fare?'

She smiled tentatively, suddenly needing to pull back from the intensity of her emotions. 'I fare very well. And you?'

He moved towards her, taking her in his arms and pulling her naked body against his. 'I'm well.'

His arousal pressed against her and the delicious aching returned.

He drew her into a kiss, opening his mouth. Her lips parted and he touched his tongue to hers. She gasped and dug her fingers in his unruly hair, holding him in the kiss.

He eased her on her back and, still kissing her, climbed

atop her. His hands stroked her. How could she have known how wonderful his hands would feel on her body? How glorious a kiss would feel?

She opened herself to him again and he entered her and drove her again to the unimaginable pleasure. While she still quivered from her release, he spilled his seed inside her.

When he lay next to her again, his arm around her, all the stress, anger and regret she'd lived with since being discovered with Marc in the cabin washed away. Like the day after a rainstorm, everything seemed fresh, bright and new. They would make this a good marriage, in spite of being forced to marry. Perhaps they had just made a baby together.

How more wonderful could life be?

Marc lay with her in his arms, sated and satisfied, but with his heart racing as if he'd just run a league. He already wanted her again, needed her again. He wanted her all to himself. Wanted their own rooms, their own household, away from his family, away from everyone.

And he wanted to flee.

The power of his need for her shook him to his core. Surely this is what his father had felt, what Charles and Lucien felt?

Thus grief still treads upon the heels of pleasure: Married in haste, we may repent at leisure.

His father's words again.

Had he married her for this—this explosive lovemaking? Was this lovemaking the pleasure in that line from the Congreve play? He cared nothing of grief and repentance. He only wanted her.

And he would do anything to have her again.

Anything.

Were these the sentiments that drove Lucien and Charles to their deaths?

Some wiser part of him threw off the covers and rose from the bed.

His abrupt movement woke her.

'Are you rising already?' she asked in a raw, sleepy voice.

All he heard was an invitation to return to the bed, make love to her again, but he needed to get himself under control.

'I had better get up.' Some hint of good sense made its way to the fore. 'Too much could make you sore.'

She patted the bed where he'd been lying. 'I do not mind.'

Good God. 'No!'

Her face fell. His sharp tone wounded her, obviously.

He dared to lean over her. 'Do not be distressed, Tess,' he managed. 'I—I sound as I do because I want you so strongly and I know we must not...' He paused, almost forgetting what he needed to say. 'Overdo.' He stroked her cheek with his finger, not willing to risk touching her with even his whole hand.

She softened again, but moved towards his touch in a way so alluring he was tempted to tell his head to go to the devil.

He straightened. 'I think I will take Apollo for a run.' He made himself smile at her. 'That should cool me off.'

She looked disappointed, but she said, 'Apollo will be happy. Will I see you at breakfast, then?'

'Better not wait for me.' Who knew how long it would take to sort himself out? 'I would not wish you to be hungry.'

She smiled. 'Hungry enough for soggy bread and cheese?'

The reminder of the cabin pierced him like a sabre thrust. 'Never that hungry again,' he murmured.

'No food ever tasted so delicious,' she said.

He gathered up his riding clothes and dressed himself, all the while very aware that she watched his every move. After he was dressed, he started for the door, but instead turned and walked back to the bed where she was now sitting up and holding the linens over her lovely breasts.

He leaned down and kissed her. She reached for him and held him in the kiss and passion throbbed inside him. He drew away.

He ought to tell her how captivating she was, how she had pleased him, but he said only, 'I will see you later.'

He hurried out and soon stepped out of the door on to the street.

The cool, fresh air filled his lungs and cleared his mind.

What was this foolishness overtaking him? Why should he and Tess not forge a happy marriage? The passion they shared should bode well for it. And she was a woman worthy of loving and deserving of happiness. Why could he not give them both that? He could make it happen. He'd do it for Lucien and Charles—and even for his mother and father. He'd be happy for all of them.

He stepped on to the pavement with renewed hope. Renewed resolve.

A man approached him. 'Mr Glenville?'

'Yes?' Marc frowned. Something in the man's manner put him on alert.

The man handed him a letter. 'This is for you. I am told it is urgent.'

Marc accepted the letter, broke the seal and unfolded the paper.

It read:

> *Come immediately. It is vital. You must come. Some-*
> *thing has happened that cannot be written in a let-*
> *ter. Do not delay. I will explain all.*
> > *Yours, etc.*
> > *Lord Greybury*

Hope turned swiftly to foreboding.

Marc looked up at the messenger. 'I will come straight away.'

He hurried on to the mews, but he'd not be riding Apollo for pleasure.

The stable boy saddled Apollo quickly and Marc set out for Horse Guards. Even the horse seemed to sense the urgency. The streets were filling with carriages, wagons and other riders, but Apollo pulled through. Marc announced himself to the sentry and handed Apollo's reins to a waiting attendant. The building seemed to be a-bustle and the air filled with tension.

He made his way quickly to Greybury's office. The clerk waved him by before he could say anything.

He knocked on Greybury's door and opened it. Two other men Marc recognised as working for Castlereagh stood with Lord Greybury. This must be something important.

They all turned when he entered.

'Ah, gentlemen, here is Renard.' Greybury gestured Marc forward.

The other men likely knew Marc's true identity, but since Greybury used his code name, it sounded like he was back on the job.

'What is this about?' Marc asked.

Greybury glanced from one gentleman to the other and

back to Marc. 'We received word today that Napoleon has escaped.'

'Escaped!'

Napoleon had been exiled to Elba after the Treaty of Fontainebleu.

'He's making his way to Paris,' said one of the men.

'Castlereagh warned the Allies this could happen,' the other gentleman said. 'He warned them.'

'We need you in France, Renard,' Greybury said. 'Napoleon will seek power again and we need to know all that transpires as a result.'

'Suffice to say that every nation on the Continent and our United Kingdom are at risk!' the first man added.

The stakes were high, that was for certain.

Marc's insides turned cold. 'I cannot go.'

Greybury straightened. 'You must.'

'I cannot,' Marc insisted. 'You must choose another man. I was married yesterday. I cannot leave my new wife.'

'You will leave her. There is no other man to replace you.' Greybury glared at him. 'Recall that you made a vow to serve your country when needed. You are needed.'

No. He could not do this to Tess. Make love to her and leave her?

Greybury leaned towards him. 'I cannot stress how vital this is. I am sorry that your private matters impinge on this situation, but your duty is to your country. Napoleon will take up the sword again. He is not a man of peace. Without the information only you can gather, countless men will no longer be able to return to their wives.'

Marc was bound by duty. He could not refuse.

'Very well,' he said. 'I can be ready by tomorrow.'

'Not tomorrow.' Greybury spoke firmly. 'Today. Now. There is a boat waiting at Dover to take you across the Channel.'

Tess would be hurt. How could she not be?

It was all his fault. If he'd maintained his distance from her, not shared his bed with her, he would not hurt her nearly as much. But, no, he let passion rule, just as Charles and Lucien had done and, because he'd done so, he'd grievously injure Tess.

How more monstrous could he be? Love her and leave her.

Better he'd lost his own life than wound her so.

Perhaps it was better not to spend another night with her. It would be cruel of him to make love to her another night.

And it would be cruel of him not to.

'Very well. Today. I can be ready in a few hours—' With hard riding, he should be able to reach Dover before nightfall.

'No!' Greybury pounded a fist on his desk. 'You must ride to Dover now.'

'Even a few hours can make a difference,' added the second man. 'We must know immediately Napoleon's whereabouts and his plans.'

'The usual network is in place,' Greybury said. 'Your trunk has already been sent to Dover.'

The office kept a trunk packed with weapons, clothing and such so he could easily slip into the role of Renard.

An announcement of his marriage would appear in the *Morning Post* this very day. As soon as all of society learned of his marriage to Tess, they would also learn he had left her. What could he say to her?

He felt sick inside. 'I cannot leave without speaking to my wife.'

'Write your wife a letter.' Greybury pushed paper and pen towards him. An inkpot was on the desk.

'No.' Marc pushed them back. 'I speak to my wife or I do not travel to France.'

Marc started for the door.

'Wait!' Lord Greybury cried.

Marc stopped and turned towards him.

Greybury stood. 'Very well. We will do it your way. Speak to your wife. But be quick about it.'

He'd take whatever time was necessary.

Greybury rubbed his face. 'Say nothing to your wife about where you are going or why, though. Remember Rosier.'

Rosier had confided in his wife, but a clever French spy tricked her into talking. Rosier's deception and his mission were discovered. And worse, Rosier and several colleagues were killed.

Marc would not tell Tess the truth. If she knew nothing, she could divulge nothing. What would he say to her instead?

'I know my duty.' Marc bowed and left the room.

After breakfasting alone, Tess spent her morning writing letters to her sisters and brother, informing them of her marriage.

Would they write her back? She'd received nothing from them so far, but perhaps not enough time had passed for them to answer her first letters. She'd tried to tell them she was well, but this morning she'd been tempted to write to them about how wonderful marriage with Marc would be. How could she put in a letter that it had been his love-making that filled her with hope? Or that something in his manner this morning brought her worries back?

If she could talk to Lorene and Genna, it would be different.

Even if there were some things she could never tell them.

Maybe they would reassure her that Marc had not been eager to be away from her this morning. Maybe they would say it was merely due to a morning mood or something.

She ought not to worry, in any event. Marc had been her steadfast protector since that moment he'd found her in the rain. He'd never failed her. Never lied to her. She even believed him about Miss Caldwell.

Hadn't she?

At least through her letter to Lorene, Tinmore would learn Tess kept her part of his bargain. If he kept his word this time, Genna and Edmund's futures should be secure.

Marc would never break his word.

Would he?

She sent a footman to post the letters and waited in her bedroom for Marc to return from his ride. If he did not knock on her door, she'd at least hear him go to his room to change from his riding clothes.

Then she'd learn her worries were baseless.

Nancy came in and out of the room, always hiding a smile and obviously trying very hard not to ask about the wedding night.

Tess blushed to think that the servants would all know she and Mark had made love. The evidence would be on the bed linens.

Had her mother been concerned about such things? Tess wondered. Did Lorene think of such things?

She could not imagine Lorene and Lord Tinmore—

She thought of the pleasure Marc created in her, a pleasure she'd never dreamed she would experience. Her body came alive again and she ached for his return.

Tess paced the room, restless and more uncertain with every tick of the mantle clock.

When the knock sounded at her door, though, she jumped in surprise.

She swung around. 'Come in.'

A last shaft of agony sliced through Marc as his hand gripped the latch. He took two deep breaths and opened the door.

'Tess!' He walked in with a firm step. 'I have something I must tell you.'

She took a step towards him, but seemed to think better of coming closer. 'What?'

'I encountered some friends of mine when I was out. At the park.'

She blinked. 'Some friends?'

He faced her and tried to keep emotion out of his voice. 'They are bound for Switzerland today and I am going with them.'

'Going with them?' Her expression turned confused. 'To Switzerland?'

He crossed his arms over his chest. 'I realise the timing is not ideal, but I cannot pass up this opportunity. I have always had a strong desire to hike through the Alps.' This was at least true. 'The possibility was denied to me during the war, but now there is no reason not to go—'

'No reason?' Her voice raised an octave. 'You were married yesterday.'

Yes. And his leaving would hurt her.

'Ordinarily I would not leave,' he explained. 'But I cannot pass up this opportunity.'

'Walking in mountains is so vitally important?'

He made himself look directly at her. 'It is what I wish to do.'

'You wish to leave me!' Her face turned red with anger.

'For a few months.' He acted as if it were a trifle. 'I do

not even need to pack much. We will purchase what we need when we reach the mountains. Sturdy boots and such. These are the same men I travelled with through Scotland. They will not make this trip again.'

'You choose them over me?' Her voice trembled.

'I am not choosing them over you.' Good God. He did not want her to think this had anything to do with her. 'It has nothing to do with you. I merely wish to take this trip.'

She swung away from him. 'I do not believe this. This does not sound like you. You would not do this to me.'

'Would I not? You do not know me.' He kept his voice steady. 'Heed this, Tess. I will do as I please. And it pleases me to take this trip. Ask my parents if I do not leave when it pleases me to leave. It is something to which you must become accustomed.'

'Must I?' Her eyes flashed.

He pretended to be severe with her. 'You will do very well without me. You've settled in here, especially with my mother and sister. Soon your sisters will be here. You will be invited to social events, events I would not wish to attend. You will be well entertained.'

She blinked. 'I do not care a fig about all that!' She swallowed, as if she were trying not to weep. 'What do you think people will say about you leaving me the day after our wedding?'

He shrugged. 'People will talk no matter what. Besides, it is not as if we can pretend this is anything more than a marriage of convenience, not when Tinmore and his guests come to town.'

Likely she would never forgive him for this. When he returned to her, what could he expect? A marriage of estrangement like his parents?

'Do not make light of this, Marc,' she shot back. 'You are leaving me to bear the scandal of our marriage alone.

And you add the additional humiliation of leaving after the wedding night.'

He cursed himself. If only he had not given in to his desire for her, her pain would not be so great. He'd been right to have been so shaken when he left her bed this morning. He ought never to have been there.

Her voice dropped to little more than a whisper. 'How could you make love to me and then leave me so callously?'

Misery swept through him. He could not answer her. He fancied he felt every bit of her pain.

'Go, then,' she rasped. 'Leave me. It is not as though I have not been left before. I dare say your absence will not be as devastating.'

Marc had no choice but to turn and walk out of the room.

As soon as he closed the door, though, he leaned his whole body against it. 'Tess,' he murmured. 'I am sorry. I am so very sorry.'

Chapter Thirteen

June 1815, three months later—Brussels, Belgium

Tess, with Amelie at her side, glimpsed the Parc de Bruxelles for the first time and gasped.

'It is magnificent!' Amelie exclaimed.

As soon as they'd arrived in Brussels, nothing would do but for Amelie to see the park. So while Lord and Lady Northdon rested in their rooms at the Hotel de Flandre, Tess and Amelie walked to the park.

The park was a magnificent space, indeed, a huge formal garden enclosed with iron rails and bordered by the Royal Palace and other grand public buildings. Inside the park were gravel walkways, crisscrossing each other in symmetrical patterns. Large, leafy trees, green shrubbery and flowers grew in grassy spots between the walkways. In every direction something interesting could be found. Statues and fountains and benches.

And men in uniforms of all types and colours, strolling with elegant ladies or conversing in groups of twos or threes.

It is madness to be here, Tess thought.

When Napoleon was exiled to Elba, the English flocked

to the Continent where travel had so long been denied them. Brussels especially had become a fashionable destination, as well as a place to live in luxury for significantly less than it cost in Britain. Now, though, all was changed. Napoleon had reclaimed his empire, and the British, Prussians, Austrians and Russians declared war, not on France, but on Napoleon himself.

Impending war brought even more people to Brussels—thousands of soldiers, their officers and others who had official duties made necessary by the inevitable war. The Allies were planning to march into France any day now.

There was no reason for Tess, Amelie and her parents to be in Brussels, though. Lord Northdon had no official duties and he certainly had no need to economise. He and Lady Northdon came to Brussels simply to indulge Amelie.

Amelie had become enamoured of a young captain in the Scots Greys to whom she'd been introduced at one of the London entertainments. The Scots Greys, a prestigious cavalry regiment, was sent to Brussels to prepare for the battle with Napoleon's forces. Amelie could not bear to be parted from her Captain Fowler, so Lord and Lady Northdon agreed they could all follow him here.

Here in the Parc de Bruxelles people seemed as festive as if this were the London Season. Was Tess the only one who worried about why the soldiers were here?

Amelie talked excitedly. 'Would it not be beyond everything if I should run into Captain Fowler here in the park? He could be here at this moment! Papa said he would send a message to him that we have arrived, but would it not be exciting if he found us here before he reads the message? He will call as soon as he is able. I am sure of it.'

Tess, too, scanned the park, but to look for Marc, not for Captain Fowler.

Because Marc, too, could be in Brussels.

The one letter Tess had received from him in the three months he'd been gone had been posted from Ostend, the port at which she, Amelie and Lord and Lady Northdon had landed just the day before. It had arrived just days before they'd left and merely stated that he was well, but was remaining on the Continent.

If Marc had been in Belgium when he'd penned the letter, he could very well now be among the English visitors to Brussels.

Apparently he was no longer in the Alps. Most likely he had never been there. He'd lied to her about his travel plans. If he had indeed been planning a hike across the mountains, he would not have taken Apollo with him.

His whereabouts ought to be of no consequence to Tess, but the pain of his abandoning her had not abated, even though she'd become very skilled at not showing it.

In London she'd had plenty of practice hiding the wounds he'd inflicted. She'd done so at every social event she'd had to attend. Either Lord Tinmore had arranged for invitations or Amelie's success at the Caldwells' party had made her a desirable guest, Tess did not know which. Amelie was quite a success wherever they went. Tess, on the other hand, received stares and whispers and sympathetic looks. At least she did not experience the cut direct as Lady Northdon occasionally did. Lady Northdon always held her head high and refused to be cowed by cruel treatment. Tess emulated her. Tess had become quite fond of Lady Northdon, who treated her as if she were another beloved daughter. Lord Northdon was not quite so generous. Tess suspected he blamed her for Marc's abrupt departure. None of them spoke to her about Marc's leaving her, though.

Tinmore brought Tess's sisters to London, as he said he would, and they were often at the same events. Her sisters insisted she explain why Marc left her. Tess told them only what Marc told her, but that was not enough for Lorene. Lorene lectured Tess on how she might have been more accommodating to her husband. Or Lorene lamented that Tess's marriage was not the sort Lorene had wanted for her. It was not the marriage for which Lorene sacrificed herself. Genna argued with both of them for expecting any marriage to solve their problems.

This was more blame Tess could leave at Marc's feet. By abandoning her, he'd widened the breach between her and her sisters. If he'd stayed, they might have at least pretended to have a successful marriage. She would not have to endure her sisters' grief for the shambles she'd made of her life. Tess and her sisters rarely called upon each other and mostly saw each other at social events where Lord Tinmore was also present. What that man thought of Marc leaving her, Tess could only guess.

Mr Welton also appeared at some of the London events, making straight for Genna, who just as swiftly sent him packing. How was it that Genna could see through Welton when Tess had been unable to? Tess could not trust her judgement of anyone any more.

She'd been so terribly wrong about Marc.

Marc's lovemaking had made her believe he loved her. Instead, he'd wanted to be a continent away from her.

No one would hurt her like that again. She built armour around herself to keep her safe and to hide how shattered she was inside.

'Shall we walk together a little?' Amelie asked, rousing Tess from her reverie.

'As you wish.' Tess smiled and tried to sound cheerful.

They strolled down one of the paths and all the men they passed paused for a moment to gaze at Amelie.

Amelie took Tess by the arm. 'Let us make our way to the centre and see the basin with the fish.'

Their guidebook said there was a huge basin in the middle of the park with silver and gold fish, but it seemed like they must pass through a gauntlet of staring men to reach it.

As they walked, Tess remarked, 'I do not see how you can be so at ease. Every gentleman turns to look at you.'

'Oh, they are not looking at me,' Amelie insisted, walking on serenely.

Was the girl that deluded? She was a beauty.

When they neared the basin, Amelie ran forward. 'It really does have fish!'

Tess joined her, acutely aware of the interest Amelie created. As Amelie circumvented the basin, Tess kept her gaze firmly on the fish and not on the staring men.

'Oh, my goodness!' Amelie suddenly exclaimed. 'He's here. Look. Look.'

Amelie ran ahead. Had she found her Captain Fowler? Tess glanced across the basin to see.

And froze.

Marc stood on the other side.

He must have seen her the instant she'd seen him. He looked directly into her eyes.

His sister reached him and threw her arms around him. 'Marc! Marc! Are you truly here?'

He embraced Amelie, but his eyes never left Tess.

When he released her, Amelie turned and called across the basin, 'Tess! Look! It is Marc!'

Tess made her way slowly to where they stood.

'Marc,' she said, trying to keep all emotion from her voice.

'Tess,' he whispered.

'So you came to Brussels, too?' Amelie cried. 'You

should have told us you would be here. We just arrived today. Where are you staying? Papa procured rooms for us at the Hotel de Flandre and Maman has been speaking nothing but French since we arrived. She cannot wait to visit the *magasins*. Every shop calls itself Magasin de— something, she said…'

While Amelie chattered, Marc continued to gaze at Tess, but he suddenly collected himself. 'Forgive me. There are others here who would wish to greet you.'

He was standing with three men and a woman.

The woman stepped out from behind one of the men. 'Mrs Glenville. Amelie.' It was Doria Caldwell, looking serene as ever. 'What a surprise. I do hope you had a good trip.'

Tess's glance darted to Marc. Had he lied about Doria Caldwell after all?

Amelie ran over to clasp Miss Caldwell's hand. 'Doria! We had no idea you were coming to Brussels, too!'

Miss Caldwell smiled at her. 'Papa was asked to come. He is assisting one of the diplomats.' Her gaze slipped over to Tess. 'We just ran into Marc a few minutes ago.'

Mr Caldwell stepped over to Amelie. 'My dear, you look as pretty as a picture. What a delight to see you here.' He turned to Tess. 'And you, of course, Mrs Glenville.'

'What a coincidence!' Amelie said brightly. 'It is almost like being back in London.'

Tess felt suddenly sick to her stomach. Her husband was here, conversing with the woman he once wanted to marry, and was about as happy to see Tess as she was to see him.

She depended upon her armour to keep her rooted to this place when she wanted to run back to the hotel and hide herself in her room.

'Good afternoon, sir,' she said to Mr Caldwell.

Marc turned abruptly. 'I am being remiss. Let me present my two companions to you.'

Tess attended to the two men standing near Marc. One was dressed as a gentleman like Marc, the other, in an officer's uniform. Marc presented them and Tess promptly forgot their names. She did notice their surprise when he introduced her, saying, 'This is my wife, Mrs Glenville, and my sister, Miss Glenville.'

Their attention quickly turned to the beautiful Amelie, though. Mr Caldwell and his daughter discreetly stepped back and she was left to speak with Marc alone.

'What are you doing here?' he asked in a gruff tone.

He'd certainly made his feelings known.

She lifted her chin. 'I am in Brussels only because your mother and father wished me to come. They are here because Amelie has a suitor here. He is the reason.'

'A suitor?'

Better to talk of Amelie's suitor than to ask Marc to explain why he was in Brussels, or why he was in the company of Miss Caldwell.

'He is Captain Fowler of the Scots Greys,' she said.

The man in uniform overheard her. 'Scots Greys? A prestigious regiment.'

'Oh, yes!' exclaimed Amelie. 'Captain Fowler considers it quite an honour.'

'You have a suitor?' Miss Caldwell asked Amelie.

Amelie lowered her lashes and looked even more beguiling. 'I suppose you could say he is my suitor.' She began to explain to Miss Caldwell and Marc how she'd met him.

Tess turned to the officer, because she did not want to be a part of Miss Caldwell's conversation. 'What regiment are you, sir?'

He bowed. '28th, ma'am.'

'The 28th is here?' Tess's eyes widened. She forgot about Miss Caldwell and Marc for the moment. 'My brother is in the 28th. Do you know him? Lieutenant Edmund Summerfield. Is he here?'

'I know him and, yes, ma'am, he is here,' the man answered.

This was beyond wonderful! 'Would you tell him his sister Tess is at the Hotel de Flandre? Tell him to call on me and ask for Mrs Glenville.'

Her brother Edmund was here! With him here she would not feel so desperately alone.

Her high spirits deflated. Edmund was here to fight in the new war against Napoleon. He could be killed.

The officer bowed again. 'I will inform him with pleasure, ma'am.'

The other man clapped him on his back. 'Come. Let us leave them all to their reunion.'

The two men bid them good day.

Amelie seized her brother's arm and pressed her cheek against his shoulder. 'I cannot believe you are actually here. And Doria and Mr Caldwell, too!'

Marc looked straight at Tess. 'This is no place for you. The Allies are preparing for war. It may become dangerous to be here.'

Was he trying to scare her away? 'Tell your father, not me. It was not my decision to come.'

Miss Caldwell broke in. 'But, Marc, the soldiers are not going to fight here. They will march to France.' She turned to her father. 'Is that not right, Papa?'

'That is indeed what is expected,' he replied.

'Oh, let us not think of the war right now!' Amelie cried. 'Come back to the hotel with us. Maman and Papa will be so glad to see you!' She turned to Miss Caldwell.

'You and Mr Caldwell must come, too. We shall all eat dinner together!'

'No, no, my dear,' Mr Caldwell said. 'We would not interfere in your reunion. But send a messenger to us at the Hotel de Belle Vue if your parents would indeed like us to join you for dinner.'

Marc looked hesitant, as if coming with Amelie and Tess was the last thing he wished to do. Or was it that he wished Tess were not a part of it?

Amelie nodded. 'We will send you a message.' She took her brother's arm. 'But you will come with us now, will you not, Marc?'

He smiled at his sister. 'Of course. I'll come with you now.'

Marc offered Tess his arm, but she acted as if she did not notice and merely walked by his side. Silent. Amelie happily took his other arm and talked on about their trip, about Captain Fowler, about the Season's entertainments she'd attended before travelling here. He'd never seen his sister so happy and so full of life.

Such a contrast to the woman carefully avoiding touching him or speaking to him. She looked beautiful in the light of the June sun on this fine Belgian day, but she was like some distant dream. Was there anything he could say or do to close the gulf his abandoning her had created?

Having her find him with Doria did not help.

When they reached the hotel, Amelie ran ahead to tell their parents.

Marc and Tess walked more slowly, still not speaking.

He'd hurt her terribly, though, and there was no way he could explain.

'How were the Alps?' she asked in a sarcastic tone.

He must lie to her again. 'Quite nice.'

She gave him a very sceptical look.

He wished he could tell her the truth.

Within two days of that meeting with Greybury in London, Marc arrived in Calais and was on the road to Paris. His task was to locate Napoleon, learn of his plans and gauge whether or not the people of France would support him. The French people, unhappy with Louis XVIII, welcomed Napoleon's return and Napoleon planned to rule France. He sent word to the Allies that he'd give up his empire, if they left him in peace.

As if the Allies would believe him.

The information Marc gathered was sent back through the network of agents scattered around the countryside and throughout the Continent. Marc learned that Napoleon had quickly raised a fully equipped army of two hundred thousand men. In fact, Marc had almost been conscripted into that army. He'd had to flee France to escape it.

Napoleon's army was readying for battle and Napoleon was intent on victory.

Marc made his way to Brussels and briefed his contact of everything he'd learned in France. His contact informed the Duke of Wellington, who had been appointed Field Marshal over the forces of British, German, Dutch and Belgian soldiers assembling in Brussels. The Allied plan was to orchestrate a coordinated invasion of France.

Marc had no hard facts, but he believed Napoleon would not wait for that invasion and he feared Napoleon would march straight for Brussels.

Now his family was here? And Tess? He must convince them to leave, but how? Why would his family believe him?

He certainly had lost his wife's trust. Tess would not even allow him to touch her.

He and Tess turned down a hallway and saw Amelie open a door to their parents' rooms. 'Maman! Papa!' she cried. 'Look who we have brought with us!'

His parents greeted him with surprise and delight, his mother kissing his cheeks, his father shaking his hand and pulling him into a hug.

'Why did you not let us know you were in Brussels?' his father asked.

'You know I am a terrible correspondent.' That much was true.

They had more questions for him to answer with evasions and lies. Through it all Tess sat at a little distance, her posture stiff, her face like stone.

As soon as Marc could manage it, he cut them off. 'I am certain I may see much of you here,' he said. 'There will be plenty of time to discuss…whatever you wish to discuss. At the moment, though, I would like some time alone with my wife.'

His father immediately stood. 'Of course.' He turned to Tess. 'Tess, take Marc to your room. We will see both of you later.' He turned back to Marc. 'You will join us for dinner?'

Marc had plans—work, actually—but he could delay until after dinner. 'Certainly, I will join you.'

'Papa,' Amelie broke in. 'You remind me. You will never guess who else we found on our walk.'

Tess rose while Amelie told of the Caldwells also being in Brussels. Marc moved to her side and gave her no choice but to lead him to her room.

She acted as if she were marching to the gallows.

She opened the door and her maid turned from unpacking clothes. 'Back so soon, ma'am?' She noticed Marc then. 'Oh! Oh, Mr Glenville!' She made a hurried curtsy.

'Nancy.' He smiled at the girl. 'How good to see you. You are looking well.'

She stared from Marc to Tess, obviously full of curiosity. 'Thank you, sir.'

Tess spoke to her in a strangled voice. 'Nancy, would you mind leaving us alone for a while?'

'Yes, ma'am!' She dropped the folded clothes she'd been holding and, glancing back at Tess, left the room.

Marc turned to her. 'Tess—'

She recoiled as if his speaking her name was a blow.

He went on. 'I hardly know what to say to you.'

She would not look at him. 'Does it matter what you say? I have lost the ability to believe you.' She walked towards the window. 'Tell me, did Apollo enjoy climbing the mountains?'

'Apollo?'

She continued in her biting tone. 'Your horse. I confess, I never knew horses climbed mountains.'

She'd surmised he'd lied about the Alps and he could not counter with the truth of where he'd been and what he'd been doing.

He had no choice but to play the role he'd created the day he'd left her. 'You may think whatever you like about my activities,' he said sharply. 'I wanted to leave, to be away. I may desire to leave again in the future.'

Her voice dropped. 'You wanted to leave me, you are saying.'

He made himself glare at her. 'I am saying I will come and go at my pleasure. I suggest you accustom yourself to that habit of mine.'

She returned his gaze. 'I've had several weeks to accustom myself.'

He wanted to ask her how it had been for her, but she would never believe he cared about such things. 'Like it or not, we are man and wife and we are together in Brussels. We must act like man and wife while we are here.'

She recoiled. 'Do not expect me to perform my wifely duties. I performed them once and you left me.'

He understood. He truly understood. It must have been excruciating to open herself to him so intimately, only to be abandoned. But he could not say so.

Instead he said, 'We will address that issue at a later date. As it is, I am housed in a different hotel. I will not require you to move from here.'

'You will not require me!' she cried.

He lifted a hand to silence her. 'Suffice to say we will make the appearance of marital harmony, if for no other reason than it will cause talk if we do not and it will upset my parents and Amelie.'

'I am used to talk.' Her chin trembled. 'I have endured much talk already.'

That was like a sabre thrust. 'Well, then, let us put a stop to it.'

She'd probably think he wanted to be rid of her if he sent her and his family away from Brussels as soon as possible. His father would never turn around and leave the day after arriving, in any event.

He took a breath. 'There is to be a ball in two days' time. We will attend together. I will see that you and Amelie receive invitations. My parents, too, if I can manage it. And Captain Fowler.'

The Duke of Richmond and his secretary were Greybury's men. Marc could manage the invitations.

'And Miss Caldwell and her father?' she asked scornfully.

'I do not include them.' Why would he? He tried to get her to look at him. 'My encountering them in Brussels was as unexpected as encountering you, Tess.'

'Possibly more welcome though,' she said.

He did not want anyone he cared about to be in Brussels now.

'You will come to the ball with me,' he commanded. 'It will be the place to be seen.'

Once they were seen together at the Duchess of Richmond's ball, the gossip should abate. He could at least give that to her.

Chapter Fourteen

Dinner was early in Brussels. Not enough time for Tess to collect herself. Oh, she had time to dress, but not enough time to master the emotions spinning around inside her.

All because of encountering her husband after all these weeks.

The Caldwells were added to the dinner party, much to Tess's dismay, as was Captain Fowler.

They supped at the Café de l'Amitié. Café of Friendship. Was that not a farce?

Tess sat at Marc's side and was forced to watch the family and the Caldwells delight in his presence.

How odd they all were, to act as if Marc had merely been on a trip to Switzerland. He had deserted a new wife, not that any of them seemed to take him to task for that.

Or perhaps they were simply on good behaviour. Lord and Lady Northdon were always on good behavior when Captain Fowler was present. They were extremely eager that Captain Fowler think well of them, even to the point of refraining from their constant bickering. They doted on Captain Fowler. If this man did not make Amelie an offer, Amelie would not be the only one crushed.

At least the conversation at dinner did not require Tess's

participation beyond the occasional expression of interest or nodding of the head. While Tess seethed inside, though, Miss Caldwell was the epitome of serenity. It did no credit to Tess to resent Miss Caldwell for it.

After dinner they all walked back to the hotel on the Rue Royale, four couples, one behind the other. Lord and Lady Northdon led the way followed by Mr Caldwell and his daughter. Amelie and Captain Fowler trailed last and Marc and Tess were caught in the middle.

Amelie called to her parents, 'Maman, Papa, it is still so fine a day. May I take a turn in the park with the captain?'

'An excellent idea!' Lord Northdon stopped for a moment, so the whole parade stopped. 'In fact, let us all walk in the park.' He turned to Lady Northdon. 'Would you like to see the park, my dear?'

Amelie looked crestfallen.

Her father chuckled. 'Do not fear, Daughter. We will not stay in your pocket.'

But they certainly could keep an eye on her.

'Marc!' his father bellowed, though they were not at a distance. 'You will come with us.'

Tess saw her chance. 'Yes, do, Marc. Take a promenade through the park with your parents and the Caldwells. I can manage to walk the few steps to the hotel alone.'

Marc did not respond to Tess, but to his father. 'Thank you, Papa. I will stay with Tess.'

Lord Northdon's brows rose, as if he could not believe Marc would pick Tess over a few minutes with his parents and his good friends. 'If you wish it,' he said tersely.

'Let them go, John. They do not wish to be with us right now.' Lady Northdon smiled knowingly, as if she thought Marc and Tess were eager to be private together. She turned to Marc. *'Adieu, mon fils.'*

While Marc said goodnight to the others, Tess started walking to the hotel. Marc caught up to her.

'You should have stayed with your parents and your friends,' she said to him through gritted teeth.

'I would not leave you,' he replied.

She laughed. Surely he caught the irony of that statement.

She did not look at him to see, though. Looking at him was too painful. It reminded her of how he had looked in their marriage bed, how he had looked upon her with his intense blue eyes, how she'd been filled with hope and happiness.

'I cannot stay, however,' he added. 'I have somewhere else I must go.'

She shrugged as if she did not care where he went.

He held open the grand door of the Hotel de Flandre for her. She entered the lobby and strode determinedly towards the stairway. He seemed to have no difficulty keeping pace with her.

She stopped. 'I am going to my room and I do not need your escort. Go on to your next…entertainment.'

He gave her a firm look. 'I will walk you to your door.'

She turned to face him. 'I do not want this attention from you, Marc. Play the devoted husband when your family is around or other people who might matter to you, but there is no need to do so when no one of consequence is looking.'

'I can still be a gentleman,' he said.

'A gentleman!' She swung away from him and quickened her pace.

'Tess!' she heard a man call. 'Tess!'

A red-coated soldier hurried towards her.

'Edmund?' Was it truly her brother? 'Edmund!'

She rushed towards him and he caught her in a hug.

Tears immediately sprang to her eyes. Her armour was no match for seeing Edmund.

'Edmund,' she repeated. 'I wanted so badly to see you!' Her brother who loved her was here!

'What are you doing in Brussels, Tess?' He sounded unhappy to see her.

She stepped back.

A furrow of worry creased his brow. 'Are you in a financial fix?'

'Not at all,' Marc answered for her. He had followed her. 'Allow me to present myself. I am Marc Glenville, Tess's husband.'

'You are the husband?' Obviously Tess's letter had reached Edmund—the one that told him she was married; she'd not followed with one that said she'd also been abandoned. 'I am Edmund Summerfield, sir, Tess's brother.'

'Summerfield.' Marc extended his hand and Edmund shook it.

'My father acknowledged Edmund and gave him his name,' Tess explained.

Marc glanced at her. 'I was not questioning his name, Tess.'

'Indeed.' Edmund shifted uncomfortably before giving Marc a puzzled look. 'Why are you in Brussels, then, if not to escape debt? Do you have an official function?'

It was a blunt question, Tess thought.

'No debt. No official function.' Marc answered without apparent offence. 'I have been here for several days, but Tess and my family arrived today.'

Why did Marc not leave? It felt to Tess as if her brother was all she had left. She did not want to share his company with Marc.

'Never mind why we are here,' she said. 'Tell me, are you well? Do you need anything? Where are you staying?'

He took both her hands in his. 'I am very well. I need nothing. And—and I particularly wanted to tell you where I am staying.'

She hoped it was nearby so she could see him often. Perhaps he would be free from duties, like the officers in the park. Perhaps she could spend a day with him.

His expression turned serious. 'I am staying with your mother.'

Did she hear him correctly? 'My mother!'

'Yes,' he responded. 'I am staying with her and Count von Osten. They have a large house on Rue Sainte Anne.'

Count von Osten was the man her mother had eloped with.

'My mother and Count von Osten.'

Edmund released her. 'I shocked you, Tess. I am sorry.'

'I do not understand.' She shook her head. 'You—and my mother?'

He shrugged. 'I discovered she was in Brussels a long time ago. I've been corresponding with her for years.'

'For years?' Tess's voice rose. 'You've written to her? About us?' About Lorene and Genna and herself?

'Of course,' he admitted. 'But mostly about me.'

'You never told us!' It felt like a betrayal.

Her mother had no right to know anything about her! Or about Lorene and Genna. How could he write to her about them? Thank goodness they'd never told Edmund about their father's financial ruin or about him stealing their dowries to purchase Edmund's commission. Thank goodness she kept the mess of her own life secret.

'Why did you find her? Why write to her? Live with her? She is not your mother!' She trembled.

A strong, comforting arm wrapped around her shoulders. Marc.

Edmund faced her. 'Your mother was always kind to me.'

'She hardly saw any of us!'

'Maybe so,' Edmund responded. 'But she always treated me well. She treated me as if I were of value and when I was a boy, I greatly needed that.'

Her mother had been charming, that was true, but she could not have valued any of them. She left them, after all.

Edmund's expression turned earnest. 'She wants to see you, Tess.'

'She knows I am here?' Tess did not want her mother to know anything of her.

'She was with me when Upton told me you were here,' he explained. 'Will you call upon her, Tess? She would like you to.'

'Call upon her!' Never.

'She even invites you to stay.' He turned to Marc. 'You, too, sir.'

'Tess is here with my parents and sister,' Marc explained.

'I am certain they would be welcomed, too,' Edmund said. 'It is a very big house.'

'No!' Tess cried.

She pulled away.

'Perhaps we should bid you goodnight, Lieutenant,' Marc said. 'Tess is weary from travelling.'

Edmund nodded. 'May I call upon you again, Tess?'

He was still her brother, after all. Even if she could no longer trust him. 'Of course you may call upon me.' She walked back to give him a quick hug. 'But I do not wish to hear more about my mother.'

'I will call again tomorrow.' He turned to Marc. 'Goodbye, sir. I hope to see more of you.'

Marc again offered his hand to shake. 'I do, as well.'

Tess hugged Edmund once more before Marc led her up the stairs and out of sight of the lobby.

She pulled away then, and turned to face him. 'How dare he! Did you hear him? He acted as if I should not mind that she abandoned us!' She started down the hallway, talking to the walls now. 'Why is it that everyone who abandons me thinks it perfectly acceptable to do so? I am expected to greet them as if they'd merely been gone an hour. Am I supposed to feel nothing?'

That day when she'd been nine, her mother came flying into the nursery, waking up her, Lorene and Genna and kissing them and saying she would see them later. Since that day she'd not sent one letter, not one message, to them. The only news they heard of her after that was through their father when he ranted about how she'd ruined his life.

'She asks to see me as if it did not matter.' Tess fought angry tears.

When they reached her door, she pulled the key from her reticule. Marc took it from her and wrapped his arms around her, holding her close.

His warmth, the solidness of his body, his scent, was comfort itself, as if he were pouring some of his strength into her. He simply held her, giving and demanding nothing. She wanted to stay in his arms forever.

But this was Marc. He'd abandoned her, too.

She pushed him away.

'Do not touch me,' she snapped.

He merely bowed and backed away. She hurried into the room, but stopped and opened the door a crack to watch him walk down the hall, away from her and to wherever it was so important he go.

Marc descended the stairway with his own set of churned-up emotions. He had indeed abandoned her, just as her mother had done.

Could he ever make it up to her? Or had their marriage been doomed from the start?

When he reached the lobby, her brother still stood there and looked surprised to see him.

'I am off on an errand,' Marc explained, walking towards the door.

Edmund walked with him. 'Is Tess all right?'

Marc met his eye briefly. 'She has had a very difficult day.'

Marc had made it difficult.

Edmund looked regretful. 'Please convey my apologies to her. I should not have told her about her mother so abruptly.'

'It is done now.' What else could Marc say?

A footman opened the door.

'I do not think Tess will call upon her mother,' Marc told Edmund as he walked outside.

'She should do so.' Edmund shook his head. 'I knew this news would be a surprise to her. I thought she might be happy about it, though. As children we sometimes talked about her mother leaving. She and my sisters always said Lady Summerfield had done the right thing.'

'Sometimes you can still hurt someone even if you do the right thing.' How well Marc knew this.

Marc liked this brother of Tess's. Edmund was loyal to Tess and caring, even if he had brought Tess unwelcome news. Marc even liked Edmund's loyalty to Lady Summerfield. Edmund had apparently forgiven her for abandoning her family.

Would Tess ever forgive him?

They parted ways shortly after and Marc walked the half-mile to Le Double Aigle at the old Halle aux Blés. It was an inn of an inferior type where he could be somewhat unobtrusive. It was also packed with billeted soldiers.

Marc climbed the stairs to his room and changed into the clothes of an ordinary Belgian.

He took care to leave the inn again without anyone noticing and made his way to a part of town where no Englishmen thought to visit. There he entered a public house, one he'd been visiting frequently. He took a seat and ordered the beer this country brewed so well. Like previous nights, he settled down to listen to the conversations of those around him. He'd stay until late at night, listening to men's tongues loosened with drink.

He suspected, though, that his thoughts would turn to Tess, even more often than they'd done before while on his travels. With any luck, he would not miss some useful information that might come his way from the many Belgians who would welcome Napoleon's return.

The next morning Marc woke early, his head aching more from lack of sleep than the beer he'd consumed. He'd promised his father he would breakfast with the family and he did not want to disappoint them. He forced himself out of bed and dressed quickly. Soon he was out in the cool morning air that finally revived him. He walked briskly to the Hotel de Flandre.

Would Tess wake so early? he wondered. Would she breakfast with the family? Would he have any time alone with her?

He would wager any amount of money that she'd not let on to his parents or Amelie or even her maid Nancy that her mother was in Brussels. He hoped she'd regained her composure.

He'd not wanted to leave her last night, but he had his duty to perform.

And she did not want him.

His night had been productive, at least. He'd wound

up befriending a couple of Bonapartists and they wanted him to meet someone this afternoon. Apparently a group of men was planning to help Napoleon gain back Belgium. Marc would shout *Vive l'Empereur* if it would help them accept him as one of them and tell him what they knew.

He entered the hotel and asked the steward to have him announced to his father. Instead of the steward returning with permission to call upon his father, his father appeared in person.

'Your mother is not yet awake,' his father said by way of greeting. 'Let us take a turn in the park.'

They walked the short distance to the Parc de Bruxelles. Even at this early hour they had plenty of company, soldiers in uniform, some arm in arm with willing women who'd undoubtedly warmed their beds the night before.

His father was silent a long time before speaking. 'I would be remiss if I did not address what you have done, my son.'

A lecture. Marc supposed he deserved it, at least from his father's viewpoint.

'You know I am not at all happy about this marriage of yours. It caused plenty of talk in town. The gossips made much of you and she being caught *in flagrante*.' He made a disparaging sound. *'In flagrante.'*

Marc sliced the air with his hand. 'We were never *in flagrante*, Papa, so say no more. I told you what happened.'

His father stopped and looked straight in Marc's eye. 'Why the devil did you leave her, then? To travel to Switzerland? God knows you've run off willy-nilly plenty of other times, but this was not the thing to do.'

'I could not refuse,' Marc said truthfully.

'Could not refuse. Of course you could refuse,' his father muttered. 'Well, you've done a lot of harm by leaving.

A lot of harm. To her and the family. What are you going to do about it now?'

'Whatever I can,' he answered honestly.

They continued to stroll down one of the walkways, passing a copy of the statue *Apollino*.

'You have to tend to a marriage.' His father's voice took on a philosophical tone. 'A wife needs your consideration.'

This was his father talking?

'You need to consider her desires, if you are married to her. And if you must do something that she cannot like, you must tell her in the gentlest way possible—'

Marc would hear no more of this. 'Papa! Are you speaking from experience? Because I have seen little of what you describe in your marriage.'

His father stiffened. 'I am not talking of my marriage.'

'Obviously not.' Marc continued walking. 'When have you considered Maman's wishes above your own? When have you been gentle with her?'

'Your mother and I should not have married!' Marc had heard his father say this many times. 'We were carried away by—by—well—those visceral feelings that lead to—to—carnal desire. She has been unhappy with me ever since coming to England where she can never belong. She blames me for it.'

'Is that so?' Marc continued. 'I dare say Tess's and my marriage began even more problematically. Before you tell me what I must do, you ought to try it yourself.'

'Your mother would not accept it.'

'Do you think so?' Marc was not letting this go. 'You and she were on excellent terms last night. Both of you refrained from picking at each other. It was quite pleasant.'

His father waved a hand. 'That was nothing. We are eager that Captain Fowler think us a good family and we are always civil in front of the Caldwells. We are anxious to see your sister well settled. Amelie seems to like this fellow very well and Fowler would make an excellent husband for her.'

Like Fowler? Amelie seemed to think Captain Fowler hung the moon and stars. And his parents had travelled to Brussels because of it.

'Did you find the evening pleasant when you and Maman were acting civil to each other?' Marc asked instead.

His father did not answer right away. He pretended to examine the busts of Roman emperors on the terrace surrounding the basin.

Finally he said, 'It was pleasant enough.'

'Then heed your own advice before you pass it on to me. Show me you can make my mother happy and I'll attempt the same with my wife.'

His father averted his gaze. 'I cannot make your mother happy.'

And Marc probably could never make Tess happy. But he could try.

He changed the subject. 'Father, I wanted to warn you about being in Brussels. It is not safe if there is to be fighting soon.'

'Ridiculous!' his father snapped. 'Brussels is as safe as London. Look at everyone who is here.'

'You should return to England as soon as possible.'

'After just arriving here?' his father scoffed. 'I have it on good authority that the march on France is a couple of weeks away at least.' He swept his arm across the park. 'Look at those men in uniform. They do not look as if this is the eve of battle. They look as if they are on holiday. Besides, your mother likes it here. We will stay as long as it suits her and your sister.'

'I realise that.' Marc felt none of the leisure of the soldiers in the park. 'But when the soldiers march, you must return to England.'

'Bah. What do you know about it?'

Marc would know more very soon, he hoped. Something was afoot and the Bonapartists he'd met in those public rooms were his best bet on learning what it was.

His father went on. 'You probably want to get rid of us so you can continue your affair with Doria Caldwell.'

He turned on his father. 'I am not having an affair with Doria Caldwell!' He tried hard to contain his anger. 'You do us all a disservice by saying so, and if you've implied anything of the sort to Tess, you are cruel indeed.'

'I have said nothing,' his father snapped, but his expression turned to concern. 'Then, why, my son? Why did you leave? Where did you go and why?'

'I went to the Alps.'

'I do not believe you,' his father said. 'You are hiding something.'

Marc looked him directly in the eye. 'Do not believe me, then. But when next I tell you to leave Brussels, take me seriously.'

His father looked back at him, his eyes widening. He slowly nodded.

Tess's sleep had been fitful, filled with dreams, not only of Marc and Edmund, but also of her mother. She dreamed of being suddenly alone in Brussels, finding her mother's house an empty ruin, but hearing her mother's laughter, watching Marc come towards her in the rain, but disappearing. She dreamed of cannon fire and soldiers on horseback galloping through the town, no one noticing she was alone.

When she'd finally fallen into a deep sleep, Nancy came in the room to wake her.

Tess sat up in the bed. 'What time is it?'

'It is eight o'clock, the time I was supposed to wake you,' Nancy said cheerfully.

Tess fought the urge to send Nancy away and burrow under the covers again. Instead she swung her feet over the edge and searched for her slippers. 'I hope you slept well.'

Nancy shared a room with Lady Northdon's and Amelie's maids. 'Lady Northdon's maid snores, but otherwise it was very comfortable.' She opened the curtains and sunlight poured into the room, such a contrast to the gloom of Tess's dreams. 'What would you like to wear?' she asked, walking over to the clothes press.

'The blue, I think.' Her blue gown always reminded her of Marc's eyes and she wore it often in the hopes that she could attach the colour to something else. The sky. The sea. Something.

Tess walked over to the washstand and poured some water into the basin. She washed herself and brushed her teeth before donning a fresh shift. Nancy brought her a corset and laced her into it, then they moved to the dressing table so Nancy could brush out her hair and pin it up. It was a familiar routine for them, even in this unfamiliar place.

'Will you see Mr Glenville today?' Nancy brushed through a difficult tangle. 'Or your brother?' Tess had confided only the bare facts of the previous day to Nancy.

'I do not know,' she answered. How could she know if she would see Marc? She did not even know the name of his hotel. If he wished, he could easily disappear again. 'I do hope to see my brother.'

In the mirror Tess saw Nancy's usual cheerful expression change to a frown. 'I know it is not my place to say, but it wasn't right for Mr Glenville to leave you the way he did and then not to let you know he was here in Brussels. He should not have surprised you so.'

'I fear it was we who surprised him.' If he'd known they were coming to Brussels, would he have left?

Nancy pinned Tess's hair into a simple knot and helped her into her dress. 'Do you remember that Lord Northdon wanted you to breakfast with them in their sitting room?'

Tess nodded.

'When will you be needing me today?' Nancy asked.

'Goodness,' Tess exclaimed. 'I have not thought that far ahead.'

'The thing is, I would like to visit the shops, if I may. The maids who work here in the hotel said that Brussels is known for its lace and I should want to look at lace.'

Tess reached for her reticule and took out several coins. 'If you see something worthwhile, purchase it, for yourself or for me. No matter what, buy yourself something.'

Nancy's eyes sparkled. 'Oh, thank you, ma'am!'

'And take one of the other maids with you. Or Staines, if you can. Do not go out alone. There are soldiers everywhere.' Nancy's sheer good spirits would attract the men to her.

'Oh, do not worry over me, ma'am. I have brothers. I know how to handle myself.' She made a fierce face. 'But Miss Glenville's maid wants to see the shops, too.'

There was a knock on the door, but it opened before Tess could speak.

Amelie stuck her head in. 'Tess! May I come in?'

She was halfway in already. 'Of course, Amelie.'

The girl practically danced into the room. 'It is such a lovely morning, is it not?'

Nancy grinned. 'Only one thing makes a girl that happy!'

Amelie gave Nancy a quick embrace. 'A man, you mean. A special man! The most handsome man you have ever seen and the most gentlemanly, too.'

'It is lovely to see you so happy, Amelie.' A man, a special, handsome man, a gentleman, was on Tess's mind, too, but to think of him made Tess feel wretched.

Amelie floated over to where Tess sat and hugged her, as well. 'I am so very happy! Captain Fowler is calling upon Papa this morning. He will ask if he can marry me!'

'Oh, miss!' Nancy exclaimed. 'That is so exciting! We must see if we can find some beautiful lace here for your wedding dress.'

Amelie plopped herself down in a chair. 'A wedding dress made of Belgian lace. Does that not sound beautiful?'

Tess could feel happy for Amelie. 'It sounds very beautiful.' But was it wise, she wondered, to become betrothed to a soldier when war was expected?

Amelie smiled beatifically. 'And now you might be happy, too. Marc is back with us.'

Tess tensed. 'Marc is in the hotel?'

'Oh, I do not know if he is in the hotel, but he is to have breakfast with us. Do you not remember?' Amelie sighed. 'I wonder what time Captain Fowler will arrive?'

Tess wondered when Marc would arrive. *If* he would arrive. She could plead a sick headache and remain in her room all day, but what good would that do? She must face him inevitably.

'I am certain Captain Fowler will arrive at the perfect time,' Tess said. Any time he arrived would be perfect in Amelie's eyes. She rose. 'Shall we go to breakfast?'

She and Amelie walked down the hall to Lord and Lady Northdon's set of rooms, which consisted of two bedchambers and a sitting room where breakfast would be served to them. When they walked into the sitting room, three gentlemen rose.

Marc, his father and Edmund.

'Edmund!' Tess hurried over to him, clasping his hand.

It was the vision that was Amelie who caught Edmund's eye, though. Tess noticed he forced himself to look at her.

When he did, he smiled. 'Your husband and Lord Northdon found me in the park and invited me to breakfast. I would never have called so early otherwise.'

'Your brother is *très charmant*,' Lady Northdon remarked. 'We were just becoming acquainted.'

'It was kind of you to include him.' Tess's gaze fixed on Marc, but she looked away quickly.

He looked fatigued, as if he'd not slept. Had his other entertainment kept him up late?

'Good morning, Tess,' he spoke in a low, smooth voice.

Amelie stepped towards Edmund. 'I have not been introduced.'

Marc spoke. 'Amelie, may I present Tess's brother, Lieutenant Summerfield.' He turned to Edmund. 'My sister, Miss Glenville.'

Edmund's face seemed full of colour. He bowed. 'My pleasure, Miss Glenville.'

'Shall we all sit and eat?' Lady Northdon said.

The breakfast was pleasant because Edmund was there and, because he was there, Tess did not have to talk to Marc or the others, even though Tess noticed Edmund's attention often strayed to Amelie. Captain Fowler joined them when the meal was almost finished and, while Amelie's and Lord and Lady Northdon's spirits rose, Edmund became more withdrawn.

Poor Edmund. What chance would he ever have with Amelie, even if it weren't for Captain Fowler? He was the illegitimate son of a disgraced baronet and Amelie was a viscount's daughter.

'Do you have time to spend with me today, Edmund?' Tess asked him.

'Later in the afternoon, perhaps.' His gaze moved to

where Amelie and Captain Fowler sat with their heads together.

'I want you to come with me this morning, Tess,' Marc said.

Tess could barely look at him. 'I have something else to do.'

Marc spoke firmly. 'No, you do not. Come with me.'

Her brother and Lord and Lady Northdon were all staring at her, waiting for her to respond.

'If I must change my plans for you, I will.' Not that she had any plans.

Chapter Fifteen

Breakfast ended. Tess, her brother and Marc quit the rooms, leaving Amelie and her captain with Lord and Lady Northdon. Undoubtedly, the betrothal was imminent.

Tess said goodbye to Edmund and she was left alone with Marc.

'Come with me, Tess,' he said. 'I want to call upon someone.'

'Who?' Tess was not willing to endure more surprises. 'I will not go unless you tell me.'

'Do you recall the gentlemen I was with yesterday in the park?'

Do you mean the gentlemen who stood with Miss Caldwell and you? she wanted to say. 'Not their names,' she admitted instead.

'One was Captain Upton, the man who knew your brother. The other was Mr Scott, who is secretary to the Duke of Richmond. We are calling upon him.'

'The Duke of Richmond?' Whatever for?

'Not the duke. Mr Scott.'

'Was he one of the fine fellows traipsing through the Alps with you?' she asked sarcastically.

'No,' he answered quietly.

Tess did not wish to call upon anyone, especially if he

was a friend of Marc's, even if he had not been a part of the fictitious trip to the Alps.

'Marc, would you please call upon this gentleman without me?' she asked. 'I am certain your mother would like for me to visit the shops with her.'

'My mother is wrapped up in Amelie and Fowler at the moment,' he said. 'Come. How many opportunities do you receive to see a duke's house?'

'How far is it?' she asked.

'About a mile,' he responded.

She acquiesced in the end.

As they set out, she had to admit that it felt good to be outside in the brisk air and to stretch her legs and walk. There was so much activity. So much to look at. All the street signs were in French and they heard more French spoken on the street than Dutch. Everywhere they walked, there were soldiers, some dressed in red coats, some in dark blue. Marc pointed out buildings of importance on the way and talked about the history of the city. It almost felt normal, like the few walks they'd taken together in London, if those could be considered normal.

They reached a very grand house on Rue de la Blanchisserie. Marc sounded the knocker and they were soon admitted to the hall. A footman explained that Mr Scott was to be found in another building. He led them to it through an anteroom and announced them to Mr Scott.

Scott strode over. 'Glenville! Ma'am.' He bowed to Tess. 'How good to see you. He gestured into the large room, its walls papered with roses and festooned with draperies in the royal colours of red, gold and black. 'This is where the grand event is to take place. The duchess has given me the task of seeing to some of the arrangements.'

Workmen were putting the finishing touches on some sort of platform. Others were carrying in sofas and chairs.

Crystal chandeliers hung from the ceiling and huge cande-
labras, taller than a man, were arranged against the walls.

Mr Scott laughed. 'Can you believe this used to be
where a coach builder displayed his wares? The children
were using it as a schoolroom—or, more likely, as a place
to play shuttlecocks—until the duchess took it over for
the ball.'

The ball? Surely this was not the ball Marc had spoken of the day before. Why would a duchess condescend
to invite Lord and Lady Northdon, or the equally scandalous Tess Glenville?

'That is why we have come,' Marc said. 'Were you able
to do what I asked?'

'I was.' He leaned forward with a conspiratorial look.
'With a little assistance from our friend.'

What friend? Of course, Tess would know nothing about
Marc's friends.

Mr Scott reached into the inner pocket of his coat and
pulled out white cards. 'Invitations for all of you. Your parents. Your sister. Captain Fowler.' He winked at Tess. 'And
you and your husband, ma'am.' His smile grew wider. 'His
Grace the Duke of Wellington promises to attend, as well.'

'We are invited to this ball?' Tess could not believe
it. 'The duchess's ball?' A ball Wellington would attend?
'Does the duchess know of our invitations?'

Mr Scott handed the invitations to Marc. 'She does, indeed.' He turned suddenly and shouted to some workmen,
'No, not there! On the other side.'

Marc put the invitations in his pocket. 'We should take
our leave. You are busy.'

Mr Scott made a wry smile. 'A tad busy at the moment. I, for one, shall be glad when this ball is over.' He
gave Marc a significant look. 'I will hear from you later?'

'Later,' Marc agreed.

They bid Scott farewell and walked back out to the street.

'Where shall we go next?' Marc asked.

Tess whirled on him. 'You did not tell me the ball I must attend would be a duchess's ball.'

Marc lifted a shoulder. 'It was an invitation I had at my disposal to arrange.'

'How could you have it at your disposal? A friendship with a duke's secretary is hardly a reason to be invited.'

'There was more to it.' He blew out a breath. 'What difference does it make, Tess? It is a very much sought-after invitation and I was able to arrange it.'

'Did you think arranging an invitation to a ball would make any difference to me?' Telling her the truth would be vastly better.

Not leaving her would have been ideal.

'This invitation will lead to others,' he said. 'It should at least please Amelie and my mother and make your time in Brussels more pleasant.'

The invitation did not please Tess. She would never have sought it. 'They talked about me in London after you left me,' she told him. 'Let them talk about me in Brussels, because you are forced to be with me.'

'I am not forced to be with you, Tess.' He paused. 'And I am profoundly sorry you were the object of gossip because of me.'

He looked at her with regret in his eyes, but should she trust how he appeared?

'Oh, how can I ever believe you?' She stepped away. 'About anything.'

He caught her and forced her to stop. 'We must learn to get on together.'

She raised a brow. 'Must we?'

He squeezed her arms. 'I know I hurt you by leaving,

but it was an unhappy accident of timing.' Caused by Napoleon, as a matter of fact.

She gave him a scathing look. 'I am certain leaving me right after our wedding night seemed like a sensible choice to you.'

'Let us drop this.' His tone turned soft. 'I have thought of another site to show you.'

They started back the way they'd come and he resumed his discourse on Brussels.

When they again passed the Cathédrale des Saints Michel et Gudule with its imposing two towers reaching to the sky, she asked, 'Why do you know so much about Brussels? Have you been here the whole time?'

He paused before answering. 'No. I have spent time here before, though.'

'When?' He'd been in Scotland before they met. Before that was the war. Who could have travelled to Belgium during the war?

'Some time ago,' he answered non-committally.

Was there no end to what he would not tell her? Secrets and lies had been a part of her parents' marriage and now it was part of hers.

They did not turn back to the Parc de Bruxelles, but continued to the Grand Place. The Grand Place was a square surrounded by buildings that might once have been grand, but now looked as if they had seen better days.

'This used to be in better repair, they say,' Marc told her as they walked through the square. 'But revolutionaries sacked the buildings a couple of decades ago.'

The buildings reminded her of herself. When she was little her life had seemed so shiny and perfect, but time chipped away at what was once beautiful, leaving mere memories of what was now gone.

She was glad when they continued past the Grand Place.

'Was that what you wished to show me?' she asked rather peevishly. Sad, neglected buildings? 'May we return now?'

'Oh, no.' He smiled. 'What I want to show you is meant to amuse.'

She wished he would not smile like that. It made her insides flutter as if thousands of butterflies were trapped inside her. He looked even more handsome when he smiled, less like a buccaneer and more like someone who could make the sun shine brighter.

She did not want to think of him as handsome. She did not want to remember how it felt for his arms to hold her, his fingers to stroke her skin. He seemed to be trying so hard to please her. It would be so much easier if he simply left her alone.

She pressed her lips together.

They turned a corner and after a few steps he said, 'Close your eyes.'

'This is nonsense,' she muttered, but she did as he demanded, mostly as an excuse not to look at him.

He led her further. 'Now open.'

She opened her eyes and laughed aloud.

Before her was a fountain made from a statue of a little boy, the water shooting out in a stream from a very particular part of his body.

'He is relieving himself!' she exclaimed.

He stood behind her, his hands resting on her shoulders. 'He is called Mannekin Pis and he has been in this spot for two hundred years.'

His hands almost made her forget anything else. She forced herself to speak. 'Why would anyone erect such a fountain?'

His voice turned deeper. 'The true meaning is lost, but

there was a statue before this one dating back to the twelfth century.'

He moved closer. Or had she been the one to move? She could feel his breath on her neck. He smelled of lime and bergamot—and a fragrance that made her body ache in response.

She did not want to feel this way. And she did not want to move away from him.

A church bell rang the noon hour.

He released her and stepped back. 'I must return you to the hotel.' An urgent tone entered his voice.

'You have somewhere else to go?' she asked.

'Yes.' He offered her his arm.

They started walking. 'Where?'

He frowned. 'To meet someone.'

Her throat tightened. Someone? If it was not a woman, then why not simply tell her?

Let him go, then! She wanted to be rid of his disturbing company.

'Why did you have me accompany you?' she snapped after they'd gone several steps. 'I do not understand at all.'

His muscles tensed under her fingers. 'We must start somewhere, Tess.'

Marc's spirits plummeted. As soon as matters calmed between them, he did something that drove her away again.

Damned meeting. He could not explain to her why it was so important or why the information he was likely to gather might help keep her and his family safe.

If he could be honest with her, it would help a great deal. The Tess he knew would understand how duty could take him away from her, even the morning after their wedding night.

He'd spent many a night thinking about her, yearning

for her and fearing he'd lost her forever because he could not be honest with her. Her delight at Mannekin Pis filled him with a little hope.

Even though she stopped speaking to him.

What would heal the wounds between them? Time? Time certainly had not healed his parents. They were as angry at each other today as when he'd been a child.

Tess held his arm as they walked, but in a perfunctory way that was like a knife thrust to his heart. He hated this silence between them, but he'd exhausted his knowledge of Brussels. What else could he talk about when almost everything about him must be kept secret?

It left too much to the imagination. His father, for one, imagined he was being unfaithful to Tess with Doria. He hoped Tess no longer believed that, but who knew what she thought he was hiding from her?

It would solve everything if he could simply tell her he was employed as a spy, that his contacts in Brussels were Mr Scott and the Duke of Richmond, that his need for secrecy had to do with duty to his country, not infidelity, not rejecting his wife. He'd come perilously close to saying too much to his father. Marc understood now how Rosier could have broken his oath of silence. It merely cost Rosier his life. Somehow Marc felt his choice, to honour his oath and do his duty to his country, might cost him something more precious. His marriage. Tess's happiness.

Was it futile to hope to win her back? As they walked together through the beautiful streets of Brussels, she would not speak to him.

He grasped at straws, or rather at a topic he knew she would dislike, but at least answer. 'Will you call upon your mother?'

Her hand tensed. 'No.'

He pushed. 'Even though your brother resides there?'

'He can call on me.' She took several steps before speaking again, but, then, it was more to herself than to him. 'I cannot understand him. She was not his mother. He was only there two or three years before she left. I never noticed her pay much mind to him at all.' She slowed and glanced to some unseen place. 'She did not spend much time with us. A visit to the schoolroom when she was home.'

'The time she spent with him meant something to him, apparently,' he said—to keep her talking.

'She was always charming.' Tess continued to walk. 'I suppose it drew even little boys to her.'

'And little girls,' he dared to add.

Her hand on his arm tightened.

'Yes,' she said in a hushed voice. 'When Mama was there nothing else mattered.'

Poor hurt little girl!

He wanted to keep her talking. 'When Amelie, Lucien and I were children, my parents were always too busy fighting each other to pay a great deal of attention to us.'

She glanced at him with a surprised expression.

He looked at her. 'Surely you have noticed that they skirmish all the time.'

'They are unhappy,' she admitted. 'But I am surprised you say they did not pay attention to you. They dote on Amelie.'

He nodded. 'I guess they do. Coming to Brussels certainly is greatly indulging her.'

She actually went on. 'They have been remarkably in concert about Captain Fowler. And they do not bicker when he is around.'

Marc was encouraged. This was almost comfortable conversation. 'What do you know of this Captain Fowler?'

'He's the younger son of Lord Ellister, a man your father esteems a great deal, apparently. From your father's
account, it is a good family.'

'No scandal?' he asked with a wry smile.

To his delight she answered in like manner. 'No scandal.'

His spirits rose.

'Do you like Fowler?' he asked.

She shrugged. 'He seems besotted with Amelie.'

He frowned. 'But you are not certain of him?'

She looked into his face. 'How can one ever be certain?'

That dagger thrust was meant for him.

They walked on.

'Is Amelie equally as besotted?' he finally asked.

'More so, I am afraid,' she responded.

'Wait.' He stopped. 'What do you mean *afraid*? I thought
you believed in such love.'

She looked away. 'Not any longer.'

The dagger twisted.

This talk of love was too painful. Tess wished he would
stop.

'Should I be concerned about Fowler?' he asked.

'Of course you should,' she snapped. 'He has the power
to hurt her terribly.' Just as Marc had hurt her. 'Love, I've
learned, has that sort of power.'

He frowned.

Did he even realise she spoke about how he hurt her?

They walked in silence after that. Good. She did not
want him to say anything to her.

But she hated his silence.

What did it matter? Soon he would leave her to meet
this mysterious someone he refused to tell her about. She
would be free of his company.

He suddenly asked, 'Do you know why my friend Charles volunteered for the Forlorn Hope?'

He'd startled her. 'Why?'

They walked a few more steps. 'Charles became besotted with a Spanish woman. He was mad for her—at least that is what he said in his letters about her.' He took a breath. 'She threw him over for another man, so he volunteered for the Forlorn Hope. He wrote to me about it. Said he might as well, because he no longer cared if he lived or died.'

How awful! She'd felt close to that level of despair because of him, not that she'd ever let on.

'Charles thought himself in love,' he said in a bleak tone. 'He was so obsessed by her, he lost all reason.'

Her brows knit. 'Sad. But why—'

He did not let her finish. 'My brother was no different,' he went on. 'Lucien lost his head over a young woman whose parents refused his suit. He eloped with her and was racing to Gretna Green when his carriage wheel broke and pitched him to the ground.' He swallowed as if it became difficult to continue. 'He lingered for several weeks. I was called home from my regiment.' He could not finish.

Her voice softened, 'So you concluded love kills?'

'Well, love killed my brother and my friend. It doomed my parents to unhappiness—' He stopped abruptly as if his emotions prevented him from saying more.

No wonder he did not believe in love.

She wished he had not shared this with her. It chipped away at her defences against him. If she allowed herself to feel his pain, her protection could vanish. She could be hurt once more.

They reached the Place Royale before she spoke again. 'Do not worry too much about your sister and Captain Fowler. They seem to have the happy combination of being well suited in temperament and situation. I suspect they will be the lucky ones.' She paused. 'That is, if he is not killed in a battle.'

Neither spoke more. They reached the Hotel de Flandre and Marc escorted her to her room.

At her door, she took out her key and put it in the lock.

He reached into his pocket and handed her the invitations to the Duchess of Richmond's ball. 'Here are the invitations to the ball. Will you pass them on to my parents and Amelie and Captain Fowler?'

She looked at him with suspicion. 'Why? Will you not be giving them the invitations yourself?'

'In case I do not see them…'

She felt her entire body turn rigid. 'Are you planning on disappearing again?'

He seized her shoulders. Their bodies were mere inches from touching. 'I will come back for the ball.'

She raised her gaze to his eyes. 'But not dinner tonight?'

He looked away. 'If I am able, I will escort you to dinner.'

She could not believe him. 'Unless a trip to Switzerland comes your way.'

She opened the door and slipped inside before he could see that holding her so close had caused her face to flush and her body to come alive with sensation.

Marc tore himself away from Tess's door. He'd not planned to hold her so close. His body had ached for more of her. Would he ever earn that right?

He hurried to his hotel to transform himself into a Bonapartist with no ties to the British aristocracy and on to the meeting where six other men gathered. One claimed to have some news from another man who was in communication with Napoleon's aides-de-camp. Marc said all the right things and was apparently accepted, because this man spoke openly.

He said they must prepare for Napoleon's triumphant return to Brussels. Napoleon might appear at any moment, he said, while the British and their Allies attended parties and staged military revues rather than preparing for battle.

His information was second hand at best, but these Bonapartists took it seriously enough to design handbills and set in stores for a victory dinner.

Marc promised he would be ready to pass out fliers or help in any way possible when the time came. There was much shaking of hands and clapping each other on the back and shouts of *'Vive l'Empereur!'*

When Marc left he was careful not to appear suspicious, or to lead them to Mr Scott or the Duke. He spent an hour visiting shops, stopping for ale and otherwise looking as if he were having an ordinary day.

Eventually he made his way to Rue de la Blanchisserie and found Scott.

Scott summoned the Duke and the three of them met in the Duke's library.

Both Scott and the Duke were grim-faced as Marc told them what he had heard.

'Can we reach you at your hotel?' Mr Scott asked.

'At my hotel or my wife's.' But would she want him to stay? He could hope. 'She is at the Hotel de Flandre.'

'If what you report is correct, Glenville,' his grace said in a grim tone, 'Brussels may soon become a very dangerous place for Englishmen.'

And everyone Marc cared about—including the woman he loved—was in Brussels.

Chapter Sixteen

That afternoon Tess brought the invitations to Lord and Lady Northdon, finding them in their sitting room. Amelie was there, as well.

'The Duchess of Richmond's ball?' Lady Northdon exclaimed.

Lord Northdon looked sceptical. 'Marc arranged this? How could he?'

'He arranged it through the duke's secretary,' she explained. 'A man who, I gather, is a friend.'

'The duke and duchess know of this?' Lady Northdon asked.

'The duke's secretary said they do.'

Amelie stared at the invitations. 'This is the most wonderful invitation I ever received. Everyone is talking about this ball and we actually will attend.' She clasped the invitations to her breast. 'Even Captain Fowler!'

Lord Northdon crossed the room to where his wife was seated. He lowered himself into the chair next to hers and leaned towards her. 'Do you wish to attend, Ines?' His tone was surprisingly mild.

Lady Northdon glanced at him in surprise. 'Do you?'

He actually touched her hand. 'Only if it pleases you.'

Amelie stared at her. 'Maman! Please say yes!'

Lady Northdon glanced from her husband to her daughter and smiled, showing every ounce of her beauty. *'Bien sûr.'*

Amelie ran over to her and hugged and kissed her, then hugged and kissed her father.

She covered her cheeks with her hands. 'What will I wear? Maman, come look at my dresses and tell me which will do for a duchess's ball.'

Lord Northdon stood and extended his hand to Lady Northdon to help her up.

She looked at him with adoring eyes. *'Merci,* John.'

Tess gaped at them. They were acting civil to each other even though there was no one to impress. Had the world gone topsy-turvy?

'If I may have your leave,' she asked, 'I should speak with Nancy about a gown for me.'

'Oui, chérie,' Lady Northdon said. *'À bientôt.'*

When it came time to dress for dinner, Tess dragged her feet. It was silly of her, she knew, because Marc would not show.

'You are quiet today, ma'am,' Nancy said as she pinned up Tess's hair.

'Am I?' She'd said nothing to anyone, not even Nancy, about Marc wanting to share dinner with her. Why would she?

Nancy twisted a strand of Tess's hair and secured it with a hairpin. 'What would you say to my sewing an overdress of Belgian lace for your ball gown?'

'In one day?' She spoke to Nancy's reflection in the mirror.

'I could do it,' Nancy insisted. 'It is just a few seams and I sew seams very fast.'

Tess sighed. 'If you wish to try.'

Nancy pushed one last hairpin into Tess's hair. 'What dress do you wish to wear to dinner?'

'It does not matter,' Tess said.

Nancy walked over to the wardrobe and pulled out the blue gown, the one that reminded Tess of Marc's eyes. Of all her gowns, why that one?

She said nothing, though. What would it matter what gown she wore?

Nancy helped her into the dress and she slipped her feet into her shoes. There was nothing left to do but appear at Lord and Lady Northdon's sitting room and go have dinner with them.

A knock sounded at the door. She was probably late and they'd sent a servant to collect her.

Nancy hurried over to open the door. 'Oh, Mr Glenville!'

Marc?

'I've come for Mrs Glenville. Is she ready?' he asked.

Nancy stepped aside to allow him to enter.

Tess stood. 'Oh. You are here.' In spite of herself her heart pounded at the sight of him.

He remained near the doorway. 'I said I would try to come for dinner.'

Tess picked up her shawl. 'Well. We should go then. Your parents will be waiting.' She turned to Nancy. 'Goodbye, Nancy.'

Nancy bobbed a quick curtsy. 'Goodbye, ma'am!'

Tess swept past Marc and crossed into the hallway. She started towards his parents' room.

He caught up with her. 'We are not dining with my parents.'

She halted and faced him. 'Not dining with them?'

He stood too close to her. 'I know you will not believe me, but they told me they were dining alone.'

'Alone?' She did not believe him. 'What of Amelie?'

'They have apparently given Captain Fowler permission to take Amelie to one of the nearby restaurants.'

She peered at him. 'Why do I think that you are tricking me?'

He took her by the arm and walked with her to a sofa at the end of the hallway.

He sat her down and his blue eyes held her in their grasp. 'Tess, I admit I have not always been able to tell you the truth, but I am telling the truth now. I want you to trust me. I want to begin again with you.'

She felt weak under the power of his gaze and his soft words.

'I will go to dinner with you,' she told him. 'But I do not trust you.'

He nodded. 'Dinner is enough at the moment. Will the Postillon be acceptable?'

'I know nothing about where to dine in Brussels.'

He stood and extended his hand to help her up. She accepted it, but he did not release her even when she was out of her seat. 'Thank you, Tess.'

She pulled her hand away and wrapped her shawl around her. They walked down the stairs and out of the hotel on to the Rue Royale.

Marc's hopes soared. He'd not been at all certain she would actually agree to dine with him. He was determined to put her at her ease.

But they'd walked halfway to the restaurant, near the cathedral, before she even spoke to him. 'Your mother and Amelie were very pleased to receive the invitation to the ball.'

'I am glad,' he responded. Mostly he was glad she decided to converse with him.

'It was odd, though,' she went on. 'Your father was quite solicitous of your mother. And there was no one about to impress, merely Amelie and me. Your mother opened like a flower in the sun under his kindness. It was quite remarkable.'

'He was kind to her? I should have liked to see that.' Had his father actually listened to him? That would be remarkable in itself. 'And they planned a private dinner? My God.'

They reached the restaurant, which was filled with other Englishmen, as well as soldiers and their ladies. There were few Belgians, probably because the hour was later than their typical dinner hour.

They ordered mussels and frites and fat sausages and large glasses of beer. They started out talking only about the food and it seemed to Marc that Tess finally relaxed around him.

'Did your sisters come to London for the Season?' Marc asked when they'd exhausted comments about the food and the surroundings.

Her expression stiffened. 'Yes, they came.'

He frowned. 'What is it, Tess? Did something happen with your sisters?'

She put her fork down and looked him in the eye. 'My marriage seems to have put some distance between us. Lorene feels I wasted her sacrifice. And I think Genna is angry because I let society dictate that I should marry. I did not tell them what Tinmore was prepared to do to them if I'd not married you.'

'And you probably could not explain why I left so abruptly,' he added.

'Who could explain why you left after the wedding

night?' Her voice was bitter. 'How could anyone understand that?'

His insides twisting in pain, he leaned towards her. 'I
did not leave to be away from your bed.'

She glanced around, as if to see if anyone heard him.
'Do not speak of it.'

He glanced down at his plate, spearing a piece of sau-
sage, knowing he was not telling her the complete truth.
He had run from her bed, had he not? He'd simply not intended to be forced to run all the way to France.

He looked up again. 'I am sorry I hurt you, Tess.'

Her face filled with colour and she lifted her beer to
her lips, taking a long sip. His words hung in the air a
long time.

The word *ball* drifted over from a nearby table.

He took that opportunity to change to a safer subject.
'The duchess's ball is a topic of conversation, I see.'

As he hoped, she accepted the turn in conversation.
'Amelie is very excited.'

They talked about the ball and the decorations they'd
seen transforming that large room into a ballroom. Soon
their meal had ended.

When they left the restaurant, Marc asked, 'Shall we
walk back through the park?'

Many gentlemen and their ladies were strolling through
the park. Lovers, Marc thought. Those in uniform would
soon be marching into battle. Tomorrow he hoped to
learn more of when that battle might occur. He hoped
he learned soon enough for Tess and his family to leave
Brussels.

They reached the hotel and walked up the stairs to her
room.

'Thank you for dinner,' she said.

On the landing, she stopped and turned to him. 'Tell

me something, Marc. Can men make love to women without loving them?'

He felt he was about to tread through brambles. 'They can.'

She nodded, looking as if she'd found a final piece to a puzzle.

She started up the stairs again and reached the hallway.

'That is the easy part,' he said. 'Making love without love. Very little is at stake—at least for the man. Love makes the whole thing more dangerous.'

'Because it can lead to death? Like with your brother and your friend?' she asked.

'Yes.'

They reached her door.

'And can women make love without love?' she asked, taking the key from her reticule.

All this talk about lovemaking—did she not realise it was all he could think of as he walked her to her room?

'They can,' he responded. 'Although for women I suspect lovemaking is dangerous whether they feel love or not.'

'Why would you say that?' she asked.

'They risk having a child.'

'A child...' Her voice trailed off.

'Do you want a child, Tess?' he asked, suddenly seeing in his mind's eye a little girl with auburn hair and hazel eyes, a little girl who would not suffer the loss of everyone dear to her.

She coloured again. 'Of course I do.'

She started to enter her room, but he blocked her way with his arm.

'We could make love, then, if you wish it.' Was he insane to even suggest this? He might drive her away again.

She turned pale. 'No. No. I—I cannot. Not after—'

He lightly touched a finger to her lips. 'Never mind. I can wait.'

Desire for her was now pulsing through him. He wanted her so much he was inches from lifting her into his arms and carrying her to her bed.

He kept himself in check.

She put the key in the lock and opened the door.

'Goodnight, Tess,' he murmured, backing away.

She disappeared into the room and the door closed.

'Patience,' he told himself aloud. At least she was talking to him now. At least she agreed to spend time with him. Time might not heal the wounds he'd inflicted, but it might help them come to some sort of truce.

He started down the hallway.

The sound of a door opening reached his ears.

'Marc?' she called.

He turned at her voice speaking his name.

She stood in her doorway. 'Stop by the hotel clerk and ask for a message to be sent to Nancy?'

'My pleasure,' he responded. 'What is the message?'

'That I will not be needing her tonight.'

He nodded, glad she'd given him something to do for her. He turned and continued down the hallway.

'Marc?' she called to him again.

He turned.

'Then come back to me.'

Marc hurried down to the clerk and arranged for the message to be delivered to Nancy. It was all he could do not to run back to Tess. He forced himself not to bound up the steps and race down the hallway to her room.

But he walked as fast as he could.

When she opened the door to him he took her in his arms and indulged in the kiss he'd feared she would repulse. His wife buried her fingers in his hair. Her lips parted and he felt her tongue touch his.

Joy filled him.

But she pulled away. 'I—I want to see how it will be, knowing you cannot love me. I want to see what love-making will be, knowing that.'

What did she mean knowing he could not love her? He did love her! That was what had driven him from her bed that first night.

But he would do this her way. She'd earned that right after what he'd put her through.

'Whatever you desire, Tess.' He took her in his arms again for another kiss.

It seemed as if her body came alive to him.

'Let me undress you,' he rasped when they broke the kiss.

'Like in the cabin?' she murmured.

He held her against him, loving the feel of her body pressing against his. 'Not like the cabin.'

He released her and untied the laces of her dress, letting it slip to the floor. He removed her corset next, this time unlacing it instead of cutting her out of it.

He stepped back, then, and peeled off his coat and waistcoat. He tore off his neckcloth. She pulled his shirt from his trousers and reached her hands beneath it to lift it over his head.

It suddenly seemed urgent that they rid themselves of the rest of their clothing. She pulled pins from her hair while he kicked off his shoes and stockings. As her hair tumbled over her shoulders, she took off her shift. He came to her again for another embrace, savouring the feel of his bare skin against her breasts. He lifted her into his arms and carried her to the bed.

He wanted to touch every inch of her, to assure himself she was real and that she was really warm and eager under his hands. He peeled off her stockings, the last barrier between them.

She reached for him. 'I am like my mother,' she said, her voice like sandpaper. 'I want this.'

Her words took him aback, but this was no time for a discussion.

Maybe she was like her mother in this regard. Maybe she was a woman blessed with the ability to enjoy sensuality. He would savour that.

He ought to be gentle, careful, slow. He ought to treat her reverently, but she urged him on, pressing her fingers against his buttocks.

He kissed her roughly and plunged inside her, his body taking over, needing to move inside her, needing to climb to the peak with her as if this were a race to be won.

She kept up with him, her breath coming in gasps, her hips rising to meet each thrust.

'Hurry,' she groaned. 'Hurry.'

He could not help but hurry. He moved faster and faster until she cried out and writhed beneath him. He felt her release inside her and his own pleasure exploded in return.

The power of his physical response to her astounded him.

This is love, Tess, he wanted to tell her. *This is me loving you.*

He suddenly understood what had driven his parents to marry, what had caused his brother to race to Gretna Green. He understood the desolation Charles must have felt when the woman he loved spurned him. To lose Tess would be devastating.

But he would not lose her, because he had no intention of ever letting her go.

She moved out of his grasp, though, but only to slide on top of him.

'Make love to me again,' she said.

Marc lost count of how many times they made love. It was as if they both needed to make up for lost time. He had no illusions about her forgiving him. He was still a long way from earning her trust, but this was a glorious start.

Sharing such pleasure together made for a very good foundation.

Unless this new war wore it away again, which it could do if it lasted ten more years. He could only be pulled from her so many times before there would be no rebuilding between them.

But for the moment he savoured holding her in his arms as dawn peeked in the windows. She looked peaceful and beautiful in sleep.

He heard a soft knock at the door. Surely it was too early for Nancy? He tried to ignore it, but it continued, louder this time.

'Who the devil?' he whispered to himself as he slipped his arm out from under her and untangled his legs from hers.

He grabbed his shirt and put it on as he walked to the door. 'Who is it?' he said as softly as he could.

'Scott' came louder through the door.

He opened it a crack and held a finger to his lips.

'You have to come now,' Scott whispered.

No, Marc protested inside. Not now. Not again. 'Wait. Let me tell her.'

Scott shook his head. 'No time. Now.'

'I have to dress.' Marc closed the door. He quickly put his trousers and stockings on and grabbed the rest of his clothes. He started towards the door, but stopped and returned to the bed. 'Tess. Tess.' He shook her gently.

She opened her eyes and blinked rapidly.

'I must go. No time to explain. I'll be back for the ball.'

He hoped he would be back for the ball, at least.

He kissed her quickly.

'No!' she cried.

But he turned away and crossed the room to the door, leaving before she could say another word.

Chapter Seventeen

Tess tried to shake herself awake.

Had he been with her? Or had she dreamed it all?

She could still smell his scent on the bed linens and she remembered the feel of him as he drove her to the heights of pleasure.

She also remembered him leaving her.

He said he'd be back, though, had he not? He said he'd be back for the Duchess of Richmond's ball.

Could she believe him?

Nancy came in the room at her usual time, glancing around as if she, too, were looking for Marc. She did not ask any questions, though. Tess could feel her wondering if he had spent the night, why he had gone. Instead she cheerfully got Tess ready to greet the day.

'The lace overdress is coming along very nicely,' she told Tess. 'It should be ready for the ball.'

The ball. Would he come? Or had he run from her again, after making love?

There had been nothing dispassionate about their lovemaking. On the contrary, they'd both been in the throes of that same sensual madness that he believed led to his parents' misery and to the deaths of his brother and Charles.

Was that why he'd run from her once again?

'Maybe after you eat breakfast, you can try on the over-dress?' Nancy said.

How nice it would be to think of dresses and lace and balls and not that your husband both desired you and re-coiled from being with you.

Everywhere Tess went that day the duchess's ball was talked of. She heard it discussed in the hotel lobby, in the park, certainly whenever she was in the company of Lady Northdon and Amelie.

The invitation list, she'd learned, was quite exclusive, limited to friends of the Richmonds and those other digni-taries, noblemen and army officers who must be included. All the more reason for Tess and the Glenvilles to have been excluded. What sort of influence had Marc, to add their names to the guest list?

Would he come?

Amelie and Lady Northdon insisted Tess accompany them to the shops early in the day for last-minute pur-chases that might be needed for the ball. Amelie bought new gloves. Lady Northdon found an elegant head piece that matched her gown. Tess purchased a lace shawl, but she spent most of her time searching the streets of Brus-sels to see if she could spy Marc.

They'd run into Miss Caldwell while out shopping, but seeing the young woman only reminded her that Marc had wanted to marry Miss Caldwell and not Tess.

When they returned to the hotel from shopping in the afternoon, Tess tried the lace overdress Nancy created. It was lovely and fit perfectly. The girl was in raptures over it, finding finishing touches to complete and new ideas to make it even more lovely. For Nancy's sake Tess pretended to be excited over it.

After she handed the overdress back to Nancy, there was nothing to do but wait for Marc. Her mood dipped near its nadir.

Tess ate an early dinner with Lord and Lady Northdon in their sitting room in the hotel. Captain Fowler, now Amelie's fiancé, was included of course. A place was set for Marc, but the setting was removed when he did not arrive.

While they ate, Tess, not a part of the conversation, became aware of a distant rumble. 'What is that sound?' she finally asked.

They were all silent until the sound repeated.

'*Alors!* It is nothing but thunder!' Lady Northdon waved her hand dismissively and continued talking to Captain Fowler.

A grim-faced Lord Northdon shook his head. 'It is not thunder.'

Tess might have been the only one to hear him. 'Is it cannon fire?' she asked.

He nodded. 'Very distant, though. Likely some testing of guns or something.' But he looked worried.

After dinner, Tess dragged Nancy away from her last-minute sewing to take a walk in the park. Tess did not want the exercise or the air, she wanted to see what was going on in the city.

Or was she looking for Marc?

The atmosphere had entirely altered from the night before when the park had been full of lovers, like her and Marc. Now people whispered together with worried expressions. Uniformed soldiers hurried to and fro.

But she did not find Marc and the cannon fire continued.

She spied Captain Upton, Marc's friend, and stopped him. 'Do you know what is happening, sir?'

He smiled with a reassurance that was not quite genuine. 'There is certainly fighting somewhere. The Prussians, likely, but it is too soon to tell. I am off to see what I can discover.'

She wanted to ask him to come round and tell her what he learned. She wanted to ask him to watch out for her brother, if they must fight a battle. She wanted to ask him if he knew of Marc's whereabouts. Could he have been caught in the fighting like he'd once become caught in that rainstorm in Lincolnshire?

'Captain?' She would ask the only question she could. 'Watch over my brother, if there is a battle.'

He made a crooked smile. 'Your brother is a good soldier. He must watch over me.' He tipped his hat. 'I beg your leave, ma'am.' Upton started off, but stopped a short distance away and turned back to her. 'Never fear, ma'am,' he called. 'The ball will still be held, they say.'

As if a ball mattered when men must fight wars.

Nancy paled. 'Ma'am, is the battle coming here?'

'It is too far away,' Tess told her.

But it was also too close for Tess to be easy.

Nancy finally begged Tess to leave the park and return to the hotel to prepare for the ball. It was to begin at ten o'clock.

Marc had until ten o'clock to show up.

After Nancy helped Tess dress, the lace overdress billowed around her rose ball gown like a cloud over the sky of a setting sun. Nancy had arranged her hair with ribbons of lace that draped over her head like cascading curls. She looked her very best, but what did it matter if Marc did not see her in it?

When it was time, she rode in the carriage with Lord and Lady Northdon to Rue de la Blanchisserie. Amelie and Captain Fowler followed behind in another carriage. The streets were crammed with carriages and cabriolets carrying guests to the ball and it took them longer to reach the house than it had for Marc and Tess to walk the distance the day before.

Once they arrived, there were footmen in livery to escort the guests through the house to the ballroom. Once they entered the ballroom, they followed other guests to be greeted by the duke and duchess. The duke and duchess welcomed them cordially, which, Tess knew, greatly relieved Lady Northdon's nerves.

The room was even more transformed than the previous day. The candlelight gave it a warm glow and made it appear as if it had always been a ballroom instead of a room to display carriages for sale. Great jardinières of flowers were everywhere, producing lovely colour and luscious scent.

'Mon Dieu!' exclaimed Lady Northdon, making some heads turn to see who was speaking French. 'It is *magnifique!*'

The guests further decorated the space. Red- and blue-coated officers. Young ladies in white and pink and pale blues and greens. Matrons in richer colours. The dancing had not yet begun, but the musicians played quietly while conversation buzzed.

The atmosphere was one of forced gaiety.

Captain Fowler whisked Amelie away to meet his superior officers. Lord Northdon was summoned by the Duke of Brunswick.

Tess turned to Lady Northdon. 'Shall we find a place to sit?' She struggled to sound cheerful.

Lady Northdon was scanning the crowd. *'Ça alors!* I

thought Marc would come. I did not think he would disappear again.' She waved her hand. '*Bien*. We may sit.'

Mr Scott approached them. 'Mrs Glenville, so good to see you here.'

She presented him to Lady Northdon.

'I know you are largely unknown here,' Mr Scott said to Lady Northdon. 'Let me present you to some of the other guests.'

He escorted them around to several of the guests, choosing mostly the French and Belgian ones for introductions. Countess D'Oultremont and her daughters took a fancy to Lady Northdon's and Tess's gowns and there was much discussion—in French—about their modiste and the latest styles.

Mr Scott, apparently satisfied that he had done enough for them, bowed and walked away. Tess realised she had not asked him if he knew whether Marc would come to the ball. Perhaps Mr Scott would know where Marc had gone and why.

She rose to follow him.

At that moment, though, pipers sounded and men of the Gordon Highlanders, dressed in their kilts, appeared in the doorway. They marched into the room and danced a set of reels to the delight of the guests, especially those who had never seen such a sight. The tapping of their boots and the bellowing of the bagpipes filled the ballroom.

After the Highlanders marched out again, Tess could no longer find Mr Scott in the crowd. Lady Northdon happily resumed talking about dresses with the countess, but Tess continued to scan the room.

She felt tension in the room. With each new set of officers who entered the ballroom, the tension seemed to heighten and the buzzing of the crowd increased. Something besides a gay ball was filling this room and Tess was determined to learn what it was.

'Lady Northdon,' she said in French, 'I am going to take a turn around the ballroom, but remain here where you are comfortable.'

She strolled through the ballroom, not acquainted with anyone, but trying to listen to their conversations. She saw Amelie still looking deliriously happy, holding on to Captain Fowler's arm.

Did the cannon fire she'd heard today have something to do with this sense of trepidation? Was the army finally going to march into France? If so, Edmund—Captain Fowler, too—would be a part of it. And all these men in uniform. The idea made her sick inside.

'Tess.' She heard a voice behind her.

She turned.

Marc!

He was dressed in formal clothes, but looked ashen and fatigued.

'Forgive me for being late,' he said.

The music swelled and the first dance was announced.

Marc extended his hand. 'Come to where I can talk to you.'

He led her back to the anteroom through which the guests entered the ballroom.

'Where have you been?' she asked, worried about his appearance.

'On the road,' he said dismissively, but added quickly, 'I need to tell you. Napoleon has marched into Belgium and his army fought the Prussians today. He is marching towards Brussels.'

'I heard the cannons.' She grasped his arm. 'How do you know this? Who told you?'

'No one told me.' He looked down at her.

'You saw them,' she guessed. He'd left town, but returned to warn them.

'I've just come back from speaking with Colonel De Lancey, Wellington's aide-de-camp. Wellington has ordered the army to march. There will be a battle, Tess, and it will be close to Brussels.'

Three gentlemen passed them and entered the ballroom.

'His Grace, the Duke of Wellington,' they heard announced.

They both walked to the doorway. One of the men who'd passed them had been the Duke of Wellington. He was tall and slender, a vigorous-looking man, much more handsome than the caricatures she'd seen of him.

She turned to Marc. 'You must be mistaken. The Duke would not be here if Napoleon was on the march.'

'He is appearing here to reassure people,' Marc answered.

One of the Duke of Richmond's daughters left her dance partner and hurried over to speak to Wellington.

Marc took Tess's hand. 'Come with me. I must find my father. My sister and mother, too.'

They found a serious-faced Lord Northdon talking to a group of men. Lord Northdon left them abruptly when he saw his son approach.

'You have heard the news?' his father asked him.

Heard the news? Tess thought. Marc saw it with his own eyes.

'I have,' Marc answered. 'This is the time to leave Brussels, Papa. Go to Antwerp, if you can.'

His father nodded. 'I will arrange it.'

Marc went on. 'You should return to the hotel now. Soon the streets will be filled with marching soldiers.'

The music stopped briefly and the distant sound of reveille could be heard.

'I'll get your mother,' Lord Northdon said.

When they found Amelie, she ran up to Marc. 'Is it true?' she cried. 'They are saying that Napoleon is at the gates of Brussels. All the soldiers must go fight!'

'Brussels is safe for now,' Marc assured her. 'But our soldiers are marching tonight.'

She ran back to Captain Fowler. 'Marc says you must leave,' she wailed. 'But I do not want you to go.'

'I must, my love,' Fowler said tenderly. 'It is as I've been trying to tell you. I must leave very soon.'

Amelie flung her arms around his neck and wept into his chest.

'We must get them back to the hotel,' Marc told him.

Fowler nodded and dragged a clinging Amelie along to where her parents waited.

'Should we not say something to the duchess?' Lady Northdon asked.

The Duchess of Richmond looked distraught. She was begging guests to stay, but the room was quickly emptying itself of all the military men. Everywhere there were couples embracing like Amelie and Fowler and saying farewell.

Her brother. Tess had hardly seen him. Now he would be going to war. She must say goodbye to him. She wanted to see him, just in case…

When Marc got his parents and Amelie out the door, Amelie was crying to Captain Fowler, 'I will not let you leave me!'

'My darling.' Captain Fowler embraced her.

Lord Northdon went in search of their carriage.

Fowler kissed Amelie before approaching Lady Northdon. 'May I walk Amelie to the hotel? These may be our last moments together.'

Lady Northdon waved her hand. *'Oui. Allez-vous.'*

Amelie and Fowler disappeared through the crowd.

Lord Northdon returned. 'Where is Amelie?'

'Captain Fowler is taking her back to the hotel,' his wife told him.

Lord Northdon looked worried, but he gestured for them all to follow him to the carriage.

When they reached it, Tess pulled Marc aside. 'I want to find my brother. I must say goodbye to him.'

'Tess, he may already be gone,' Marc told her.

'Or he may not.' She stood her ground. 'Direct me to Rue Sainte Anne. He might be there.'

'Your mother's house?'

'Tell me how to find the street. Please, Marc!'

His father snapped, 'We must hurry!'

Marc walked over to speak to him. His father shook his head, but climbed in the carriage after his wife and it went on its way.

Marc walked back to Tess. 'I will take you to Rue Sainte Anne.'

It was near two in the morning but the streets of Brussels could not have been more filled with activity. Everywhere was the sound of reveille, the pounding of marching boots, the wailing of women and children saying goodbye to loved ones. Tess did not know how she would have made it without Marc holding her hand tightly and pulling her through.

Her mother's house was not a great distance from the Duke of Richmond's. It was, however, more grand. Lamps shone in the windows and the door was opened by a footman almost immediately after they knocked.

'Lady Summerfield's daughter to see Lieutenant Summerfield,' Marc told the man.

The footman ushered them in and quickly closed the door. 'Wait here.'

'He did not ask why we called in the middle of the night,' Tess remarked.

Marc still held her hand. 'This night follows no rules.'

Tess expected her brother to appear. Instead a beautiful woman descended the stairway in her nightdress and robe, her blonde hair down upon her shoulders.

'My dear girl!' the woman cried.

Tess had a memory of her mother coming in the nursery in the mornings dressed just this way. She'd hug and kiss Tess and her sisters and ask them their plans for the day.

'My dear girl! You are here!' She walked directly up to Tess and took her hands, clasping them to her chest. 'Oh! My little girl. You have grown into such a beauty!'

'Mother,' Tess managed, pulling away. 'Where is Edmund?'

'Edmund will be down shortly,' her mother said. She turned to Marc. 'Is this your husband? Edmund told me you were married. Trust my daughter to pick a handsome one.'

Marc bowed. 'I am Marc Glenville, ma'am.'

'It is a pleasure to meet you.' Her smile still charmed. She turned back to Tess. 'And Lorene is married, too, is she not? She is Lady Tinmore now. How unexpected. Such an old man.'

Tess leapt to Lorene's defence. 'It was what she wanted.'

Her mother waved a finger. 'No young woman wants to marry an old man, even if he is a rich one.'

'You are an expert on marriages?' Tess asked, her voice sarcastic.

Her mother's eyes flashed. 'I am an expert on men and on falling in love, my dear, sweet girl.'

Marc stepped forward. 'Lady Summerfield, my wife is very eager to see her brother.'

'Glenville.' Her mother pointed her finger at Marc. 'Now I remember! Your father married a Frenchwoman.'

'Yes, Mama,' Tess said. 'You have likely heard the stories. Where is Edmund? Does he know I am here?'

'He is almost done packing.' She took them both by the arms. 'Come. Let us wait for him in the drawing room. Is it not terrible? Napoleon at our doorstep! Edmund leaving to fight battles! I cannot bear it. We were awakened from our sleep with the news.'

She led Tess to a sofa upholstered in pale green brocade and sat next to her.

The door opened and an elegant gentleman walked in. His hair was now peppered with grey, but Tess recognised him. He was Count von Osten, the man who took her mother away from her.

'Ossie, my love.' Her mother reached out to him. 'Come greet my beautiful daughter Tess and her husband.'

'This is Tess?' The count smiled warmly. 'My gracious, you have grown up to be almost as beautiful as your mother.'

He offered his hand and Tess felt she had no choice but to accept it. Instead of a handshake, he blew a kiss over it.

'I remember you, Count,' Tess said tightly.

Marc stepped in and introduced himself and drew the count aside.

'Where is Edmund?' Tess asked her mother. 'I came to see him.'

Her mother patted her hand and spoke soothingly. 'Do

not worry, pet. He will not leave without saying goodbye. He knows you are here.'

'Some brandy?' Count von Osten offered Marc. 'Sherry, ladies?'

'So thoughtful, Ossie,' her mother cooed. 'Yes, we will have sherry.'

Her mother chattered on as the drinks were poured and handed out. Tess drank hers gratefully. Seeing her mother shook her badly. She felt as if she were nine years old again, so excited to have her mother notice her, so despondent when her mother left.

All Tess wanted to do was see Edmund before he went to battle. Where was he?

Finally the door opened again and Edmund walked in. Tess left her seat and ran over to him. 'I could not let you go to battle without saying goodbye.'

He hugged her. 'Tess. My dear sister.'

She held him tight. 'Stay safe, Edmund. Do not do anything foolish. You must come back to us.'

'Do not worry over me.' He released her. 'I must go.'

He turned to Marc and shook his hand. 'Take care of my sister.'

Marc nodded.

The count clapped him on the back. 'Fight well, Edmund.'

He turned to Tess's mother. She enfolded him in an embrace that made Tess ache with remembered loss. 'My dear boy. I will be so angry with you if you do damage to yourself.'

Edmund laughed. 'Then I have no choice but to return in one piece.'

He came back to Tess, holding her one more time.

When he finally released her, Marc came to her side

and put an arm around her. Edmund gave them all a smile of bravado. 'I am off, then.'

He turned and walked out of the room.

Tess tried to stifle a sob. It helped that Mark's arm was around her.

Mark felt Tess's worry and grief as if it were his own. She might suffer yet another loss, her brother this time. Her brother might be killed in battle the very next day.

'My dear girl,' Lady Summerfield murmured, coming close and patting her cheek. 'You must stay here with us. We will have a room ready for you in an instant. I'll find you a nightdress and anything you need.'

Marc felt Tess bristle. 'Understand, Mother. I came to see Edmund, not to reconcile with you. I do not see how I can reconcile with you. You left us. You forced Lorene to become older than her years. Genna was only six years old. You left us to our father, who resented us.'

Her mother looked wounded. 'My only regret was leaving my children.'

'But you left anyway,' Tess accused.

Her mother seemed to grow older in mere moments. 'Stay here, Tess. Give me time to explain it to you.'

'No. I will go back to the hotel.'

Marc spoke up, 'I must take her back, ma'am. My father will be arranging carriages to take them to Antwerp in the morning.'

'Antwerp!' Lady Summerfield exclaimed.

Marc turned to the count. 'You might plan to leave, too, sir.'

'Leave Brussels?' Count von Osten's eyebrows rose. 'I think not.'

'We will stay,' agreed Lady Summerfield. 'Nothing will come of this, you will see.'

'As you wish.' Mark lifted Tess's lace shawl and wrapped it around her shoulders. 'We need to leave now.'

'We will have our carriage sent around,' Lady Summerfield said.

'No!' Tess instantly replied.

Marc quickly added, 'The streets are too crowded. We will make better time walking.'

Lady Summerfield took Tess's cheeks in her hands and kissed her. 'My darling girl.'

Tess shrank back. 'Goodbye again, Mother.'

They were soon outside and the streets were even more filled than before. Mark grasped Tess's hand again and they threaded their way through.

Reaching a relatively open area, he paused. 'Are you warm enough, Tess?'

'Yes,' she said distractedly.

They finally reached the hotel, which, even so late, was busy with people going to and fro in the lobby. They walked up the stairs and reached the hallway where her room and the rooms of his family were.

Marc stopped her. 'Tess, you must get what rest you can. I suspect my father will be leaving early.'

'For Antwerp,' she said.

'Yes. You will be safe there.'

She nodded, but still seemed in a daze. At the door of her room she removed her key from her reticule. He took the key and placed it in the lock.

He wanted to kiss her, but feared she'd already had enough for one night.

'Goodbye, Tess,' he said. He did not know when he would see her again.

She looked stricken. 'Where are you going?'

'To my hotel.'

She shook her head. 'Do not leave me.'

* * *

Tess opened the door and stepped aside so he would enter first.

'I am too tired to argue with you,' he said as he crossed the threshold.

'Oh, you are here!' Nancy rushed over to her. 'Mr Glenville. You are here, too!'

He nodded to the maid. 'I'll just sit for a moment. Do what you need to do.' He took off his coat and waistcoat and lowered himself into a cushioned chair.

Nancy turned back to Tess. 'Have you heard the news? Of course you have. You have been out. I was so worried about you! The others came back so long ago and you were not with them, but Staines told me that Lord Northdon said I was to pack your things. I just finished. Except for your nightclothes, that is.'

Tess kicked off her shoes. 'Help me out of this gown, would you, Nancy?'

Nancy unpinned the lace overdress and took it off. 'Do you think Napoleon will march into Brussels? The Belgian maids say that is what will happen and that no English-woman's virtue will be safe from his soldiers.'

Surely Wellington would not allow that to happen. 'Napoleon would have to defeat our soldiers first,' Tess said.

Nancy unbuttoned the long row of buttons at the back of the dress. 'Lord Northdon will take us to Antwerp tomorrow where it will be safe, Staines said. We are to be ready at six.'

A mere two hours away.

'Then there is no sense of my dressing to sleep.' Tess stepped out of the ball gown. 'Let me change into a travelling dress.'

While Nancy laced up the dress, Tess pulled the pins from her hair and put it in a plait. 'You must pack your things, as well, Nancy. And try to get a little sleep.'

'What about Mr Glenville?' Nancy turned to him.

His eyes were closed and his head rested in his hand.

'I will attend Mr Glenville,' Tess told Nancy. 'Do not worry.'

Nancy curtsied and hurried out of the room.

Tess turned to Marc.

He was sound asleep in the chair.

There was so much she wanted to say to him. Twice he'd left her after making love to her. She wanted to tell him she finally understood that he did not want those intense emotions that rose up between them, the sort of aching emotion that he believed led to his parents' unhappiness and the deaths of his brother and friend.

She also wanted to thank him for returning to warn them about the French advance, for taking her to her brother and helping her endure meeting her mother.

She wanted to tell him she forgave him for abandoning her, because he came back.

She wanted to tell him all of that, but he needed sleep more than her words.

She bent down and grasped his arm. 'Wake up, Marc. You need to walk to the bed.'

His eyes opened and fixed on her. He smiled.

'Come on,' she coaxed. 'Stand up.'

She placed her shoulder under his arm. He stood and allowed her to lead him to the bed. He climbed in it and immediately settled into sleep. She pulled off his shoes and climbed in next to him. She wanted to lie next to her husband.

He rolled over and spooned her next to him. 'Tess,' he murmured.

There would be no passion between them this night. The need for sleep was too great. They would share this bed as they had shared the cot in the cabin. Then and now he made her feel warm and secure and safe.

Chapter Eighteen

Tess closed her eyes just for a moment and must have slept, because the next thing she knew, Nancy was knocking on the door. 'Mrs Glenville! Mrs Glenville. Lord Northdon wants us in the lobby. Are you awake?'

She sat up. 'I am awake.'

'Come now!' Nancy cried. 'Leave your trunk and portmanteau. Staines will see they are brought down.'

'Everything is ready,' Tess answered. 'We will be down in a moment.'

Marc groaned. 'Must we rise now?' He put his arms around her.

She would like nothing more than to remain in his embrace. 'We must hurry. Your father is waiting in the lobby.'

He held her tighter. 'I am not going with you, Tess.'

It was as if the wind had been knocked out of her. 'You are leaving me again?'

He drew away. 'I must.'

She climbed off the bed and thrust his shoes at him. 'No. You must come to Antwerp with us where it will be safe.'

He frowned as he put on his shoes. 'I cannot. I—I must be elsewhere.'

She peered at him. 'You are going to the battle.'

'I am not saying where I am going,' he countered.

'You are going to the battle. You want to be a part of it.' Tess's throat constricted with emotion. She'd heard of men who craved such excitement.

She slipped her feet into her half-boots and tied the laces. She wrapped her plait in a knot and put a bonnet over it. She picked up her shawl and a pair of gloves and felt as if her world was crumbling around her.

'Are you ready?' he asked.

She nodded.

They walked out the door and started down the stairs to the lobby, which was filled with more people than usual, even at its busiest time of day. Tess felt as if she were marching to the gallows.

He stopped her on the landing. 'I dare not take the time to bid goodbye to my family.' He clasped her to him and held her tightly.

'You are leaving me again, Marc,' she cried against him. 'To go to a battle. You are not a soldier. You do not have to go. You could be killed. I'll never forgive you if you leave me again.'

He still held her. 'I must go, Tess.'

'You choose to go. Just like before.'

He released her. *'Au revoir.'*

She covered her mouth with her fist, stifling a sob as he made his way across the lobby. She watched until she could see him no more.

Wiping away tears, Tess walked down to the lobby and searched for Lady Northdon. She finally found her. Amelie stood with her, red-eyed and pale.

'Ma chère,' Lady Northdon said to Tess, 'where is Marc? Your maid said he was with you.'

'He left,' she managed.

'*Pfft!*' his mother exclaimed. 'He is always leaving! I wanted him to come with us, although he would have had to ride on top of the carriage. John says we will ride in two carriages. One for you, me, Amelie and John.' She used her husband's given name. Twice. 'The servants will ride in the second one.'

Lord Northdon worked his way over to them. 'Staines is collecting the luggage.'

'Marc is not coming with us,' Lady Northdon told him. 'He is disappearing again, Tess says.'

Lord Northdon muttered under his breath. 'Not disappearing. Working.'

Tess heard him.

'Maman, may I sit?' Amelie looked ready to collapse.

Lady Northdon walked her to some chairs and sat with her. They were out of earshot.

Tess turned to Lord Northdon. 'What did you mean by *working*, sir?'

He shook his head. 'I ought not to have spoken.'

She faced him directly. 'What did you mean?'

He leaned down and whispered in her ear, 'Working for the Allies.'

She felt the blood drain from her face. 'Marc told you he worked for the Allies?'

He leaned down again. 'No. He told me nothing, but I am certain of it.'

Her hands shook. 'Will he be in danger?'

'I fear so,' he said. 'I fear he has been in danger more times than we ever knew.'

He'd not left her to hike through the Alps. He'd been called to duty.

The hotel door opened as two carriages rolled up.

Staines ran in from outside. 'These are our carriages, sir,' the footman said.

The streets were nearly empty except for a stray officer here and there who apparently was getting a late start. Peasants with their carts filled with cabbages, green peas, potatoes and other produce rumbled leisurely past the hotel. It seemed a peaceful, normal day.

Lord Northdon nodded. 'Let us get the trunks loaded as quickly as possible.'

While they waited for the luggage to be brought to the carriage, Mr Caldwell and his daughter entered the hotel.

Mr Caldwell carried a portmanteau. 'My lord, there you are. Are you leaving the city?'

'I am taking the ladies to Antwerp,' Lord Northdon answered.

'Might I beg a favour of you, then,' he went on. 'I must remain in Brussels, but might I prevail upon you to take my daughter with you to Antwerp? I would be most grateful to you.'

Lord Northdon looked to his wife. 'I am not certain we have room in the carriage.'

'John,' Lady Northdon said. 'We cannot leave the girl. We must take her.'

'Very well, Caldwell.' Lord Northdon turned to his wife. 'I will sit on the outside.'

Lady Northdon looked aghast. 'You will do no such thing. We will simply squeeze into the seats.'

Miss Caldwell, looking very stressed, gave them a wan smile. 'Are you certain of this?'

'There will be room for Miss Caldwell.' Tess raised her voice. 'I am not going with you. I am staying here.'

'Tess!' Amelie cried. 'You cannot!'

'I will stay.' She thought quickly. 'My—my mother invited me. She is here in Brussels. My brother has been staying with her.' Although Tess had no intention of accepting that invitation.

Lord Northdon faced her, a look of concern on his face. 'It may become dangerous here.'

'Count von Osten will protect us.' She did not explain who the count was and none of them asked.

Lady Northdon peered at her. '*Ma chère*, are you certain?'

Tess answered her in French. '*Oui, madame. Je suis certaine.*'

Nancy spoke up. 'I will stay, too.'

Tess walked over to her and put her arm around the girl. She knew Nancy was afraid. 'You will do no such thing. You must go to Antwerp and help Lady Northdon and Amelie. You may attend Miss Caldwell.'

'But you will be alone!' Nancy cried.

'I will not be alone. I will be with my mother and she has dozens of servants. I will be safe. I promise you.' She turned towards Lord and Lady Northdon. 'I want to be here to see my brother. I will also look for Captain Fowler and send you word of him.'

But most of all she wanted to stay in Brussels for Marc, because it all suddenly made sense. Why he left without any notice. Why he sent no letters. Why he lied about where he'd been. Mr Scott. The Duke of Richmond. Were they involved in this, as well? Marc would come back to Brussels to report to someone, she guessed, if not them.

If he came back.

Marc was no longer running away from her. He was running into danger.

Nancy said a tearful goodbye to Tess before she climbed in her carriage and it pulled away. The first carriage carrying Lord and Lady Northdon, Amelie and Miss Caldwell had already left. Tess returned to the hotel lobby and informed them she would still be their guest. Her trunk and portmanteau would be returned to her room while she ate a quick breakfast in the hotel's dining room. There were a few other guests like herself with worry written all over their faces.

At a table near her were two officers seated with two young women and another man—their brother by the family resemblance. Why had the officers not yet left? she wondered.

'Nothing will happen today,' one said confidently. 'We may be assured of overtaking the regiment at a place called Waterloo where the men are to stop to cook.'

Tess hoped they were right. She hoped no men would die on a battlefield this day.

She ate only a little and returned to her room to sleep, removing only her hat, gloves and shoes and lying down in her clothes where she'd so recently lain with Marc.

She woke to cannonade, louder than the day before. Yesterday's had come from a battle between Napoleon's army and the Prussians. Where was today's cannonade coming from?

She rose and did what she could to neaten her hair. Again donning her bonnet and half-boots, she left the hotel and made her way to the park in hopes of learning some news.

The park was a different place than it had been that first day when she and Amelie saw it for the first time. Gone was the gaiety and sense of anticipation. It was replaced by strained expressions on the few people walking there. The cannons boomed over and over, like a death knell. How many men were fighting at this very moment, how many men were falling injured, how many were falling, never to rise again?

Where was Marc?

'Dear God,' she prayed. 'Keep them safe. Keep Marc, Edmund and Captain Fowler safe.'

She saw the two women and their brother from the hotel. Their soldier companions were no longer with them.

She approached them. 'Pardon me. Do you have any news? Do you know where they are fighting? Do you know anything at all?'

One of the women smiled sympathetically. 'We have talked to many people. Some say the battle is six miles away; some say it is twenty miles away. Someone told us our army won a complete victory. Someone else told us our men were completely cut to pieces. It is all rumour. We do not know anything with certainty.'

Tess thanked her and walked on.

A few minutes later she saw Count Von Osten crossing the park at a brisk pace. There was no way to avoid him.

He recognised her and hurried to her side. 'Tess! We thought you would be on your way to Antwerp.'

'The others went. I decided to stay,' she said.

'Where is your husband?' he asked.

'Gone.' What more could she say? 'I am alone.'

'Alone?' His brows shot up.

'Yes. Alone,' she responded. 'Do you have any news of the battle?'

He looked concerned. 'What? You should not be out walking unescorted. The town is not safe.'

'Do not worry over me. Have you any news?'

'Well,' he finally answered, 'I just spoke with Scovell who was at the battlefield. Our army was attacked when only two of the regiments were at the ready.'

'Which regiments?' she asked.

He looked sympathetic. 'The 92nd and 42nd Highland Regiments; the 28th —Edmund's regiment—and the Royal Scots joined the fighting later.'

Tess's heart shot into her throat at his mention of her brother. 'Is there any word of Edmund?'

'No casualty reports yet, I'm afraid. We know nothing of Edmund.' He frowned. 'The good news is that our boys held their own. There was no victory, but no loss, either, and the entire army will be ready for what comes next.'

It was not over.

Two Belgian men, obviously inebriated, staggered towards them.

'What have we here?' one said in French. 'Come with us, miss. We will show you a better time than that old man.' He grabbed her arm.

That old man, Count Von Osten, flew into action. He rapped the man's fingers with his walking stick, so hard that the man let go. He beat on both men with his stick until they turned and ran.

'Are you all right, my dear?' he asked Tess.

She nodded.

He offered her his arm. 'Come with me. You need protection. I am taking you to your mother's house.'

She was so shaken that she agreed.

'We will go directly to your mother,' he said. 'I will send one of our servants to collect your things from the hotel.'

As they walked, the cannonade continued. 'It is not over,' she said more to herself than to the count.

He made a worried sound. 'Apparently not.'

When they reached the house, the count sounded the knocker, but the door did not open. Instead a voice from inside shouted, 'Who is it?'

'Von Osten,' the count called back.

The door opened a crack and the footman who had greeted them the night before opened the door.

Lady Summerfield spoke from the top of the stairs. 'Is it the count, Jakob?'

Von Osten answered as he entered the hall, 'I have brought you your daughter.'

'My dear girl!' Lady Summerfield rushed down the stairs and threw her arms around Tess. 'You have come back to me!'

Her mother's affection was painful. 'It seems I needed a safe place to stay after all. The rest of the family have gone to Antwerp.'

Lady Summerfield released her. 'Why did you not go to Antwerp, sweet one?'

Tess swallowed. She could not explain about Marc or about how she needed to find him when he returned to Brussels. 'I—I wanted to stay. For Edmund.'

Lady Summerfield pressed the back of her hand against her forehead. 'Oh, Edmund! I have been so worried about him! Did you hear those cannons today? But, come, we will have our best bedchamber prepared for you. Have you eaten?'

Tess shook her head.

'Then we must feed you, as well.' Her mother put an arm around her and walked her into the drawing room. 'And give you a nice, warm bath.'

Tess was pampered as she had never been pampered before. Bathed. Clothed. Fed. It was as if her mother was trying to make up for all the years she'd been absent. Every word, every kindness, only reminded Tess of how it felt to be abandoned by her. She appreciated her mother's efforts, but was not ready to forget how it felt to be abandoned by her.

Her mother kept trying, though.

* * *

The next day in the afternoon, Tess extricated herself from her mother's solicitude and had some relief. She sat on a window seat in her bedchamber overlooking the street, which was still busy with people rushing here and there and carriages rumbling past.

As she sat storm clouds gathered, like harbingers of doom. The heavens opened and rain fell in thick sheets, finally clearing the street. Tess watched the rain and listened to its roar and remembered that rain of only a few months back. This rain was as thick, as loud. She remembered again the sight of the horseman appearing through the grey curtain of rain, the horseman who rescued her and became her husband.

Where was Marc now? Were he and Apollo caught in the downpour, like on that fateful day? She shivered, remembering the cold. For Marc's sake she was grateful the temperatures this day were not so dangerously frigid.

So much had changed since that rainstorm and, Tess suspected, much would change after this one. Armies would clash. One would be the victor and the other, vanquished, but not before many men would die.

She gazed up at the bleak sky. 'Please keep them safe,' she prayed. 'Edmund, Captain Fowler—' Her throat tightened. 'And Marc.'

Chapter Nineteen

Marc was where he was supposed to be, behind the French lines. He'd reached his position in the night, carefully moving past the tents of the French soldiers, acting the part of a Belgian citizen, changing his bearing and expression as he'd also changed into Belgian clothes. No one stopped him, however. No one had come close enough to notice him. He supposed it was due to the rain. Uncomfortable as it was, it acted as a shield.

He discovered a place that seemed deserted, a thicket of trees and shrubs where he and Apollo concealed themselves and waited for dawn.

The night, the rain, all made him think of Tess and remember how they'd been caught in rain this thick. He was chilled to the bone, but nothing like he'd been that February day. He spent a miserable night.

When dawn broke, Marc ate some food he'd carried with him. He walked up the slope through grain as tall as he was, reaching a ridge.

Below him was what looked like the entire French army, waking, like him. Soon popping sounds broke out all over the valley. The men were clearing their muskets of the charges that had lain in them all night.

There was no doubt he was behind the French lines, all right. His task was to keep watch, follow the army if they fell back, report any potentially useful information and create mischief, if he could—anything to help the Allies. He had an excellent vantage point of what he'd learned would be the battlefield, if Napoleon decided to attack. Wellington had chosen the ridge of Mont St Jean, a narrow space for a battle, only two and a half miles, by the look of it. On Marc's right was a farm, La Haye Sainte; on his left, another one, Hougoumont. Wellington had men in each.

Marc glanced around him. He seemed to be alone at this spot. It gave such a view of the field that he expected to see Napoleon himself ride up to use it as his command base, but no one was near. He took out his field glass and looked down at the French army. There was no command post that he could see. His first order of business, then, was to find Napoleon and his generals.

Without getting discovered.

That second morning at her mother's house, Tess waited in her mother's sewing room, waited for the sound of cannon to reach her ears, but none came. She wished it would rain again so the battle could not be fought, but the sky cleared and the sun shone. Out in the street wagons of wounded soldiers rolled by. Count von Osten sent Jakob the footman out to discover where they were from. They were from the first battle at Quatre Bras. Some wore the uniform of the 28th Regiment, but he'd been unable to discover if Edmund had survived Quatre Bras.

Count von Osten had gone out himself to visit the Place Royale in hopes of getting information. Tess's mother, who insisted on keeping her company, seemed determined to talk about anything except the impending battle. She asked incessant questions about the people she'd known in Yardney, about the servants at Summerfield House, about the house itself. Did it have new furnishings? Had her garden been changed? Whatever happened to her portrait that used to hang in the drawing room?

Her mother did not ask how it had been for three little girls to be abandoned by her and left with a bitter man for a father. She did not ask who arranged for their education, who taught them how to be young ladies, who tended their cuts and scrapes and injured feelings. Tess had no opportunity to explain how much those tasks fell to Lorene, who'd still been a child herself.

But her mother was not the only one who avoided questions. Tess did not ask her mother whether she found it easy to leave her children, or why her mother had never written to them or tried to see them or tried to discover how they were faring without her.

It was nearing eleven o'clock in the morning and her mother had been chattering for almost two hours. Tess's mind kept straying to some unknown battlefield where her brother and Captain Fowler would fight. Where would Marc be? Would he be in harm's way?

'Did you know I met the count at Vauxhall Gardens?' her mother asked. 'What a lovely night that was! We slipped away and walked together on the Dark Walk…'

Her mother, of course, had been married at the time and Tess's father had been left wondering who his wife had run off with this time. Tess had heard her father's version of this event many times.

'I know it may be hard for you to understand, but we loved each other. It was love at first sight.' Her mother's tone turned more subdued. 'There was no denying it. We needed to be together.' She glanced aside and smiled, but the smile was not meant for Tess. 'We still do need to be together.'

'Is that so?' Tess managed to keep her voice bland.

Her mother reached over and grasped her hand. 'But you have a love match. You must understand.'

'A love match,' Tess repeated. 'Why do you say so?'

Her mother laughed. 'Why do I say so? Your husband dotes on you. You are very lucky, you know. It makes life so much easier to love your husband and for him to love you.'

Easier? Tess wanted to scream. Realising she loved Marc made nothing easier, not when he might be killed this day.

Boom!

She and her mother both jumped.

Boom!

'The battle has started,' Tess whispered.

Marc found Napoleon's headquarters only a mile from where he had viewed what would be the field of battle. He'd seen the great man himself and his generals in conference at an inn called La Belle Alliance. Oddly Napoleon seemed to have chosen to remain at the inn, but surely his aides could have found the same location Marc had found with its perfect view.

Marc watched the inn for as long as he dared, but, though the generals had ridden off, Napoleon stayed. It was safer to return to the ground where Marc could watch the battle, though he would probably not be of any use to the Allies on the French side of the field.

It would be hard to watch the battle and not be in the thick of the fighting, to witness men dying and not be down there doing his part.

The sun was high in the sky when the French advanced on Hougoumont Farm, the first action of the battle. Marc had been in battle before his brother's injury and he knew he'd witness carnage this day and be helpless to stop any of it. Yet he also knew he could not take his eyes away.

He watched the French attack Hougoumont Farm. The fighting looked hard, but the Allies held on.

French guns pounded into the British line, which remained on the far ridge, mostly out of view. Through his glass Marc could see Wellington on his horse, riding from one end to the other, issuing orders, surveying the battlefield.

No comfortable inn for Wellington.

The French cannons stopped firing but their smoke put a haze over the field. Through it, though, Marc saw the French infantry go on the march, straight for the middle of the British forces. It was a magnificent, terrible sight. Thousands of soldiers, marching in column, like a human battering ram ready to pound down the British door. Their drums beat the Pas de Charge.

Could the British hold?

The French came closer and the Allied guns fired on them. Men fell and were left like litter on the field as the mass moved on.

'The guns are not making a dent,' Marc said aloud.

He had to stay low, lest he be seen, but he wanted to pace, to shout orders.

He wanted to fight.

On the crest of Mont St Jean, the British line fired their muskets, one volley after another, until the French infantry broke into retreat. Marc nearly whooped with joy to see the cavalry giving chase. He put his field glass to his eye again. The Scots Greys were among them, he could tell by their beaver hats.

Amelie's Captain Fowler would get his chance at glory, Marc thought, trying not to envy him.

It took only moments for the glory to turn to devastation. The cavalry had ridden all the way to the French guns, but it was too far. Fresh Cuirassiers cut off their return and Marc witnessed slaughter.

Few Scots Greys made it back to the line and likely Fowler was not among them. Marc memorised the ground where the cavalrymen fell, where he'd search for Fowler.

Later in the afternoon the cavalry charged again, this time riding in full force for the British line of infantry. Surely this was a mistake? The infantry formed squares that held, though the squares became smaller and smaller as men were wounded or killed. But this time the French cavalry suffered great losses, being fired upon from the squares. Through his glass Marc found the 28th holding their own. Tess's brother would be one of the officers on horseback in the middle of a square. It was where Marc would have been, had his brother lived. He and Charles might have fought this battle together—if things had been different.

Marc shook those thoughts from his head. Instead, he analysed the tactics on each side.

The whole of Napoleon's strategy seemed like a mistake. Why attack the centre and not the more vulnerable flanks? Why commit so many men to the siege of Hougoumont? Why attack in column and not in line, which would have given them so much more fire-power? Still, with all these mistakes, Napoleon's forces were close to victory. The Allies were straining to hold on. The field was awash in bodies and blood and evening was approaching.

From Marc's right, another army approached. His heart sank. French reinforcements? If so, Wellington was doomed. He put his glass to his eye once again, but these regiments were still too far away. He kept his eye to the glass as they marched closer and closer.

Marc's spirits soared from the depths to the heights. The Prussians were marching towards the battlefield. They'd arrived to support Wellington!

He swung his glass to the battlefield again. His elation was short-lived. Napoleon sent in the Old Guard, his finest soldiers. They churned across the field towards a very thin British line. The Prussians would be too late by mere minutes.

The drumbeat of the Pas de Charge pounded in Marc's ears. The Guard advanced. Marc could almost taste their triumph as they fired upon the poor line of redcoats.

But just as Marc despaired, thousands of British soldiers rose up as if by magic, all firing round after round into the Guard. Many fell. The others broke and ran.

Marc bounded to his feet and cheered.

The entire French army broke and ran with the Allies at their heels. Marc stuffed his glass in his pocket and hurried to where he'd left Apollo. The fleeing soldiers were running towards him, and if he did not get out of there, he'd soon encounter a multitude of panicked, desperate men.

A more horrid day, Tess could not have imagined. When the sounds of the battle reached Brussels, even her mother's determination to talk of other things failed. They sat, silent and worried, while the booms of the cannons went on and on. Count von Osten went out every couple of hours in search of information, but nothing reliable came his way. Each time he returned to the house, he said he'd heard both that all was lost or that Wellington was victorious, but neither report could be believed. At one point, a whole regiment of Belgian soldiers rode through the city, declaring the battle lost, but messengers from the battle-field did not confirm that, and the cannons kept firing, indicating nothing was finished.

It was near nightfall when the guns finally went silent and von Osten left once again. It was midnight before he returned. He burst into the sitting room where Tess had endured the entire day in her mother's company.

'My darling!' he cried. 'Tess!'

They both rose to their feet.

'He has done it! Wellington has done it! The French are in full retreat and the Prussians are chasing them all the way back to France!'

'How wonderful.' Tess's mother flew into his arms and he swung her around in a joyous display.

'Are you certain?' Tess asked cautiously.

He'd come home so many other times saying first one thing, then another.

He smiled at her. 'I was at the Place Royale when the dispatch came in. There is no doubt!'

Tess sank back in her chair, suddenly exhausted. 'Thank God.'

'Ossie,' her mother said, 'we must celebrate. Drink a toast to our fine soldiers. Let us bring out the champagne and gather the servants to be given some, as well. Champagne! It is perfect for toasting a victory over Napoleon!'

He ran out of the room and returned a few minutes later with a bottle of champagne and three glasses. 'There is celebration in the servants' quarter, never fear. This bottle is for us.'

Tess's mother stood up and took two of the glasses from him. He'd filled them to the brim with the bubbly wine.

She handed one glass to Tess. 'Be more cheerful, my darling girl! We have won.'

Tess accepted the glass, spilling a little over her fingers. 'I will be more easy when I know Edmund is safe.' And Captain Fowler.

And Marc.

Where had he been during the battle? Had he been in danger? Was he safe now?

The count's expression sobered. 'There were many casualties, they said.'

Some of the exultation evaporated.

The count put his hand on Tess's shoulder. 'Do not worry. Tomorrow I will take the carriage to the battlefield and see what word I can find of our dear Edmund.'

'May I come with you?' she asked.

'To a battlefield?' He looked upon her kindly. 'I think not.'

Marc changed back into his own clothes before riding to where the soldiers were bivouacked for the night just steps from where they'd fought the most desperate battle he could imagine. It had not been possible to follow Napoleon in his retreat. The vanquished emperor was swallowed by the desperate men clogging every road, running over the countryside, all trying to reach the safety of home. Darkness was falling fast, making it even more difficult. Besides, with no more army, where would Napoleon go except Paris?

Marc instead would search among the survivors for Tess's brother and Amelie's fiancé. Exhausted men sat around small campfires, haunted expressions on their faces. The battlefield was in their view, but it was now a macabre sight of bodies that appeared no more than grey mounds in the darkness. The stench of blood and death was inescapable and the cries of wounded and dying men and horses pierced the air.

No one dared come to their aid. The looters, the most

ruthless and heartless of men—and women—moved among the bodies, stripping them of clothes, pulling out their teeth, taking anything that might bring money. Looters would think nothing of killing anyone who tried to stop them. But every cry that reached Marc's ears hit him like a sabre thrust. Were they Edmund's cries he must ignore? Or Fowler's?

If Marc found them among the survivors, he would not have to search among the dead and dying when dawn broke. He started with the 28th. Edmund's chances of making it through were a lot greater than Fowler's.

And Marc did not want Tess to suffer yet another loss.

It took him hours but he finally found Edmund.

Among the wounded.

Edmund lay on the ground outside a house where one of the army's surgeons was occupied with amputating limbs. Edmund's uniform was stained with blood.

'Glenville?' he mumbled hazily as Marc knelt next to him. 'What the devil are you doing here?'

'Tess would want me to be here,' Marc told him.

The day after the battle was even more stressful for Tess, if that were possible. The count went out early, but returned almost immediately because the roads were too crowded with the wounded pouring in to Brussels, some in wagons, some on foot. He left again, this time to return to the Place Royale to see what names were on the lists of killed and wounded. Tess went out herself, then, much against her mother's wishes. She walked to the main road over which scores of wounded soldiers travelled and asked any soldiers from the 28th Regiment if they knew what had happened to her brother.

The sight of countless men so terribly injured was heart

wrenching. Some of the injuries were so terrible that she did not see how the men were still alive. She suspected they would not survive long. Where would they all go?

She spied another wagon with men wearing the red coat with yellow facing and the stovepipe shako that identified them as being in the 28th. She ran alongside. 'Excuse me, gentlemen, do you know Lieutenant Edmund Summerfield?'

One man answered, 'We know him.'

She did not mince words. 'Is he alive?'

Two of the men shook their heads. 'Don't know, ma'am.'

'I saw him fall,' said a third. 'Didn't see him rise again.'

'Dead?' She stopped.

The wagon rolled on.

A bitter taste filled her mouth. She ought to continue, ought to search for Captain Fowler, but her vision blurred with tears.

She wiped her tears away with the back of her glove. This was no time to weaken, when these men had endured so much worse than she could imagine. She could still do her duty to Amelie and find Captain Fowler, no matter that she'd lost her dear brother.

And, possibly, Marc. How could she search for Marc? She did not know where he was or if he would return.

But she knew someone she could ask.

She turned around, trying to get her bearings. Using the towers of the cathedral to guide her direction, she started to walk to the Rue de la Blanchisserie, to the home of a duke and duke's secretary, who undoubtedly would know more about Marc's whereabouts than anyone else.

She tried to cross the street.

Two wagons rumbled by. A crowd of wounded men staggered behind them. In the midst of the crowd was a lone horse carrying two men on its back. The crowd parted

for a moment and Tess could see that a man not in uniform led the horse.

It was Marc! The man leading the horse was Marc!

She ran into the street, trying to reach him, blocked by
the poor wounded soldiers.

'Marc!' she cried when she came close enough. 'Marc!'

He glanced up and stopped.

She ran towards him and threw herself in his arms. 'You
are safe! You are safe!'

He hugged her close while men flowed past them. 'Tess.
Tess. You were supposed to be in Antwerp.'

She clung to him. 'No. I stayed. I feared you would not
come back.'

The sea of men washed around them, but it was a while
before he broke the embrace.

'I found them,' he said.

She did not know what he meant at first, but he turned
to the two men on the horse. On Apollo. One man held the
other, a man wrapped in a blanket.

'Captain Fowler.' He looked like death itself.

The other man said, 'Hello, Tess.'

She looked up at him. 'Edmund.' It was like seeing a
ghost.

She ran to him but could only hold his leg. 'Edmund.'

He flinched. 'My leg, Tess. It is injured.'

She jumped away.

'Bring them to my mother's house,' she said.

Chapter Twenty

Marc could not believe Tess walked next to him through the streets of Brussels, or that she stayed in her mother's house.

When they reached it, her mother took immediate charge. She directed rooms to be made ready for Edmund and Captain Fowler. Water was heated; food prepared. The men were bathed, fed and given clean bedclothes as well as clean bed linens. Their wounds were dressed. She'd sent for her physician and surgeon, but neither came. Too many wounded to be cared for in Brussels; too few surgeons and physicians.

Edmund suffered a ball through the shoulder, a sabre cut to his torso and another through his leg. He was feverish, but there was every chance he would recover completely. Captain Fowler, whose wounds were many, hovered near death and was insensible. Tess's mother did what she could for both of them.

Marc had to leave Tess again that afternoon, this time to call upon Mr Scott and the Duke of Richmond to make his report. Afterwards he collected his portmanteau from his hotel. Wherever he went there were wounded men.

They were on the roads, still walking from the battlefield or riding in wagons. They sat in the pavement or in the parks. They hung out of open windows.

How many more would die before daybreak? A vision of the battlefield, of the dead and dying, came back to him, sickening him all over again. He'd forced himself to walk through it to search for Captain Fowler and he'd carried Fowler back.

He felt sick anew.

That night he dreamed of the battlefield again, again seeing the faces of the dead and dying. He woke with a start.

The battlefield vanished and there was only Tess lying next to him. He held her closer and buried his face in her hair to erase the memory.

She turned to face him. 'Something woke you.'

'A bad dream,' he murmured. 'It is gone now.'

She nestled in his arms. 'I cannot believe you are here next to me.' Her soft breath warmed his skin. 'I thought you would not come back.'

'From the battle?' Waiting, not knowing what was happening must have been its own sort of hell.

'Not the battle,' she responded. 'Although I was afraid of that, too. I meant I thought you would not come back this afternoon. I thought you might be sent away again.'

'Sent away?' He sat up.

She sat, as well. 'You went to see Mr Scott, did you not? To make a report?' She met his eye. 'A report on the battle, I suppose.'

She was not supposed to know this. How could she know? 'Do not make guesses like that, Tess. Making up guesses like that could—could be dangerous.'

'Do not fear.' She touched his face. 'I have said nothing to anyone.'

'That is because you know nothing, Tess.' He tried to be emphatic.

No one knew what would happen next. Was Napoleon vanquished? Or would he and his army rise to fight another day? Marc was not yet free of his duties and it still could be lethal for his clandestine life to be revealed.

She smiled. 'Your father guessed. He guessed you were not simply running off; you were off doing a job.' She held the covers over her nakedness and looked down at him. 'It all suddenly made sense why you left and why you made up the story about the Alps.' She sighed. 'And here I thought you left me because of the lovemaking.'

'Because of the lovemaking?' Leaving her bed had been wrenching.

'You explained it to me,' she went on. 'You thought making love to me would bring us unhappiness, like your parents, or death, like your brother and your friend.'

'That is correct, Tess,' he admitted. 'I did not know of any man who felt so powerfully for a woman who did not experience disaster.'

'It pains me to say it, but I believe the count and my mother have not experienced disaster,' she repeated. 'I mean, my mother hurt me terribly by running off with him, but look at them. They are still besotted with each other. They are happy.' She spoke sadly of their happiness.

'They might have managed together, but they left children without a mother,' he said.

She nodded.

He sat behind her and held her tight. 'I thought I lost you, Tess. I thought you would never forgive me for leaving you again.'

She twisted around to look into his face. 'You were only doing your duty.'

He held her face in his hands and kissed her, a long, lingering kiss, and felt the passion flare between them again.

'I love you, Tess,' he said.

She rested her forehead against his and smiled. 'I have my love match after all.'

Epilogue

February 1816—Lincolnshire, England

Marc had insisted upon bringing Tess back to Lincolnshire after they'd spent Christmas with his family in the country house. Lord Tinmore was hosting another house party to which they'd been invited and Marc had convinced Tess they must accept. It was a chance to see Lorene and Genna and Edmund, so Tess acquiesced.

They'd left Brussels as soon as Edmund and Captain Fowler were well enough to make the journey. Edmund healed well. Fowler returned to his parents and, his health still poor, had broken his engagement with Amelie. Amelie had become depressed and her parents had taken her to the country house to recuperate.

Marc and Tess had the house on Grosvenor Street to themselves. For all the turmoil of their meeting and marrying, the life they'd settled into was quietly wonderful. No longer did Marc disappear now that Napoleon had been exiled to St Helena. He and Tess spent much of their time together.

Spending Christmas with his parents at the country house had been their first trip together. This was their second.

Marc had suggested they make the trip on horseback—
he, riding Apollo, she, riding her Christmas gift from him,
a sweet mare she'd named Artemis. Somehow they'd taken
a wrong turn. Instead of familiar roads, they wandered
places that she could not recall ever having seen.

'I cannot believe you got us lost,' she complained.

'*I* got us lost,' he countered. 'You are from here. You
should know where we are.'

She glanced around at the fields on each side of her. 'I
have no idea where we are. We could be in the Alps, for
all I know.'

'The Alps? Very amusing, Tess.' He looked up at the
sky. 'Well, we had better find Yardney or Tinmore Hall
or some place soon, because it looks like it might rain.'

'Wonderful. We are going to be caught in the rain
again,' she said sarcastically. 'I cannot believe our luck.'

He grinned at her. 'I, too, cannot believe our luck.'

The roads turned this way and that and became narrower and narrower.

'Marc, I am starting to worry. What if we do not find
our way?' She remembered how it felt to be lost and caught
in the rain. At least this time she would not be alone.

Apollo pulled ahead of her a little distance and Marc
turned down an even narrower path.

'Marc!' she called to him. 'This cannot lead anywhere.'

He did not heed her.

The path led to a small cabin with a small stable next to it.

Tess laughed with joy and cantered up to ride next to
him. 'It is our cabin!'

He grinned. 'I've arranged for us to spend the night.'

They settled the horses and walked to the cabin door.

Marc put a key in the lock. 'I have the real key this
time.'

She blinked. 'How did we get in last time?'

'My skeleton keys.'

He opened the door and she stepped forward to enter. He stopped her. 'Last time I carried you.'

He scooped her up in his arms and carried her over the threshold.

She gasped at what she saw. The table was set with bread and cheese and biscuits and tarts. There was a tin of tea and bottles of wine. A fire already burned in the fireplace and their chairs and the cot were arranged the way they'd left them.

'I cannot imagine how you arranged this!' she cried.

He put her down and enfolded her in an embrace. 'My luckiest day was when I found you in the rain and we wound up here. I wanted to celebrate it.'

At that moment lightning flashed, thunder rumbled and rain pattered the roof.

Marc swung Tess around as they both laughed in delight.

They stopped and stared into each other's eyes.

Tess touched his face. 'It was my luckiest day, too.'

He leaned down and took possession of her lips as the sound of the rain filled their ears.

* * * * *

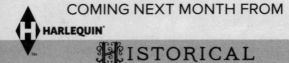

REQUEST YOUR FREE BOOKS!

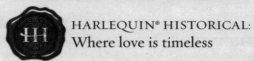

HARLEQUIN® HISTORICAL:
Where love is timeless

2 FREE NOVELS PLUS 2 FREE GIFTS!

YES! Please send me 2 FREE Harlequin® Historical novels and my 2 FREE gifts (gifts are worth about $10). After receiving them, if I don't wish to receive any more books, I can return the shipping statement marked "cancel." If I don't cancel, I will receive 6 brand-new novels every month and be billed just $5.44 per book in the U.S. or $5.74 per book in Canada. That's a savings of at least 16% off the cover price! It's quite a bargain! Shipping and handling is just 50¢ per book in the U.S. and 75¢ per book in Canada.* I understand that accepting the 2 free books and gifts places me under no obligation to buy anything. I can always return a shipment and cancel at any time. Even if I never buy another book, the two free books and gifts are mine to keep forever.

246/349 HDN F4ZY

Name	(PLEASE PRINT)

Address	Apt. #

City	State/Prov.	Zip/Postal Code

Signature (if under 18, a parent or guardian must sign)

Mail to the **Harlequin® Reader Service:**
IN U.S.A.: P.O. Box 1867, Buffalo, NY 14240-1867
IN CANADA: P.O. Box 609, Fort Erie, Ontario L2A 5X3

Want to try two free books from another line?
Call 1-800-873-8635 or visit www.ReaderService.com.

* Terms and prices subject to change without notice. Prices do not include applicable taxes. Sales tax applicable in N.Y. Canadian residents will be charged applicable taxes. Offer not valid in Quebec. This offer is limited to one order per household. Not valid for current subscribers to Harlequin Historical books. All orders subject to credit approval. Credit or debit balances in a customer's account(s) may be offset by any other outstanding balance owed by or to the customer. Please allow 4 to 6 weeks for delivery. Offer available while quantities last.

Your Privacy—The Harlequin® Reader Service is committed to protecting your privacy. Our Privacy Policy is available online at www.ReaderService.com or upon request from the Harlequin Reader Service.

We make a portion of our mailing list available to reputable third parties that offer products we believe may interest you. If you prefer that we not exchange your name with third parties, or if you wish to clarify or modify your communication preferences, please visit us at www.ReaderService.com/consumerschoice or write to us at Harlequin Reader Service Preference Service, P.O. Box 9062, Buffalo, NY 14269. Include your complete name and address.

HHI3R

*Taking refuge with an ally, rebel Bao Yang accidentally
compromises the man's daughter when they're
discovered alone. To save her honor, he must marry
the beautiful Jin-mei immediately!*

Read on for a sneak preview of
A DANCE WITH DANGER,
a thrilling new offering from
USA TODAY *bestselling author* Jeannie Lin,
linked to her previous novel THE SWORD DANCER.

As she ducked through the curtain to her sleeping area,
she heard her name spoken softly. So low that the sounds
resonated against her spine.

"My warrior woman."

Yang came from the darkness and his arms circled
around her. Suddenly she was pressed tight against him.

Their first embrace should have been awkward, all
hands and limbs and not knowing how they should be
with one another. But as Yang pulled her close, her body
molded to his. Her lips parted to say something. She
didn't know what, but it didn't matter because she was
caught in a kiss that was hard and urgent and made her
knees go soft.

"Yang."

She meant for the utterance to be a protest or at least
a question, but it came out the sigh of his name, deep in

her throat and unexpectedly sensual. She had never been kissed like this before. She had never been kissed at all. His mouth pressed against hers, urging her response with so much passion that there was no opportunity to doubt or question. It was like the rush she'd felt during their match, but so much faster and stronger. By the time their lips parted, her head was spinning.

"Hold on to me," he said.

Her hands grasped the front of his robe while she stared at him, confused. Her heart was beating hard and every part of her felt flushed.

"Hold on to me," he repeated in a low murmur against her earlobe. He bit into the soft flesh and heat flooded her veins.

Jin-mei hooked her arms around his neck and held on tight. If she hadn't, she would have crumpled to the floor. He lifted her with his arm secured around her waist and another hooked beneath her knees. The ship spun around her. She found herself with her back against the hard wood of the berth, though it somehow seemed more welcoming with Yang's weight pressed against her, shoulder to hip. *Made to fit one another*, Lady Yi had told her.

Don't miss
A DANCE WITH DANGER by Jeannie Lin,
available May 2015 wherever
Harlequin® Historical books and ebooks are sold.

www.Harlequin.com

HHEXP0415

THE WORLD IS BETTER WITH

Romance

Harlequin has everything from contemporary, passionate and heartwarming to suspenseful and inspirational stories.

Whatever your mood, we have a romance just for you!

Connect with us to find your next great read, special offers and more.

f /HarlequinBooks

🐦 @HarlequinBooks

www.HarlequinBlog.com

www.Harlequin.com/Newsletters

◆H HARLEQUIN®

A *Romance* FOR EVERY MOOD™

www.Harlequin.com

SERIESHALOAD2015